The Dragons' Chosen

Gwen Dandridge

Copyright 2016 Gwen Dandridge, All rights reserved.
Published by Hickory Tree Publishing
HickoryTreeBooks.blogspot.com

Library of Congress ISBN: 978-0-9893157-6-0

www.gwendandridge.com

Cover illustration ©2015 Carol Heyer
Cover design ©2015 Siri Weber Feeney
Inside layout and illustration by Carin Coulon

First Hickory Tree Publishing Edition

Also by

Gwen Dandridge

The Stone Lions

Coming soon

The Jinn's Jest

This book is dedicated to Phyllis Schimel
For all her many kindnesses

Chapter 1

The sky was songbird blue, the sun golden; a light breeze brushed my cheek, cooling me down following the uphill gallop. Beneath me, my mare, Flight, shifted her weight as she pawed the ground. Nothing could be better than this.

I turned in my saddle as Crown Prince Theo from Gowen, my third suitor this month, thundered up behind me. My reverie ended as he hauled his mount to a stop. Oh yes, there was one thing that could perhaps be improved.

"You bested me." He nodded to my victory. His eyes lowered, though not before I saw the sullen glint in them.

Once again, I'd let my pride rule when I should have stroked my suitor's self-worth. I used my smile to soften his loss. Mother had sent us off, properly chaperoned by my ladies and guards, but they fell behind once our challenge began. As good a horse as the prince rode, I had no doubt I would win. These were my lands. Flight and I had traversed them together since my father gifted her to me in honor of my fourteenth year. We knew every hillock, fence and ditch.

But, I shouldn't have beaten him. I knew Mother hoped he would confirm his offer for me today. And that I would stop finding excuses to reject courters and accept.

"It was but chance; you are much the better rider." I slid my gaze to my reins so he could not read the lie in my face. Mayhap he would see my behavior as a young maiden's modesty.

He brightened then, throwing off his bad humor. He was pleasant and attractive, though somewhat too sure of my answer to be flattering.

I didn't understand my parents' sudden push to get me engaged. I wasn't likely to die an old maid, not at the age of sixteen and crown princess of Verdeux. Nor were we on the verge of war and my troth needed as the price for peace.

Flight still pranced in place beneath my hands, as if pleased with herself for besting Theo's large bay hunter, Lion Heart.

Theo dismounted, walked over to me and placed his hand on Flight's bridle. "Genevieve." His other hand wrapped around mine as if in ownership.

Here it comes, I thought. I knew I would say "yes." There were no more reasons to refuse. He was nice enough, wealthy enough, royal enough, and his lands abutted ours. I couldn't protest that he was ill-favored or unsuitable.

Father had approved this union and my mother was eager to see me affianced.

Most of all, it was my duty. How I had been trained all my life.

Still I wished for something more … romance, even love, perhaps. A small sigh escaped from my lips. What a foolish thought. A princess shouldn't wish for these.

I looked out to the fields beyond. Across the field came one of my father's riders on a mission, a cloud of dust blossoming in his wake.

Noting my distraction as the rider joined my guard, Theo squeezed my fingers. I wouldn't let my family down by refusing. I curled my fingers in his, smiling, showing him nothing but a girl delighting in his presence.

"Genevieve," he repeated. "I would…"

"Your Highness." A voice called as three guards charged up the hill. My ladies remained milling around near the tree line below, too timid to brave this route.

A frothed horse and rider broached the hillside. "Princess, you must return immediately. Your father wishes you to attend him."

"What is this about?" Theo demanded.

The rider brushed the sweat from his face. "I wasn't told, My Lord. Only that the Princess must return."

Theo's hand slid from mine. As he mounted his horse, I blew him a kiss. A little wait would do him good. He was too sure of me and I was not so sure of him.

Whatever Father wanted, I was grateful for the reprieve.

I sailed into court followed by the kittenish antics of my ladies-in-waiting. I no longer remember what they were saying that made me laugh out loud as I came before my father's gaze, but I stopped suddenly at the quiet—and the look on his face.

I scanned the room, hoping for some clue to the disaster that must have hit my kingdom. Our priestess, Mother Morigan, perched like a bird of prey in the shadows, which was ominous in itself, as she only appeared in court when tithes were gathered or someone died.

I wondered then if someone *had* died. It certainly felt so. The three traveling musicians played a melancholy tune in the corner. The handsomest one with a neat beard cut to a point stared at his feet as I walked past, no shy smile as usual.

My sister, Danielle, was leaning into my mother's shoulder, sobbing. My two little brothers, Harold and Bartholomew, stood with their tutor by the sidelines, alarmingly still. I searched my mother's face and grew more afraid. She was rigid, her face splotched, the queen who never wore her emotions in public.

My ladies held back. I walked forward to kneel at my father's feet. Mother Morigan moved to stand by my side. As my head rose, I felt her place a delicate chain about my neck. I lifted it up to see a dragon etched in a round gold coin. My question was answered.

It was I who had died.

Chapter 2

I wasn't at my best that afternoon. My head throbbed, my gold coronet pressed on me like iron slag and my nose was clogged from squelched tears. Hovering near, two of my ladies-in-waiting leaned upon each other and sobbed; another stroked my hand as if I were some tabby cat from the stables. Cupped in the palm of my hand, the gold coin with its etched dragon icon looked harmless, but it marked me as *chosen*.

The dragons had returned.

Five, some reported, three, according to others, or maybe as many as ten. They were seen circling high above the Perpinan hills east of Tine.

I knew the history of our land, though my mother had tried, ineffectually, to keep this particular piece of it from me. The likenesses of fourteen young women, girls almost, lined the farthest gallery in the castle. Portraits and statues depicting princesses from across the nine kingdoms of Gaulen. I had looked at those images, stricken by the sadness I imagined in their eyes, wondering at their stories. But the only secrets given up were their names, their kingdoms and a year inscribed in each frame.

No one was descended from them; they left no bloodlines to be memorized and recited. They had simply disappeared. No tutor would answer my questions about them, and the history books mentioned them only briefly. *Daughter of King whomever*, the books pronounced, *chosen*, though for or by whom they never said.

I had looked for answers, and at thirteen, the same age as my sister was now, finally found them in a moldy leather-bound history I discovered deep in a chest in a far reach of the castle. Age had rusted its iron corner pieces. Across the center was a raised bronze medallion with the tarnished image of a dragon, wings extended in mid-flight, etched into it. The book's pages were stuck together, and water stains blurred the writing. I read a full page before I pushed it from me, sick with horror.

Each of these princesses had received a token a handful of months before her seventeenth birthday. After which she was delivered to the cliffs of the Crystal Mountain and left (tethered, I read, to prevent the unfortunate princess from accidentally getting lost in the wilderness).

The next day all would be gone—the dragons, the princess—nothing was left. Each century the dragons came and a princess was given up.

It couldn't be true, I had thought. No one I knew had seen a dragon, nor were there rumors of them. They hadn't been heard of for one hundred years; surely they must all be dead.

I replaced the book, closed the chest and never looked back.

That happened four years ago; I was turning seventeen in two months' time.

I knew that word was spreading like a flood. News of the dragons' return coursed throughout the court, into the towns and marketplaces and out into the least hovel of Verdeux. Already horsed couriers and rock doves were racing messages out to far reaches, bringing comfort for other royals: their daughters were safe—until the next time, generations from now.

The cool golden coin burned my hand as I reread the inscribed word *chosen*, and the blood chilled inside my veins. I must be taken to the mountain in two months' time or the dragons would come in force. No negotiations, no substitutes. My mother was, without a doubt, still pleading with the priestess for divine intervention to rescue her daughter. Father, whose strength of arm matched his sense of duty, was incapable of sacrificing the kingdom for anyone, even a beloved child.

I had always known that I was a chess piece, destined to be married for the good of the kingdom, wed to someone like Theo. My hand in marriage a prime talking point at negotiations among kingdoms; I was valuable, a political prize. Royal wedlock wasn't a romantic ballad to titillate love-sick girls. It was a bond to unite kingdoms and secure borders.

But I was also loved by my parents, and as such, had some say in my future. But now, with the flick of dragon's wing, I had none.

A stream of horsemen clattered into the courtyard below, and I roused out of my melancholy musings. I drew my hand away from Clara's irritating stroking.

Perhaps she was only trying to soothe herself, since her position at court would end in two months.

Felicity continued sobbing into her embroidered handkerchief.

Melody held up a gown. "Do you think this dress is sober enough for tonight? Verdigris is such a good color for you. It sets off your crimson hair."

Her inappropriate gaffes no longer surprised me. Melody was another of my mother's attempts to flatter a noble by making his daughter part of my entourage. This morning I would have cared what I wore and even been mildly offended by her calling my hair crimson.

This morning I would have overlooked her words. I only wish that my troubles remained so petty.

I glared into her eyes and she hastily fell silent.

It was these three girls' sole job to attend me, to keep me in good company and cheer. Normally they had, but now the task was beyond anyone's abilities.

Lost in these thoughts, it was no wonder I was distracted when the strange girl first materialized in my bed chamber. I thought perhaps my eyes were blurring from unshed tears. Clara's shrill scream brought me to my feet as the blur whirled and transformed itself into a creature.

What was this? One of the dragons' minions or something very different? It looked like a woman, young perhaps, with straight long hair the color of cinnamon that had never seen curling tongs or hair net. Spanning her nose were two glass-like oval shapes held by dark brown bars that disappeared into the fullness of her hair. Her clothes were immodest at best. She wore trousers of some kind, made of rough blue material that belled out from her knees to her feet. A short, unbuttoned vest of multiple colors lay over a thin, ill-fitted white chemise that proclaimed in garish purple letters "Free the Chicago Seven." One of her hands held a single card, as if she had been playing a game and had stepped away from the table for but the pause of a breath.

She stood looking at me, shifting the eyepieces back upon the bridge of her nose. Her gaze skipped from one part of the room to another, taking in my maids cowering now behind the dulcimer, then rested with a frown on the blue and red tapestry on the wall before alighting on me once again.

"Uh-oh, Toto. I guess we're not in Kansas anymore," she said in a soft, oddly-accented voice. Though her voice didn't quaver, there seemed a tightening about her eyes that might have been cunning, but I wondered if it was fear. Her forehead wrinkled as if puzzled as she scrutinized the card she held. Then, with a twist of her hand, it disappeared beneath the folds of her clothes. When she looked up, her face was ashen, highlighting the unpowdered freckles scattered like pollen across her nose. For a moment, I thought she might flee. The hairs on her arms stood up as if she was cold, though the sun had been pouring into the room all morning.

I stood my ground and ventured a guess, in the hopes she would deny it. "Are you a witch?"

She frowned, cocking her head slightly, then bit on the nail of one ring-less ring finger as if contemplating. "No, are you?"

"Of course not." I hesitated, waiting for one of my ladies to intercede. Behind me, there was a thud. I assumed it was Felicity. She had an unfortunate tendency to faint given the least provocation. I took the chance to glance behind me. Clara looked as if she was preparing to have a fit; Felicity was definitely down, with Melody crouched beside her, trying to rouse her. It was not looking hopeful that my ladies would perform the introductions.

The strange young woman nodded as if something had been confirmed. "I didn't think so." She looked down at her shoes; brown peasant's sandals with exposed toes in dire need of grooming. We settled into an uncomfortable standoff. She shivered.

Remembering some smidgen of her training, Clara took a step forward. "You are in the presence of the Princess Genevieve of Verdeux, daughter of Wilheim and Camille." She burst into tears. "And she is fated to be eaten by the dragons."

I could see we needed to revisit protocol and appropriate behavior at court. The strange woman looked me in the eyes and I pulled back at the intensity of the connection.

I flashed Clara a frown.

My distress and irritation must have registered with her, because Clara's hand flew to her mouth. She curtsied, her head bowed. "Your pardon, My Lady, my words were thoughtless and ill considered." Clara took a step closer to me, watching the apparition as if she were a rabid animal that might charge without thought. Tears crawled down Clara's rosy cheeks. "The people of the Kingdom praise your intelligence, beauty and charm. Surely your parents won't allow you to be given to the dragons and…" She should have stopped there but her cupid bow lips kept right on moving. "Even if they do, I'm sure, er…I hope, er…maybe they won't be hungry this time."

Felicity, now recovered from her faint, roused herself enough to deliver a screech that could be heard in the next kingdom. The door opened and five guards rushed in, took in the scene and surrounded the oddly dressed woman.

She … well, she vanished.

Chapter 3

That evening was necessarily sober. Time has a way of sharpening reality. With each hour, the knowledge of my fate tumbled from my head down into the core of my body.

At supper I sat between Clara and my mother. Theo and three of his men sat a table over. I couldn't fathom his thoughts, nor did I care.

The dragons were never far from my mind. Almost as if to reinforce the point, two of our sentries entered the hall and stopped before my father.

One bowed before addressing him, "Sire?"

My father nodded, and all attempts at small talk ended, as everyone up and down the tables strained to listen.

The sentry continued. "We have confirmed sightings of dragons crossing our borders and penetrating deep into our lands. Three were seen by a miller and his son not fifty miles from here."

Father held himself tight. "Lower your voice, man."

In a stage whisper, the sentry spoke again. "Two others were seen circling near the kingdom of Brigathe before they veered off eastward."

Hushed words of sympathy caught my ears. I turned inward, grabbing for anything to distract myself.

I thought of the bizarre young woman to fixate on a safer image than my delivery to reptilian flying monsters. Was her arrival connected with my…future?

My mind was in a daze of disbelief. I jumped as my mother reached over. She placed her hands over mine and gently extracted the shreds of a cutwork napkin that I had been absently ripping. Her touch felt like ice.

She and Father locked eyes across the long walnut dining table.

A quick look showed me that everyone seated was mesmerized, watching me tear the thin linen cloth into ever smaller strips.

Several guests at the table murmured, their eyes avoiding mine, but I heard my name whispered and a responding "Shhh" from various table companions. If I was an item of discussion, I would at least shape the talk.

Before my hands betrayed me again, I lifted my head and stood. Digging my nails into my palm to gain control, I projected my voice down the length of the table. "To Verdeux!" I raised my wine glass. "The royal family is part of the land. If it bleeds, we bleed."

I learned the strategies of politics and diplomacy at the same time I was taught to curtsy and ride a horse. While I might be a chess piece, my parents made sure that I also acquired skill at the game of royals, assuring me that I would never be cast aside as if I were a pawn— though in this case perhaps tossed out as a morsel might be the more appropriate metaphor. But overnight my game board had been brushed away, trampled by mindless beasts. While inside I trembled, I refused to surrender my dignity as well as my life to these animals.

I stiffened my back and continued, "During times of famine or battle or hardship, we call on our people to sacrifice—to sacrifice their land, their sons, their children for the common good. Your princess can do no less."

Our butler stood at the door as he had for twenty years, longer than I had been alive, his nose now pink with emotion.

One of the maids flung her apron over her face and rushed from the room.

I have no idea what I ate that evening. In the background, I heard my sister sobbing but I didn't look her way. I couldn't. Instead I forced my hands to steady and carefully deliver food to my mouth.

The traveling minstrels entertained us with music for our supper. A fortnight ago I had found them charming and handsome, and had bantered with them. Now I couldn't spare the energy to chide Melody and Felicity for the sugary glances they sent the trio's way.

Their bard, Trill, got halfway through a ballad of unrequited love when his exquisite baritone voice wavered. Across the distance, his eyes met mine and I looked away. I wasn't interested in his pity.

Fortunately, the lute and mandolin player covered for him, playing a musical interlude while he composed himself.

Even my younger sister, Danielle, and our two brothers, Harold and Bartholomew—aside from a minor incident with two frogs—were quieter than usual. Father had an extra glass of fortified wine.

Uncle Castor, who was past his prime and known to be one helmet short of full armor, kept saying in a louder and louder voice, "Genevieve going off to the fens? Not a good time for that. You never know what kind of creatures are out this time of year." His wife leaned over to him, whispering. He rallied like an old war horse that pricks up his ears at the sound of the battle drums and fifes. "From beyond the fens, are they? What do they want with our little lady?"

Aunt Matilda tugged at his sleeve and whispered again.

He raised his voice even more, calling out, "Genny, good for you. The royal house needs new blood. You will do us proud with those…"

He turned back to his wife. "Who did you say they were? Well, no matter, our Genevieve is no fragile flower, not her. You can be sure that she knows her worth. Those people will be dancing to her tune before long." He looked around the table, oblivious to the open mouths and shocked looks from the others.

"I am surprised that Wilheim is considering betrothing Genny to someone from such a far-off kingdom." He nodded and winked at my ashen-faced mother. "Thought King George's boy from Gowen, Tad, Thomas, Theo, whomever, was the one that Camille had set her sights on for Genny. I always thought him too much a fop for her."

I heard a gasp of indignation from Theo's table, followed by a titter of laughter that was stifled abruptly.

Amidst all this, a small window of my mind kept turning over the image of the inappropriately dressed woman with purple lettering across her bosom. I felt somehow, though I could not yet say how, that our fates were joined.

Chapter 4

I couldn't sleep. I curled up in the chair on my balcony, looking out across the courtyard into the night sky, casting my mind past the soft gray of our tall castle walls and out into the blue-gray hills, to the patchwork of golds and greens in the fertile meadows beyond. The wind tickled my face. The scents of fall wildflowers from the valley mixed with the spicy lavender of burning candles wafted across me. I sat listening into the evening. The hunting dogs in the kennels barked at some real or imagined prey. The drawbridge creaked and chunked as the guards pulled it up for the night. I loved it all. Here I had spent my whole life. My father's people, *my* people, slept safely in their homes.

During the day, long forgotten legends had whipped through town of past dragon attacks, of monsters in the Fandrite Mountains. Of land burned so thoroughly that nothing grew for decades, of crops destroyed, of hunters who never returned. The stench of blood and smoke was all that remained, clinging like fog over charred ground. Whether those stories were true or not, I couldn't say. But there were dragons and they wanted me.

I thought of running away. I thought of ending my life. I thought of many inappropriate and unworthy solutions. If I were to run away and disappear, the dragons would come. If I died, the dragons would come. If I turned into a hen and started laying eggs, the dragons would still come. I saw no solution that didn't involve me riding off under armed escort, trussed like a stuffed goose, to the Crystal Mountain beyond the fens. My going was the only way for my kingdom to survive. No one could war against a single dragon, much less many. If I ran away or ended my life, peace would be a thing of the past. My legacy would be the destruction of all I loved.

My death by the dragons was the only way for them to live.

My hands shook as I thought of my end. I hoped the dragons would be quick. It seemed likely with so many. I didn't wish to linger among them. I lowered my face into my hands as tears streaked my cheeks.

A small breeze brushed my hair. Behind me I heard a gasp and the creak of my bed. I turned, preparing to rebuke whoever had disrupted my solitude.

The mysterious girl who'd appeared in the morning sat cross-legged on my coverlet, one hand laid across her lap, the other again clutching a card before her as if it were a candle. She looked around, appearing bewildered, before dragging one fingernail across my lace bedcover as if testing for substance. My nightgown rustled as I sat up straight, unsure of how to address her.

Leaning forward, she spoke. "So what was all that about dragons?"

It took me some time to respond. Her audacity, her attempt to quell her curiosity at my expense, would have shocked any of my ladies or even the lowest servant. They would have escorted her away before she closed her mouth. But still I hesitated; it would not do to offend a gift from the Goddess or even a witch, if such she were.

Nonetheless, I noticed her sandals were on my bed. I left my balcony for a closer look at this person.

Yet another ill-fitted chemise clung to her body, a rather brilliant orange this time, with white lettering that insisted, "Be the change you want to see in the world" and a hastily-sketched portrait of a man. Underneath, the artist had signed his work in large cursive letters, "Gandhi." A woman who appeared and disappeared was not normal, not covered in the rules of court etiquette. I took in her clothes, her hair and even her demeanor once again. She was not the kind of female my mother would have chosen to attend me. She was an unknown with no social standing, no one to foster for political gain.

"Who are you? And why are you disturbing my privacy? If you are not a witch, then what are you? Are you come from 'beyond,' come to escort me to the dragons?" Even in my distressed state, I heard the pleading in my voice.

She let out a big sigh, much as my younger brothers would when questioned about some particularly outrageous exploit of theirs as if it was too complicated to explain.

"Oh man, you really exist. Here you are, beribboned and be-jeweled, truly the quintessential Barbie."

I listened to her speak this nonsense as I tried to invent some context for her presence. Surely her appearance couldn't be ascribed to the coming "event," but why else would she appear at this particular time? I hadn't read of guides come to accompany the princesses into the den of the beasts, but it did make sense that such might be provided—someone to bestow wisdom and reflection on a royal sacrifice. From her looks it seemed unlikely that this girl could provide either of those qualities. Nevertheless, I ventured a cautious guess.

"Are you here because of my...." I couldn't finish that thought. "Because of the dragons?" I managed to whisper.

She nodded as if confirming something. "I heard right, then. Your friend, she did say dragons." She paused.

It was hard to look calm and regal with the tearstains I knew were on my cheeks. Still I held my head high and nodded.

"Okay, this may seem silly, but this is the same day, right? Time hasn't warped here or anything?"

"It's the same," I answered wearily. "You were here a mere six hours ago."

She nodded again as if something was clarified, then stared out at the night sky and back at me as her fingers drummed a restless beat on my coverlet. "You're planning on going through with this, aren't you? Dragons! They're a story, *a myth.* They don't exist." She caught herself and seemed to reconsider, "And even if they do, you can't just deliver yourself like a steak."

I frowned, finding the steak reference too close to my own thoughts. "You obviously don't understand. I am the sacrifice, this century's shield. My going will protect my kingdom for a hundred years."

"Bullshit."

My face flushed with anger.

She knelt, bouncing with agitation. "What are you, all of a hundred and ten pounds? Do you truly believe a dragon will be content for a hundred years on that?"

"Many dragons, and they have been before."

"Okay, many. That's even more silly." She sat back, pushing up the glass things on her face and then chewed at one already ravaged cuticle. "You need to rethink this." She looked up at me, again assessing. "Have you ever seen a dragon?"

I lifted my chin, trying to appear serene and wise. "No. I told you they only come every hundred years or so. I'm sixteen. Even a peasant such as yourself can count and figure the likelihood of that. But others have seen them, and recently."

This was not going the way I had hoped. While I could see her point, it didn't matter if I saw them only for a moment, or not at all. It was still necessary for me to go—and end there.

Her eyes narrowed. "Really. Well, even someone as frippery as you look can't believe that dragons would come here for a mere floofy lace-covered mouthful. And," she looked me up and down, "dressed like something out of a Disney B-grade movie."

While I didn't understand the exact meaning of her words, the sarcasm was crystal clear. I had on a truly lovely nightgown with lavender and silver trim down the sides, a favorite of mine. Small white seed pearls covered the hem and sleeves. I looked again at her scruffy clothes, immodest and cheap, no, worse than cheap—tawdry. She sat there almost naked, in barely a shift and pantaloons, and criticized my clothes?

I hoped the Goddess had not sent her, but if she did, I fervently wished that she would take her back and keep her there, wherever that was, for a long, long time in a small dark cell. I knew I should call in the guard. No one, no one spoke to me like that. Not ever! But unlike my ladies and most everyone in the castle, she spoke honestly of what was coming; and we both knew it was my death. I turned my head so she wouldn't see the single tear overflow onto my cheek.

"Besides, I'm not a peasant; I'm a freshman at Berkeley."

"Please spare me the details of your family's trade." My face reddened as soon as the words leapt from my mouth. My parents had schooled me that the least member of our kingdom was significant, and that we depended on the peasants and the tradesmen.

She raised one eyebrow at my words, though for what reason I couldn't fathom. One side of her lip curled up and then the other. Gradually, I smiled in response. She burst out laughing, not covering her mouth, her head thrown back. It was infectious—common, but infectious—and I, too, laughed. Tears of laughter streamed down my face until they dissolved into real tears.

I sat beside the apparition and wept.

Once I stopped sobbing, I noticed her watching me with a puzzled look as if unsure of how to proceed.

"Okay, let's start again, Genevieve something or another. I remember, princess in some weird country that feeds its women to dragons, one every hundred years." She raised an eyebrow again.

"But we know this doesn't make any sense." She looked at me for confirmation. "Not from an ecological point of view. I mean, given the body mass of that many dragons and, uh, you. Wait, why you? Do you have any enemies? Are there any siblings or other relatives they could have asked for instead? What about other princesses?" I noticed her tapping her sandaled toes against my satin tufted footboard. "Once per century. Is there a special day or year?"

I shook my head. "No one knows when they will come. From what I've heard, it varies considerably. Is that significant?"

"Oh yes. My name is Chris, by the way." She held out her hand. Instinctively, I stretched mine out to meet it. She pumped my hand up and down once and released it.

Chris. Her name was Chris. What an odd name for a girl. Fascinated, I leaned toward her. She suddenly slapped the palm of her hand to her head.

"Ha! Wait. How do the dragons communicate?"

"I don't know that they do."

"Well, how did anyone know that they particularly wanted you?"

"A missive was sent along with a gold coin." I pointed to the token that lay like a viper on a nearby table.

She barely glanced at it before scoffing, "So do dragons have really, really huge pens and pencils? Do they mint coins? Maybe there is some other, more rational explanation—like a human who is doing this?" She looked up with growing skepticism in her eyes.

I was still trying to make sense of the word "pencil" when, with a clank and thunk, a small armored figure struggled up onto my balcony yelling at the top of his lungs. A voice I knew.

The woman named Chris disappeared again. No farewell, no curtsy, no poof of smoke—just gone. I stared at the space where she had been.

On the balcony, there was another crash as the armor-covered form ran into my half-open balcony door.

I walked over to help. He was struggling in armor much too large for him.

"Harold, this isn't kind. Mother told you not to disturb me this evening. You know she did."

"No, I'm a knight. Sir Harold, the bravest, the mighty dragon slayer, the most daring, the—"

A knock sounded at the door and a voice spoke, "Genevieve,

darling? I hate to disturb you, but I thought I heard Harold. Is your brother in there?"

Harold whispered, "It's Mother. Hide me."

Chapter 5

"These rituals are to prepare you for adversity—by walking in the Maze of the Goddess, you will gain understanding and comfort. You are favored, blessed, to have been chosen."

With these words, the priestess, towering over me in her silk vestments and a self-important expression on her lips, marched me to the entrance of the tall shrubs. Her hands pressed me toward the seldom-used metal gate that now swung ajar. Her shaved forehead glistened with perspiration. I forced myself not to recoil, nor allow her to push me forward. I walked with a feigned lack of fear toward the opening. A wind had risen and was rustling the topmost leaves of the tall green bushes that formed the ritual maze. The maze smelled of flowers and cloves. Perhaps this would be less a trial than a reprieve.

The priestess continued prattling, "This is an opportunity, neither an end nor a beginning, but rather think of this as a circle." She grabbed both my hands in hers. "You've always been a rational child. Our people of Verdeux will praise your name. How many people have saved their kingdom?"

Fourteen of them, I thought, as I extricated my hands. I knew all of their names now, and I guessed that she knew not one of them. She continued her speech, caught up in the fiction of her own importance, but I noticed she couldn't meet my eyes for any length of time.

"We, in the church, pray for you. Every night we light candles and burn incense in your honor. Know that your gift, your sacrifice, will be remembered and revered throughout time."

In a moldy book hidden in a back hall, I thought, lowering my eyes so she couldn't guess my thoughts. Through my lashes I saw her eyes flicker over me as if she recalled the annoying detail of my presence. "Whatever I can do to make this time easier for you, the least service, please let me know."

I sighed, just under my breath, but she heard me. She looked away, clearly annoyed that I wasn't as swayed by her rhetoric as she wished.

She was a coward, a manipulator, but fortunately, neither clever nor insightful. I turned my eyes, innocent, green and guileless, on her. "Oh, Mother Morigan, thank you. Your support means so much to me. Might I ask for your presence on the journey to the Fandrite Mountains? It would be such a comfort to have you by my side."

She blanched. "Child, while it would be my heart's wish to lend what support I could on your journey, my responsibility is to those left behind. But be comforted. You'll have someone with you to protect your honor."

I felt a bit giddy. My honor? As if that could be of any importance now. The breeze picked up and I smelled sawdust, copper smelting and, overall, the cloying scent of incense. What new chambers were they building? A monument to me, perhaps?

I launched in with a winsome smile, taking some satisfaction in her discomfort, though I should have felt guilty teasing the poor woman. She would never come and I certainly didn't want her. "I'm sure Father would be happy to ask the church to give you dispensation to travel. He would find someone, obviously not as skilled as you, to fill in the four or five fortnights you would be away."

She stuttered a bit and then forged ahead. "No, no, I couldn't risk your safety by taking a position better served by one of the guards. We must think of your protection; your father knows how dangerous the Fandrite Mountains can be."

I thought not.

Mother Morigan changed the subject. "But here we are at the maze. " She resumed her droning speech. "This walk represents your steadfastness and dedication to the Goddess. She will stay by your side." She breathed deeply in. "I feel her presence. Her perfume envelops and consoles. Fear not that you will be lost and alone; I will be at the end, waiting there in prayer until you complete your time with the Goddess." She gave my hand a limp squeeze. "The true path will *shine* if your heart and mind are true. Breathe in her serenity." She gave me a bit of a push toward the opening. "Remember your way will *shine*."

I took a couple of steps forward and had to head right or walk into a bush. I thought of her last words: the path would shine. She had emphasized this, twice. Was there a reason? She had never been a particularly subtle person. I looked down. The path was three feet wide and covered with a crushed glittery stone. The shrubs on either side were about twenty feet high and very thick. The air felt cool, moist. The shadows made it seem like twilight, as the sun couldn't quite reach down onto the shaded path.

I started forward again and came almost immediately to another decision point. Right, left or forward? To the left the path dulled, as it did straight forward, but the right was aglow with sparkling stones embedded in the path. Ah, that was it. It was not a test of anything but the ability to see the obvious trail markers. I laughed to myself. In the last two weeks, I had wanted time, time to think, to be by myself, and always I was surrounded by people. Even at night, one of my ladies slept by my side.

I hadn't seen that oddly dressed and oddly named girl, Chris, since the evening after I was chosen but I thought often about what she had said. I believed, I wished, she might be right. Could there be a mindful being at the end, someone with whom I could negotiate and turn this to a better outcome? Surely someone must have sent the message. Would it be possible to survive this and have the dragons leave without either my death or the destruction of my land?

I had so little to go on, but now there was the whisper of an alternate outcome, and I grasped it as a child would a treasured toy, a talisman to protect against night terrors. I looked at the path again and walked left, away from the glowing stones. Here, neither my ladies nor my family nor tutor could intercede. I could consider my fate and whether I could change it with no one around. There was nothing anyone could do about it. After all, I walked in the sacred maze. No one could disturb my time with the Goddess. I wandered in the soft light for about an hour, always straying away from the path that led out.

As I rounded yet another corner, Chris stood examining the dark green leaves of the shrub, a card sticking out of her waistband. She looked over as I approached, frowning in that evaluating way of hers.

"Oh wow. There you are. I figured you had to be near. You're always close when I arrive, aren't you?" This time her chemise was black with stars and the moon painted on it. The bold lettering made no sense but spelled out, "I was born at night, but not last night."

I smoothed down my taffeta dress with its delicate lace insert, awaiting her curtsy. It didn't come.

"What is this place?"

I debated not speaking, as she hadn't shown any sign of proper deference, but court manners seemed wasted on her.

"It's a maze, Chris, though not a very difficult one. It belongs to the Goddess. If you follow that trail," I pointed to a way covered with glitter, "you will come to its end."

I waved my hand at the greenery. "It's part of the ritual before my journey. It is said to impart wisdom and strength of mind."

"Goddess?" she asked.

"Yes, the giver of life. The mother of us all."

"Hmm." Chris said, looking around at the high shrubs. "Allowing you to be fed to a dragon doesn't seem very motherly."

She clearly didn't understand. Chris didn't seem to be a spiritual person. It was an awkward moment.

She stood there twirling a lock of her hair. She could be pretty, I surmised, were she properly coiffed and attired. Certainly, her face could be considered attractive, with wide-set gray eyes and pointed chin, though she had been overly out in the sun. And her figure, well, she was comely built. It was hard not to compare her to myself as little was left to one's imagination in that thin chemise. She seemed somewhat taller than I, with a flatter derriere and slightly larger waist than mine. Her bosom was high and full, perhaps a smidgen over-developed. She must be accustomed to hard work, for I could see muscles in her arms and legs, but she had all her teeth. An enigma.

Again, I wondered at her appearance so close to this time of trial and distress. Surely there must be a connection, some reason she had arrived. I prepared to query her but she spoke up again, seemingly starting right where we had left off the last time she appeared.

"So about the alleged dragons, what reasons could there be for someone or something to want a princess? Could there be some weird form of counting coup by an indigenous people here? Is there anything unusual about you, some strange blood type or an odd personality quirk or anything?"

I cringed at the image of blood. Truly, the woman behaved as if she were a hound on the trail of a deer. "Blood type? It's red like everyone else's. Is it different for your people?" I asked.

She puckered her lips. "Oh right. That wasn't identified until mid-1900's. Yours is clearly a pre-enlightenment culture. I can't figure out if I'm falling back in time, or entering some other world entirely. Because in my world, dragons don't exist."

I inhaled deeply as I searched for a common thread between us.

"Perhaps we should start somewhere else. How did you get here? This maze is barred but for those whose path might be—shortened"—I grappled for the right words—"by heroic events."

She slid to the ground, sitting; her feet sprawled out in front of her like a three-year-old, picking at a loose stone on the path with her chipped fingernail. "I'm not totally sure." She removed the card from her waist, holding it up for me to see. "This is the catalyst, at least I think so. My great-grandmother left this for me." She turned the metal card over in her hands. I saw a woman's image embossed into the rectangle, a shiny golden card that reeked of magic, the instrument of witches and seers— carnival fortune tellers.

"It came with a little rhyme. A silly thing actually or…" She looked at me. "Perhaps not so silly." She gave a small, nervous shrug.

I moved closer. "Is it my future you see in your card? Is that it?" Logically, my future looked fairly straightforward. Short, messy, and soon to be over.

"It's not a tarot card. At least not any that I know." She frowned, re-examining the card. "But I think it must represent you in some way."

I looked at the card closely. A narrow interlace border marked its edges, rubbed so by hands over the years, so the design was now barely raised. The center was clear—a girl wearing a crown sat erect on a throne high in the sky, pillowed by clouds. A border of five stylized birds, or maybe they were swords suspended in midair, encircled her. I shuddered. Underneath three couplets were written:

> Across the seas of land and life
> Across the sands of mind and strife;
>
> Beyond the mountains of my fears
> Beyond the valleys, white with tears;
>
> Back and fro between these stand
> The journey to a distant land.

When I could again speak, I asked, "You are not a seer, then?"

She shrugged again. "Like I said, I'm a Berkeley student." She looked around and bit her lip. "In California. You know, America." At my increasingly confused look, she added with a nervous glance around,

"In nineteen-seventy-four." She chewed on a tattered fingernail. In the intervening silence, I tried to think of any principality with the unlikely name of Berkeley.

"What is your king's name?"

"There are no kings in America. We're a democracy."

I looked at her in disbelief, but then I reflected on her clothes, her posture, everything about her. Truly, there was no place in my world where such a woman could exist.

"I'm a freshman, first year. I'm majoring in Anthro and Women's Studies."

We stared at each other for a span. I attempted a translation. "A finishing school for women with deportment and tatting?" It didn't make sense. A peasant like her wouldn't need that.

She frowned. "No, of course not. Berkeley's a university—you must have those. I'm studying the history of women. Their contributions to our world, the cultural manifestations of being the second sex." She looked at me to see if I was following, which I wasn't. "And not just women there; Berkeley is co-ed. My dorm is even co-ed, both men and women." She added this as if clarifying.

Neither of us spoke.

I think each of us was trying to decipher the other. I knew I was. She couldn't have meant what I heard her say. Surely men and women of her age didn't study together.

When next she spoke, it was so low I almost didn't hear.

"How much time is left?"

"Time?"

"Before you leave." She stared directly at me.

I looked down at my lace sleeves, making a conscious effort not to fiddle with them. "Less than a fortnight before I set forth, just under twelve days, and then one month's time to arrive at the place designated by the dragons. I have to be there by my birthday on the sixteenth of October. Time seems to move with increasing speed since this has happened," I admitted in a shaky voice.

"You're truly planning on going, aren't you?" Her voice was incredulous.

"Yes," I answered, proud that my voice didn't quaver.

Chris's voice rose. "This is beyond stupid. It's medieval." She shook her head as if something she said caught her attention. "You don't need to go. There are lots of other options: you can petition your rulers, your religious leaders, your people. Anything but serve yourself up as a before dinner canapé to a dragon."

"This is my kingdom. I have no choice."

She raised her arms over her head and let them fall into her lap. "You always have a choice," she shouted.

I cocked my head at that. It was true in an absolute sense, but for me there was no honorable alternative. I tried to smile but I don't think I expressed it fully. "Yes, and this is mine."

Chapter 6

The week before I was to leave, I sat for my portrait in a gown of royal blue with my hair pulled up into a high tower of braids. Around my neck hung the gold token, lest there be doubt that I was our kingdom's sacrifice. Eight copies of the portrait were destined for other castles' remote galleries.

My mother sat across from me as the painter did his task, her face frozen into a mask of pain. Nothing I could say would ease her. She offered to go in my place, to refuse the dragons, or to hide me in exile. So many solutions that couldn't be. I could not betray my honor and, in her heart, my mother knew that.

Too soon, much too soon, my last day arrived. The clatter of activity swirled about me. Father stared steely-eyed just above the heads of his men, barking instructions to a thick-mustachioed man on a roan horse. My siblings were dressed in their royal best, manners polished and shined for the sending off. Danielle's face, splotched from tears, made her freckles stand out. I, personally, had checked Harold and Bartholomew for hidden creatures—mice, frogs or crickets—before we left the palace. My final undertaking as their elder sister. Harold was still insisting that I call him Sir Harold, the Dragon Slayer. So much so that he begged to dress in armor for my going, but Father spoke to him so harshly that he left off, disappearing in the keep of the castle before I could say goodbye. Bartholomew clung to my side, not truly understanding what was to happen, but knowledgeable in the way small children are of unstated distress.

In the midst of all this chaos, I kept my emotions tightly bound, allowing none of my inner turbulence to cross my countenance. Every piece of me was groomed as if for a coronation. My hair was tightly bound and coiled; my riding dress, a cream velvet with pale green insets in the sleeves. There were no tear streaks on my face. I would not have it said that I left distraught and broken.

Mother refused to come, saying she could not watch me ride off to my death. She had held me tightly before I left her rooms, repeating that she would help me escape. Pleading with me that even now at the eleventh hour, it was not too late.

But it was. The play was written and sealed with the message that had arrived the month before. Though resigned to this journey, I had not spent the last two weeks exclusively in self-pity. Every waking moment was spent planning and analyzing any possible preparation that I could set in action to survive this.

Chris had disappeared once again in the Goddess's maze, when a large calico cat, yowling at the top of her lungs, skittered across our path. The cat was probably just in heat but Chris had blinked out of sight. She hadn't returned, not that I expected her to. Still, she had given me hope. Some of the theories Chris suggested that day sounded plausible. Unlikely perhaps, but plausible. Did I truly know what awaited me at the end? Not really; or at least I was willing to fool myself into that self-deception.

Three of the men loaded the chair I had requested onto a cart. I swore that I would meet my end sitting regally as befitted a princess, not tethered and helpless as I imagined my predecessors. Perhaps, for all my plans, I would find the same fate waiting for me, but bringing a seat of power did give me a sense of control and kept me from throwing myself from the castle walls.

To add to the spectacle, a squealing and unhappy pig was tied behind, though I rued the image it might carry to passersby.

The pig—well, that was based on one of Chris's outlandish theories. While she was gone, perhaps never to return, I found myself clinging to her suggestions as if to a lifeline.

A small hunting knife I also brought, eight inches long, hilt to point, the bone handle cunningly carved. The bard, Trill, handed it to me as he and his musicians departed late one night. He bowed before me, pressing the gift into my hand, saying cryptically, "Despair not, Your Highness. Sometimes it's dark because it's night, and sometimes because your eyes are closed."

Then he left, with a hastily muttered goodbye and a kiss to my hand that lingered a touch long. Another time I might have blushed, but now I could hardly rouse myself to express my thanks for yet another platitude. After he passed, only a faint scent of spice remained.

The last look in his eyes was one of guilt; the same emotion I saw in the eyes of my ladies, my parents and everyone around me. How could they not feel guilt, sending their princess off as a sacrifice? I understood and knew it had to be.

Lastly, I packed the book—the one that spoke of the fourteen princesses—as a talisman, a connection to them, however remote.

Father assembled ten men-at-arms for the journey, four weeks of riding through some of the kingdom's most impenetrable country. Places with names I had only heard spoken in fables and songs: the great river Daine that spilt out across the Lorne Valley, the hills of Perpinan, the fens, the Fandrite Mountains and there, the Crystal Caverns where the dragons waited.

I brushed my hands down my riding habit, feeling the bumps of the green braid under my fingers. An adventure, that's how I must see this, until it was either proved true, or it was no longer possible to hope.

I winced as Lucinda, the scullery maid, lumbered forth. My newest chaperone. For my part, I didn't see that a chaperone was essential for me traveling to my likely end. It seemed unlikely that my continued maidenhood had any value to the goddess or anyone else where I was going, but Mother Morigan insisted.

Lucinda curtsied to my father, an awkward, feeble gesture, lacking any grace. "Your Majesty, the supplies are loaded. All is readied."

I turned my head to the side to spare her my look of discomfort. I'd known birds with a wider vocabulary—and better configured. But, as Father had said to me, she was a tough woman, made of strong peasant stock—someone who could endure a ride to and from the Fandrite Mountains and beyond. I stood up straighter, painfully aware that next to Lucinda, with her massive arms and thick waist, I must appear small and vulnerable.

My father nodded, looking over at me; extended speech was too great a burden for either of us right now. Father pressed a small chess piece into my hand, curling my fingers around it, "Genevieve, if a pawn can fell a king, surely a princess can outmaneuver a mere passel of dragons." A fierce light shone in his eyes. "Don't concede the game."

There was so much to say, but one more word and I would dissolve into tears. I refused to show my people a face splotched and despairing.

I cradled the pawn in my hand. All my memories spilled forth of our evenings playing chess, two strongly focused wills bearing down on the game board. I remembered his patience teaching me to play when I was four and still letting me win when I was seven. My pride was unbounded when I beat him fair and square at ten.

I curtsied low and turned to leave.

Captain Markus led over two horses, a rangy gray gelding with long legs, a ewe-neck and a roached mane, and a sturdy brown with wide hoofs and a broad back, both some mixture of draft and mountain stock. It appeared someone had hastily run a currycomb across the brown's coarse coat, as I could see traces of harness marks across his shoulders.

I stood there for some time before I realized the captain intended those horses for my journey, one for me and one for Lucinda. I felt as if I'd been splashed with cold water. My gaze roamed across the broad backs and stiff bristled manes. I almost laughed bitterly. Not even out of my kingdom and already my status reduced.

I had said my goodbyes to Flight this morning. She was fifteen and a half hands high, burnished copper with a white blaze and four matching white socks. Many mornings I would lean against the fence, watching her trot around the pasture, her dainty feet lifting high over the grass. Astride her I was every inch the pampered and spirited princess.

She obviously wouldn't be bearing me on this journey. "Thank you, Markus. I'm sure they will do wonderfully. Do they have names?" I asked.

He patted the gray. "Winter. He's a good horse, one of the best for covering ground quickly and smoothly, a trifle skittish but solid."

"And the other?" I looked up at the huge placid beast.

He lowered his eyes, unable to meet mine. "Dumpling. Perhaps you might wish to rename him. He's very reliable, tough and sound." *Much like Lucinda,* I thought. "Nothing short of a dragon will cause him to bolt." At my sharp intake of breath, he did look at me. "Your pardon, Your Highness. It's a saying. I meant no harm."

I mounted the gray gelding. Markus helped Lucinda up on Dumpling's wide back. There was no crowd to see me off. Mother refused to allow this to become a public spectacle, excluding everyone but my family.

My carefully prepared speech rattled through my skull as we headed out the gates. *This duty is mine. No one else can do it, and I go willingly, if sadly. I ask that each of you remember me, and remember the others who went before so that our land is safe and fruitful.*

As we trotted through the castle gates, I wondered how many of the other princesses had prepared an equally worthless speech.

Chapter 7

Word travels fast in a small kingdom, and I was hard to miss. My hat with its buttercup rosettes and green ribbon kept the sun off my face, but didn't prevent me from seeing people shy away at our approach or from hearing the whispered conversations. I missed my parasol. It could have afforded me a respite from all the furtive looks.

At midmorning, Captain Markus turned his roan gelding. "At the top of this rise, we will stop." He seemed on the verge of saying more but the clip-clop of hoof beats from behind us arrested his attention.

"Waaaait!"

I knew that voice and could picture the piebald pony that bore it. We stopped. Not long after, my brother Harold caught up to us. He dismounted badly, entangled with some mismatch of chain mail, saddlebags and Father's favorite sword. His pony stood head down, legs apart, his froth-covered sides heaving. Harold trotted up to us, the tip of the sword dragging behind, leaving a snakelike trail in the road. There would be trouble over that sword when Father found out.

"Harold!" I leapt down and gave him a quick hug before scanning the road for his steward. "Where are your guards? What are you doing out this far?"

He dislodged himself from my embrace, bowing until he almost toppled from the ill-fitting armor, which fell to his knees.

"No, remember? I'm Sir Harold now, slayer of dragons, protector of the Princess Genevieve."

He looked up at me, confident of my approval. "Don't worry, I'm here now. I'm your protector. I won't let the dragons take you."

I wouldn't cry, I just wouldn't. Nor could I laugh at such determination and love. I bent down, kissing his forehead.

"I am honored, Sir Harold, that you come to me in my time of need. Your valor is noted and your courage unparalleled. You are my hero, my knight. With your arrival you have vanquished my sorrows and given me a gift beyond price." I put my hand beneath his chin and looked into his eyes. "But now you must do me yet another favor and return, telling Mother and Father that I am well and at peace with my choice. In a few years, you will become a king yourself. You will need practice dispensing wisdom and information."

"Aren't you coming back with me?"

"In spirit, yes, but I can't leave quite yet. There is something I need to do, but I wish you to have this." I pulled one of the yellow silk rosettes from my hat. "This is a token for you, Sir Harold, of my gratitude and admiration. I charge you with returning it safely to Mother's hand with my love. Will you do this for me?"

He nodded and saluted me prettily—much better than could be expected from an eight-year-old.

I reached down, hugging him to me as I whispered, "And next time, your next adventure, leave a note, please, so as not to worry Mother."

He nodded, his eyes serious.

After some short time, oh too short, three of the men escorted the heir back toward the castle. He waved goodbye to me from the saddle behind one of the men, leading a tired little pony.

The rest of the day, I rode in silence.

The men spread along the road in clusters of two and three. There wasn't much to do while riding; each mile looked much like the previous one. It was mid-Fall when we headed out, the fields covered with the stubble of harvested grains. That first day, everything I looked at reminded me of my fate. At one stop, I watched the death struggle between a praying mantis and a green and yellow beetle. The mantis ended the exchange by stuffing the unfortunate beetle into his mouth and biting down. I looked away.

I was losing my family, my life and my future. I lived inside my head arguing over this choice. I ignored the men. Lucinda was a silent drudge who shadowed my steps.

Occasionally I noticed our journey. Initially, the road was well traveled; merchants going to town, craftsmen and women driving carts laden with goods, peasants heading to market with eggs and vegetables. Farmers looked up from their reaping and stared.

I stood out. Ten rough men—no, eight only, with the rest accompanying Harold—a cart laden with my chair, one large chaperone on an even larger horse, a very unhappy pig, and me.

Lucinda's silence was an unexpected break from the prattle of my ladies. She saw to my needs, provided a buffer from the men, and was generally helpful. I hoped that she wasn't aware I hadn't wanted her to come.

Winter proved to be a good choice as a mount. His trot was smooth and his manner willing. I watched him carefully, but he showed no sign of shying.

As we rode, I took to listing their names—the lost princesses—in the order of their disappearance: Teresa, Anisette, Ophelia, Isabelle, Nicolette, Chantal, Alexandra, Penelope,

Sophia, Elsbeth, Rosalind, Willa, Lynette, Victoria, much like a children's rhyming game. There was some comfort in doing this, though I could not bring myself to add my name to the end.

The first night we stopped at an inn, "The Horned Owl." The sparse room with a roughly woven woolen blanket laid across the narrow bed reinforced the end of all that I knew.

In the cramped room, Lucinda's sleeping bulk blocked my door. No one spoke to me. None met my eyes. I could already be gone. It no longer mattered that my silk riding gown was the envy of six townships, that my skin had been compared to the color of fresh cream or my hair always remained perfectly coiffed after a long day's ride. Nothing mattered. I was as good as dead.

The men who escorted me were a mixed lot. The Captain was old, almost fifty, his skin hardened from years of riding beneath the sun. There was a ribbed scar on his right hand that started at his knuckle and disappeared up his sleeve. His lips were drawn in a tight line. I never saw him smile.

Aside from Captain Markus, I recognized only three of the other royal guardsmen accompanying me. George had been a sentry for my father for years. He had a cheery nature, gray-brown hair that never stayed in place without a liberal application of hair oil, and rounded cheeks burnished brown from the sun. He whistled as he rode.

Samuel and Michael I also knew. Samuel sported a tidy ocher-colored beard of which he seemed particularly fond, stroking it absently as we rode. He was bald and lean, wiry really, all muscle and nothing extra; two black slashes of eyebrows ran across his face, and what little remained of his hair was in a thin braided queue at his neck. Michael had the shoulders of an ox and the bandy legs of a goat, but a kinder man I had never met. All three were old enough to be my father.

The others were unknown to me, younger men from among my father's soldiers. Perhaps I had seen them from afar and passed them by without a glance. My mind had been focused elsewhere: on politics, on court relationships and on my place in them.

"May I take your horse, My Lady?"

I jumped. What a picture I must make staring off in the distance. So wrapped in my head, I hadn't noticed one of the men standing at Winter's side. I wondered how long he had been there waiting.

I forced myself to focus.

"Yes, thank you," I said. It was George. He was the one who placed my chair out for me each evening, unloading it from the cart and placing it alongside the fire. An unacknowledged kindness. My chair, with its carved arms and scrolled back, the extra burden carried to pamper me, for my comfort.

I dismounted and handed him the reins. He started to lead Winter away.

"Wait." It shocked me that I had become so lax. There was never an excuse for ignoring your retainers.

He turned to me, a question in his eyes. "George. Thank you," I repeated, but this time I meant it. "Thank you for coming. It means much to me to see a familiar face on this journey."

He stammered something about his duty and walked away with Winter.

A few feet over, Lucinda hovered, her arms crossed. Watching as if there could be some indiscretion between us, as if my purity mattered to anyone now.

It was silly. None of these men appealed to me. They were too old, too coarse or too uneducated. Nothing like Theo, the young prince of Gowen, with his tawny good looks, or the Duke of Armon, or even the bard Trill, whose eyes seemed to focus on me when he sang.

Not that any of my father's men seemed particularly interested in me either. I was a task, an assignment to complete, none of their business. But, still, Lucinda watched.

There was no one to talk to, not really. Nothing to do except ride on the dusty road that led to the Fandrite Mountains.

But each night I fell asleep reciting the names of the chosen princesses like a prayer:

Teresa, Anisette, Ophelia, Isabelle,
Nicolette, Chantal, Alexandra, Penelope,
Sophia, Elsbeth,
Rosalind, Willa,
Lynette, Victoria.

And some nights, when the stars disappeared behind the clouds, I whispered my name too.

Chapter 8

A week dragged by, and after many less than stellar accommodations in local country inns, we arrived at Castle Ilmington at the edge of the wilderness; beyond stretched the Lorne Valley, where only a few isolated villages dotted the plain. After safely delivering Harold to my parents, who must have been frantic, my three men had returned. We were again the happy party, I thought, and rolled my eyes.

The evening we arrived, people lined the roads to view me, the doomed princess, portrait perfect— my spine straight, my head high. We—my escort, I and of course, the pig—were the talk of the town. No doubt, the royals across nine kingdoms were breathing a sigh of relief that their daughters were spared. I was certain my mother remained unmoved from where I last saw her in her tower room, staring at the door where I exited, willing me to stay.

Ilmington was not a pretty castle, rather too stiff and squat for elegance, but well fortified against wolves and marauders. It was set on the south shore of Lake Nessen, crouched like a large toad on the top of a promontory, dull gray stones forming the wall with rounded turrets adorning each corner like warts. Once we were near enough to be seen by the sentries, we heard horns trumpeting our arrival. We crossed the drawbridge, dismounted, and walked the horses through the low opening.

Here we were welcomed and given proper lodging. My men were promised a tankard of ale and taken to the soldiers' barracks. They deserved it. I was put up in royal quarters, a well-appointed sleeping room with a thickly ticked mattress and cerise brocaded curtains hanging from the canopied bed. My clothes were unpacked, brushed and aired, my hair washed and rinsed with rosemary and lavender. The bath that night was glorious, deep enough to sink my shoulders into, and hot. Really, really hot. I slept soundly for once, awakening to the smell of hot chocolate and warm flaky pastries set on a tray near my bed. But for the trivial fact that there were dragons on my horizon, life felt almost normal. I did find myself missing George's cheery whistle and Michael's booming laugh, but these were fleeting thoughts.

Our hosts had arranged a dance for the next evening with visiting nobles attending. I was more than ready for the distractions of music and dancing. I knew there would be covert glances and whispers behind fans, but for this last chance for pleasure and gaiety, I would sweep them away as if they were dust motes. This was my final opportunity for polite company and gaiety before entering into the wilderness.

Chapter 9

Frederick pressed a kiss to my hand. He was a pretty man, a viscount only, but charming and amiable. We'd been introduced before at my parent's court. He was part of the throng of the young demi-nobles that circled social events. I had always found him pleasant, full of life and daring. He had a ready smile, dimples and molten brown eyes. I looked up at him as a lock of golden hair fell over his brow. How could I not allow myself to be entranced? It was for but an evening. He asked me to dance, and again and then again. The rules that I had adhered to all my life no longer bound me. How could it matter if I danced with the same man twice in a row and flirted with abandon?

Lucinda, dressed in an ill-fitted mustard yellow dress, frowned as I whirled by. Flounces didn't suit my chaperone. She seemed determined to hold to the conventions from my previous life, ones that I no longer saw as relevant. A young page, after a knowing look at Frederick, bumped against her, spilling punch across the shoulder of her dress. Lucinda ineffectually wiped at the dark splotch as it spread down her chest. Frederick smiled and gave me a wink as two serving maids whisked her away amidst a flurry of fussing.

That dance ended too soon for me. As the music started up again, Frederick tucked my arm under his and pointed out at the balcony. "See that? I had the moon delivered 'specially for you. Come, let us enjoy the evening."

My last chance at life, at love and romance, at being a girl with someone to flirt with—I nodded. As the dancers spun around, we stepped into the shadows. No one noticed us standing at the edge of the dance floor; we ducked outside.

The cool air felt refreshing after the heat from the ballroom; I smelled jasmine and lilacs mixed in a heady night perfume. Paved stone turned into grass as we wandered beyond the towering yews that enclosed the gardens.

"You are beautiful. Of course, you know that. Your mirror must have reflected that to you all your life." He smiled at me. "Songs have been written about your hair, your green eyes—your neck." He lightly touched the nape of my neck. "Even now ballads are being written for you." He lifted my hand to his mouth and nibbled gently at the tips of my fingers. "Have you heard the latest song written about you? It's being sung in taverns and castles. Some traveling bard created it, but everyone is singing it, 'The Lost Lady with the Sea-Green Eyes.'"

He kissed the inside of my wrist. "Would that I could compose something for you, an ode to your beauty or a thesis to your intelligence. What should it be?" He smiled, pulling slowly at one of my curls that had escaped my net. "If I could but be the golden net holding your scarlet-fire hair. Oh, to provide a service to you, even the most simple as this."

I blinked. Not that again. "It's auburn."

"What?"

"My hair—it isn't scarlet or crimson or copper, it's auburn." I know this is a small point, but I disliked the tired exaggerations about my hair color. Never anything new.

He held the lock up to the moonlight, running fingers across it. "Ah yes, so it is."

I was lulled once again, lapping up the attention like a kitten.

He leaned over and kissed the corner of my mouth. I breathed a sigh of pure pleasure. His arms encircled me and I could hear music. Well, yes, it was from the ballroom, but it seemed they were playing just for the two of us.

He wrapped one arm around me, murmuring into my ear, and kissed my lips.

I hesitated, twisting my head aside. "I think we should go back in."

"Just a few minutes more. You take my breath away. You are my princess, and I naught but your devoted slave."

I shook my head, but he obviously didn't notice. Another minute, I thought, and we'd return. I felt warm and dreamy and loved.

His mouth mashed against mine.

By the end of five increasingly vigorous and imperfect kisses, the music stopped for me. I was disenchanted and tried to pull back.

I should not have left the party. This had gone too far.

I could hear his breathing in my ear. "Tomorrow morning we will marry. Your honor will be uncompromised."

What was he talking about? The music was back, but now the

discordant clanging of bells replaced the harps and violins. "No. I'm flattered, of course, but that is not possible." I tried to squirm away. "We need to return now; people will be looking for us." I couldn't marry him. I couldn't marry anyone, and he was but a viscount.

I had to get back to the party before someone noticed, before there was talk. This couldn't go any further.

Frederick pulled me tighter. "Be patient, my sweet. It will take but a few moments and then all will be better. It's said that the dragons never take a deflowered princess." I felt three buttons on my bodice pop open, his tongue roughly enter my mouth.

"What!" I endeavored to push him away, but he didn't seem eager to leave. I struggled anew. My temper rose; the music replaced by the deep boom of war drums.

"Shhh, just relax," he insisted, his hand grabbing for my breast. "Trust me. Even if you get with child, it won't matter. Will it?"

Four more buttons went the way of the first ones. This was not noble behavior, not what I expected from a peer.

"Release me now!" We both tumbled down on the grass. I could have sworn he tripped me.

He seemed to have sprouted multiple arms and legs. I shoved him harder, but he didn't seem to notice. Frederick initiated a full-fledged assault on my person, holding me down. I fought back with elbows, hands and nails. Both of us abandoned the mannerly behavior of courts. This was no longer the behavior of an overzealous seduction, but an attack.

"Stop it! How dare you, you, you poxy brigand. Stop!" I commanded. My full skirts were tangled and I could feel the chill night air on my legs. He outweighed me by four stone and he wasn't listening.

I bit him. He reared back for a split second, saying something quite unbecoming.

"Ahem."

Two large men lifted Frederick bodily off me.

"I believe the princess said she wants to go inside now. Isn't that right, George?"

"Aye, that's what she said."

"You're looking somewhat mussed," Michael added as he shook Frederick hard enough to rattle his teeth and shoved him toward George.

"Here, let me dust you off before you return to the castle." George held Frederick's arms and Michael doubled him over with a punch to his stomach.

"Much better, don't you think?"

I stood, holding my bodice together, shaken, bruised, a smidgen wiser and very, very angry.

George's eyes glittered with rage, but his voice oozed concern for Frederick as he spoke to him. "Yes, you should go inside now. You're looking a little under the weather. If I were you, I might get out of the night air. It isn't good for you."

"I'll have you hanged," Frederick sputtered, gasping for breath as he tried to straighten up.

I don't believe he could see the fire in my sea-green eyes, but he should have thought this through. "I wouldn't if I were you. You've accosted a princess."

Anger warred with sense. I wanted him punished, publicly humiliated, but not at the cost of my name, my honor. I didn't wish rumors of this spoken behind furled fans, people laughing at my inexperience and naïveté. My family having to deal not only with my death, but also my dishonor.

Honor won. I gritted my teeth.

"Let us agree that you won't be drawn and quartered, and they won't be charged with mussing your person." I watched his face, defiance and pride competing with the beginnings of trepidation. "And, to ensure your continued health, make very, very sure that no word of this is ever mentioned. Not even whispered." I willed myself to stand there, to speak clearly and carefully though I shook with fury and shock.

"So that you comprehend this lesson, I will send off a message to my father tonight for my men's safety and the safety of any other females you might feel the need to write an ode to."

Frederick snapped, "Well, you're going to die a virgin. I hope that is some cold comfort to you."

I stood stock-still and then turned to my men. "Please escort Frederick to his lodgings." I turned my back for a second and then reconsidered. "And, if you would, make sure, make very sure, that Frederick is completely 'dusted off' before he enters his room. I wouldn't want this lesson to be wasted."

I retreated to my rooms, quickly throwing a shawl across my gown to disguise the damage done and to cover my missing buttons. I would not have my last days marred by this incident. I took out the chess piece that my father had gifted me and tossed it in my drawstring purse for courage. I tucked my hair back into my net, smoothed the creases from my green gown and put on my best smile. Once again I joined the party. I was charming, or so I hoped. I chatted with my hosts, interacted with the matrons and flirted with three or four men ranging from age from thirteen to sixty-three. I was bright, clever, and did everything but wag my tail like a hunting dog retrieving a grouse.

But beneath it all I shivered. My name and position no longer shielded me. A man had thought to take advantage of my situation. And I had bitten someone, protected myself with nails and teeth. This was not like sparring with the weapons master. I was flooded with emotion: embarrassment, shame, and yet, strength. It was distasteful that I was reduced to such, but I now knew that I would defend myself if attacked, and not just with words.

And through it all, as the music played, I smiled and charmed.

Mother would have given me her nod of approval. Frederick was not to be seen; I hoped he had taken his lesson to heart.

I had learned mine.

Lucinda watched my performance from the sidelines with no expression on her face. Later that night, as she helped me dress for bed, she still said nothing, though the bruises on my body were obvious in the candlelight. She held my arm out, examining the dark spots, before rubbing it with an herbal mixture that smelled of camphor and mint.

I slept, dreaming of dragons who rode the wind, nobles who sprouted fangs and a woman who wore writing on her chemise.

Chapter 10

We left early the next morning, well before I was prepared to be awake.

I quietly informed Captain Markus of George and Michael's gallant behavior, though the details didn't bear recounting. As Mother was wont to say, self-pity is so plebian.

Riding along the dusty road, I reviewed the previous night: thinking about my folly with Frederick; how he had taken advantage of my situation, not for love, or even lust, but for power. None of my peers had looked for me, nor come to my aid. My rescuers had been my father's men, George and Michael. It came to me that I hadn't expressed my appreciation to them, taking their rescue as my due. An uncomfortable thought crossed my mind; what must they think of me, not only naïve and reckless but ungrateful also.

An opportunity for reparation came at our midmorning stop. George held Winter's reins as I dismounted. Nearby, Michael checked his mount's feet for stones, both of them acting as if nothing had happened the night before. Lucinda busied herself with Dumpling's saddlebags, pretending not to hover.

When I didn't leave, George raised his eyes to mine, questioning. I reached over, patting Winter's mane to cover my embarrassment. "I never said thank you."

George exchanged a glance with Michael before speaking. "Nothing to speak of, My Lady. We protect our own. We could see he was up to no good."

"But you didn't have to. You should have been off enjoying a pint of ale."

George nodded. "We have daughters too. He's not worth the backside of a bullock's bastard." He flashed a discomforted look at me. "Begging your pardon, My Lady."

Impulsively, I grabbed his hand. "George, you do not need to beg my pardon. If anything, I need to beg yours. It was my inattention that put me in that situation."

His ears reddened. "No, My Lady, 'tis nothing to mention. At your age I got into foolish scrapes way worse." His whole face and neck turned a dull red. "Not that I'm thinking we're alike in any way, or that you were foolish," he stammered.

I fixed him with a look. "No, you're right. I made a foolish choice."

George protested, "It was something anyone might have done, My Lady."

Anyone who hadn't been raised as had I, perhaps.

"I'm no longer who I was. Please, you don't need to be so formal."

Michael looked at me from beneath his shaggy eyebrows. "You're our princess—for the duration of this journey and beyond."

Something snapped inside me. This journey also affected these men. Men whom I had all but ignored.

I stood tall, comprehending. Yes, I was going to my death, but they would take the guilt back with them, living with it day after day, year upon year.

"And you need to know that while I am your princess, you are my men. Not my father's—mine."

At their glance toward the captain, I clarified. "Oh, not to command. But in my heart. All of you are held there. For this journey and beyond." I placed a single kiss on each of their cheeks.

Captain Marcus called for us to mount up, jerking the three of us back to the open road.

George hovered near me for the rest of the day. He whistled merry tunes, winking at me in comradeship each time he trotted by on his horse. After our exchange, I exerted myself, engaging the men in simple pleasantries, embarrassed by my recent discourteousness. Small changes, a polite hello and thank you; simple recognition of the men who were part of this endeavor. I pushed myself to stop acting listless and aloof and instead to see, really see, the others in this group. I made it my task to enquire after my men by name, to ask their opinion, to ask for their thoughts. In the days after leaving the Castle Ilmington, I saw them looking at me differently, as if seeing me not as a duty but as someone worthy of conversation.

At one stop, a small posy of wildflowers appeared upon my saddle. Michael and Jeremy stood nonchalantly nearby, bright yellow pollen dusting their shirtfronts. As the days passed, a dozen kindnesses lifted my spirits. One afternoon, slices of dried apple mysteriously appeared on my folded cloak, and that night five of the men entertained me with an impromptu mummer's play. The following evening, a chessboard was unrolled, like a tiny carpet, as it had on many nights, but this time *I* was challenged to play the winner. Even though I worked hard not to beat Ethan too badly, they tormented him all the rest of the evening.

"Losing to a slip of a girl," Jeremy snickered, but now, I was one of them. These men, commoners all, extended themselves, sharing their private stashes of supplies with me, for no recompense. They knew my destiny but shed no false tears and spoke no soothing words to feed my sorrow. These men weren't looking for an opportunity to further their own status through me. There was no favor to curry in seeing me to this end. And still they gave of themselves, and I felt honored—and loved.

With a single unpleasant incident, many of my assumptions had collapsed. It became clear to me that not all nobles were, well, noble, and that some of the common people were—noble, that is.

Halfway into the week, George trotted up alongside me. Lucinda watched him with a warning set to her eyes. He whistled as if nothing were on his mind. "Your Highness," he finally said.

I nodded, waiting for him to continue.

"Just thought you ought to know, all men aren't like that. That's all." He tipped his hat and cantered off. As I watched him lope away, some of the strain of the week peeled away.

I had never spent much time in the company of men, never noticed how truly different they were. As I emerged from my initial fog of despair, I started to observe them. Their hearty camaraderie was not much different from Harold and Bartholomew's, a pleasant change from my dithering ladies-in-waiting. I loved to hear them guffaw, snort and chortle, none of the polite tittering behind an open fan. Once they relaxed around me, my language expanded in interesting ways.

I found observing their antics habit-forming. Watching them became my entertainment, my distraction. George stayed sunny and optimistic. Michael, Jonathan and Sam argued constantly about the best way to hunt boar, whether with hounds or beaters or both. Each endeavored to get me to side with them in the debate. Ever serious Ethan with his high forehead and narrow nose confided to me his worries about his young daughters.

Lawrence, Jeremy, Charles and Douglas were forever playing

pranks and teasing each other. I was hard pressed not to laugh when Charles tied one of my pink satin bows on the tail of Captain Markus's horse. Oh yes, I had given him the bow.

What sympathy, guilt or anger the men felt at my situation, they hid it well, showing me their caring with smiles and kindness.

It was hard to stay frightened all the time.

The dragons were waiting, I knew, and I wondered what, if anything, the beasts thought. My thoughts veered to them more and more often, not out of self-pity but from true curiosity about those huge creatures. I knew next to nothing about them. I didn't know where they came from or how long they stayed. Ever since Frederick's ending remark that I would "die a virgin," I wondered about the dragons and myself.

Did dragons prefer virgins? It did bring up questions. There was the book hidden away in my saddle bags. I wondered if those ancient pages answered any of these questions. Part of me wanted to know and part wished to remain ignorant.

During the days when the sun was up and the morning was soft with dew, I could escape and pretend I was on a lovely jaunt into the woods.

Mostly, I watched the sky, patted my horse, sang little songs in my head, and observed the exchanges between the men. Each evening around the camp's fire, the whines of the cicadas harmonized with the snorting, spitting and snoring of the men. Their risqué jokes had me laughing aloud as we sat eating our evening meal. Lucinda glared at them but they were unrepentant.

I told no one of my nights when all my terrors surrounded me. Sleep would come and with it dreams of sharp, tearing teeth and claws. I would awake sweating and trembling, my breath coming fast and hard as if I had been running. I would cradle the pawn my father had given me; smooth out my official signed documents; and try to envision a different end game. But the dreams kept coming and I would greet daybreak with the joy of one for whom a pardon is received moments before the executioner raises his axe.

I was lost in thought when Captain Markus called a halt to rest the horses. The afternoon sun was scurrying westward. A beautiful meadow, strewn with orange and purple wild flowers, stretched out before us.

I dismounted and handed Winter's reins to Jeremy. Lucinda

clambered off her horse, landing heavily with a nasty twist to her ankle. She shrugged aside Malcolm and Douglas' offers of help and went on about her duties, cooking supper, laying out my supplies while the men set up camp. I sat stitching my embroidery as Lucinda limped by.

At our evening meal, she hobbled over with my meal: some unfortunate rabbit one of the men had shot, together with a lovely fresh trout. Not royal fare, but truly wonderful after a full day in the saddle.

I put my plate down, observing my entourage. How could I have overlooked this? They were also tired and hungry. I noticed Malcolm, bedding down Winter and Dumpling, and Michael's weary yawn as he went about setting up my tent.

Lucinda hobbled back with the tea kettle. "Sit down," I said. "You need to rest."

She shrugged, pushing a mug of tea into my hand and made her way back to the fire. I got up and followed her. Enough. No longer would I sit as if behind canopied stands. This, for now, was my life.

"You'll do me no good if you don't take care of yourself." I practically dragged Lucinda to the side of the fire and sat her on a log, propping her leg up. "Sit here and rest. Tomorrow, well, we'll see," I said. She shook her head impatiently and started to get up again.

I placed my hand on her shoulder. "No, truly, I wish you to rest. This is only the beginning of the wilderness. You must heal so that when I need you—and I will—I can count on your strength." She relented then, her face ash-white with pain.

I poured her a cup of tea from the kettle, burning my finger in the process.

By the next morning, Lucinda's ankle had swollen up like a gourd. Captain Markus examined it, declaring it a bad sprain but nothing more. I rose early, restless, and yet more awake then I had ever been. I stirred the fire and put on a kettle of water as I had seen the men do. Lucinda limped over, using a stick to balance. I firmly pointed back to the log and shook my head.

No longer was I the fragile princess who required everyone to wait on her. She was gone and would never return.

Winter whickered as I brought his morning bran. He plunged his head deep in the bucket once I placed it down. Dumpling stamped his feathered hooves and nudged me with his huge head, encouraging me to hurry with his food.

It was a good thing that Dumpling was steady. He snorted once as the air before him spun when Chris materialized almost under his nose. I stood still, holding Dumpling's feed, not sure what to say or do, though the relief and distress on my face must have shown. She rushed to my side, wearing a sleeveless chemise that declared, "Women who seek to be equal with men lack ambition." A shawl of some kind wrapped around her arms. Her legs were bare from knee to thigh with a short strip of clothing above that one couldn't call a skirt, and boots that laced up the front to her knees.

She looked at my face. "I'm sorry, I'm sorry. I was so caught up with exams and papers, then I couldn't find the card and…."

I couldn't stop a tear from trickling down. Here was the only person who had given me reason to hope.

From the corner of my eyes, I saw my men gather about us but my attention remained with Chris.

Her voice lowered to a whisper, a plea. "I couldn't accept that you were real. I'm so sorry." She grabbed my hand and I let her, her hand so tight on mine she almost snapped in half the golden card she cradled within her fingers. It seemed silly to stand on formality under the circumstances.

"Step away, Your Highness." The captain's voice interrupted our reunion. I could see him evaluating her, an unknown, dangerous element compounding the complexity of his task. He glared at her and flicked his fingers to ward off evil. "Begone, witch."

Chris held on to my hand. My fingers ached from the strength of her grip. I waved the men back. "A friend, not a witch." I smiled, pleased with that sudden awareness. I did have a friend. I looked at the men around me; perhaps more than one.

The captain's hand now on his sword, he moved closer, no more than a foot away. George and Samuel were a half step behind him with grins on their faces as they watched the stand-off. Ethan, Laurence and the younger men looked at Chris with a mixture of embarrassment, terror and interest.

"Captain," I repeated. "She's a friend from the land of Berkeley, but nonetheless a friend. She is not a witch. Not a danger to me or to you." He fondled his sword handle, his fingers easing it out of the scabbard. "Captain," I insisted yet again. I moved in front of Chris, still holding her hand. "In this you will heed me."

Captain Markus finally nodded, not convinced, but unwilling to gainsay me. He moved his hand off the sword. "Well, whatever she is, witch, demon or friend, if she is a comfort to you she can come. But get some clothes on her before we have a riot."

"Perhaps 'uprising' would be the better word," Jeremy muttered and the other men chuckled.

Chris grinned, blowing a kiss to the men before dismissing the captain with an under-her-breath "fascist pig." I was too relieved and distracted to decipher yet another of her odd expressions, but it didn't sound complimentary. As he left, she turned to me. "Who died and made him God?"

I attempted an explanation. "Markus is an honorable and capable warrior; a fine commander, but he has been a soldier all his life. He's neither accustomed to women or to magic. It can't be easy for him."

"That is such a cop-out." She frowned, following him with her eyes. "But speaking of pigs," Chris looked about her, "you did at least bring one, didn't you?" she asked. "I don't see any here."

I sighed. "Yes, she's tethered over behind the horses. I don't think this will work. No one, not even a particularly dim-sighted dragon would mistake a twenty-five stone pig in a ball gown for me. Besides, every time we try to put a hat on her, she tears it to ribbons."

Chapter 11

Chris gritted her teeth as she struggled onto the saddle. Captain Markus had rearranged the supplies, mounting her on a tall cow-hocked gelding with the unlikely name of Glory. An uglier riding horse I hadn't seen, with masses of coarse brown mane, a thick shaggy coat and an unfortunate braying whinny. Chris immediately renamed him Janis after a heroine of hers. Dressed in one of my riding skirts and a large inelegant jacket of Lucinda's, Chris wasn't likely to set fashion. And no matter what I did, her straight hair escaped my third best snood.

Much to Chris's annoyance, Jonathan and Malcolm told everyone who would listen about her attempts to mount from the wrong side. Jonathan argued that the horse couldn't tell the difference between Chris and the supplies the pack horse had recently carried, but Malcolm insisted that he had seen sacks of meal that rode with more grace. Fortunately, Glory, or Janis Joplin as Chris persisted in calling him, appeared indifferent to his new burden, placidly following nose to withers with my horse, Winter. We kept to a fast walk most of the next morning. My men took bets on how soon Chris would fall.

We rode through a forest of oak and ash that spilled out to a stand of willows clustered by the side of a stream. Every few miles the landscape opened, and the hills of Perpinan appeared, and beyond, wrapped in a cloak of mists, the Crystal mountain of Fandrite. A frisson of fear crept down my back as we neared my destiny, and I was glad that Chris rode beside me.

Chris kept her eyes pinned to Janis's neck, her fingers entwined in his mane as if that might help her stay on. Where could she have been raised that she rode so badly, worse than any peasant? I had so many questions about her and few answers.

My gaze flitted over her, trying to fit the puzzle piece that was Chris into my circumstances. Something that could explain Chris to me, to understand her better. I ventured a guess. "Is your card a family heirloom? Something handed down from a seer ancestor?"

She gingerly extracted one hand from Janis's mane and reached inside the folds of Lucinda's jacket. "It was a gift from Nana, my great-grandmother. She was known as a bit of a firecracker but never a seer." She held the card out for me to reexamine. I had seen it once before: the girl sitting on the throne supported as if by clouds. Across the top, an interlocking design framed the illustration. I frowned; something niggled in my brain.

"Nana died during the holidays. The card was left for me. Part of my inheritance: money for college, the small enamel box that contained this card and the poem written in her curly script."

We both looked at it again.

"When I was little, she kept it near her, though she would never let me touch it. She would sometimes look at it and I thought she might cry—longing and pain or whatever. I never understood."

I tried to concentrate on her speech. It was difficult to parse out and there were concepts that I didn't understand. I tried to shape her words into something I could comprehend but I found my mind wandering. Something about the design on the card distracted me; it seemed familiar.

She shook her head, tucking the card back into the jacket. "That day, the first time I saw you, I had cupped the card in my hand. And I felt pulled, drawn in. The words on the note whispered themselves to me and I heard myself repeating them like a mantra—the next thing I knew, I was there in your room." She waved her hand at the landscape.

Janis lifted his head and jogged for a few steps. Chris grabbed back onto his mane. "Each time I hold the card and say the words, I'm here with you. Wherever you are." She looked around, with some peculiar expression of contemplation and study. "She meant for me to be here. I'm positive of that. But I am not sure what I am supposed to do!"

She shrugged off her train of thought.

"So what's our plan?"

I rearranged my riding skirts. "There is no plan, we arrive in a fortnight."

A little sound of air escaped her mouth. "You can't be serious."

I patted Winter's neck before I spoke. "I must go. You're a comfort to me and I value your thoughts, but there's no way out of this. You must know that."

"Well, actually, no, I don't know that." She relinquished Janis's mane and waved her hands. "Look at what you're doing. Don't you have any sense at all? Can't you see what your people are doing to you? They're sending you to your death." By this time she was so upset she was sputtering. "Your own father sent you to die."

I held my composure against this onslaught, trying to make her understand. To put it right. "No, it isn't like that. Those are my people, my responsibility. Father is king. It is his burden. We both know our duty. There is no honor in causing our towns to be burned to the ground, thousands killed. That's what would happen if I'd stayed. Someone had to go, and I was the one chosen. One life, one princess of royal blood—one instead of thousands."

I thought back to a conversation with my father two weeks before I left. "Genevieve, I never thought I would rue my kingship. Here I stand bound, wishing that I were but a farmer, with no obligation, no duty to my kingdom." He had reached out, placing his hand on my shoulder and spoke, misery heavy in his voice. "We're two of a kind, both of us confined by duty and honor. I wish it were different."

Tears had brimmed in my eyes, threatening to fall if I moved. He pulled me close, rocking me gently. The tears did spill then. We both knew the cost to our land, our people. I shivered, thinking of the devastation that dragons would wreak on our land.

He had moved away, pacing back and forth. "As a king, you steel yourself to the loss of your children—your sons, perhaps to war, and your daughters to distant marriage, but this…

"We don't really know what happens at the Crystal Cave. Perhaps there is some hope. Perhaps—no, no, I'm fooling myself." He sank into a chair, his head buried in his hands.

I had remained silent, grieving for him and for me. When next he spoke, looking up, it was with such despair that I could hardly bear it.

"Your mother is taking this hard. Her own great-aunt, Victoria, was one of the chosen. Your mother sits for hours in front of the gallery of chosen princesses, looking at her great-aunt's portrait, looking at the portrait of you now also gracing the wall." He held out his hand. "I will abide with you as long as I am able." I folded myself up on the floor next to him, resting against his knee, and we sat silently there for the better part of the night.

Chris stared at me in dismay, probably wondering at my sudden silence. I realized there was no way of instructing Chris, who hailed from a land bereft of kings, of the obligations of royalty to their people. I turned my head away so I didn't have to address her lack of understanding. We rode awhile in uncomfortable silence.

"Might I ask why you disappeared so abruptly in the Goddess's maze?" I asked after some time.

"Oh, um. I was startled before. I think I have a handle on that now. My karate instructor says that self-awareness is the beginning of discipline. That even the most fearless person can flinch." She looked at me. "You know, that second before you leap into action when your focus wavers?"

"No." I shook my head, utterly confused by her comments.

Chris shrugged, "Oh, well, it can happen."

A screech came from above and we both looked: a falcon kiting, beating its wings to stay in a single place. The falcon dove, rising with some small luckless mammal in its grasp. Lately, I watched predators and prey with a new fascination. I had never before felt myself to be in the prey category. But now that my status had moved from princess to entree, I had a new empathy for them. Chris poked her foot at me.

"Look, we don't have much time. We have to talk."

I listened for over an hour as she explained the dynamics of scapegoats throughout the history of her land. It didn't make much sense to me, but then not much about Chris did.

The terrain closed in once we passed the Daine River. Trees loomed, forming dense woods, and little rivulets crossed and re-crossed our way.

We rode side by side, weaving various theories of dragons and schemes into a patchwork of solutions. Not that any would work, but it was comforting to pretend, to indulge Chris's faith. She was still displeased with my decision and she railed against my continuing on this journey.

"My professor of Women's Studies says this kind of thing happened all the time. It's cultural, men sending women off to their deaths. In Hawaii, women were dropped into the mouth of the volcano to appease the Goddess Pele; in India, they were placed on their husbands' funeral pyres and burned; the Inuit deposited their unwanted women on icebergs when they tired of them. Your people ship them off to dragons."

Chris swatted at a biting fly on her horse's withers and Janis jogged a step or two in response. Chris was so focused on her diatribe that she forgot to clutch at Janis's mane as she continued talking. "You need to stop this madness. Take a stand! I still say we dress the pig up in your clothes and tether it. The dragons may be very happy with pork, happier even. It isn't like they are kosher or anything."

I frowned at her odd language but refused to respond. We'd been over this four times just that day.

"Even if they notice, maybe they'll think of it as an hors d'oeuvre. We could slather the pig with rat poison. Arsenic? I know, dragon's bane! Do you have any of that? I bet that would mess with a dragon's digestion."

I had heard this before also. In fact, I was becoming quite an expert at the tribal practices of her land and on her various proposals of how to kill dragons.

I answered her again as I had these past days. "It is my duty." I watched her mouth curl into a sneer.

I looked away, and she erupted. "They're using you, and you're letting them."

"So tell me," I shot back, my voice now heated. "Would you abandon your people, your family and lands to war and destruction to save one life, your life? If it meant the death of thousands, would you?" I looked at her, then whispered, "I can't."

Chris was still and finally spoke, "Ok, I see your point. Maybe I wouldn't. But I would want to be absolutely positive that it was necessary. That there was a valid need."

I forced myself to speak normally. "Let's go back to thinking of solutions. Ones that don't involve my running away and losing my honor."

"Oh, for frigging sake, you are so holier-than-thou."

I looked at her, startled. "I'm not particularly religious, no more than most."

Chris rolled her eyes. "Do you always have to be so literal? It's just an expression."

I resigned myself to being forever confused when with Chris. She was my only confidante, but there was no understanding the woman.

Chapter 12

At night we stopped, camping out under the stars. Lucinda's ankle was slowly healing but still I insisted she rest. Chris, while obviously not a horsewoman, eagerly helped around the camp once she recovered from her saddle stiffness.

With Lucinda injured, Ethan took over the cooking. I was checking Winter's legs for burrs when I witnessed a small tussle between Chris and Douglas about a bucket of water and an axe.

Water sloshed as Chris and Douglas vied for ownership. Chris's brows lowered into a frown. "Let go. I can do this myself."

Douglas tugged on the bucket, ineffectually trying to pry it from her hand. "Oh no, My Lady, allow me. It isn't right that you should haul water and chop wood."

"I have it already. And don't call me 'My Lady.' I'm not your lady." In the heat of their discussion, the bucket dropped and the water poured upon the ground. I was grateful it wasn't the axe that fell.

Douglas picked up the bucket, still trying to redeem himself in her eyes. "My Lady, er, Chris. Let me do this for you. Allow it as a favor to me."

Chris glared at him. "I don't need some muscled male to carry firewood or water, thank you very much! Now, since you've been so helpful, I have to go all the way back to the stream again." Chris angrily yanked the bucket away from him.

At that point I interceded, and Douglas retreated with his gentle feelings hurt. Douglas and Lawrence both were sweet on Chris. All of us noticed but Chris. She was friendly with the men, winking and grinning with everyone except the captain, though she could go from joking to combative with the blink of her eye. The men were fascinated by her. Her cinnamon hair was often loose, pushed casually behind her ears, her face bare of embellishment apart from those strange eyepieces. There was a power to her, a sureness that came not from rank but from within. She backed down from none, holding her own in ways that I had never imagined. She took their teasing and teased back. Once she even sparred with Charles, flipping him to the ground right before she herself was felled by a quick move that sent her buttocks over teakettle. She got up and shook his hand, saying, "Good job." And that was that.

It was all beyond me. I sat quietly with my embroidery, but drawn to that easy way she had with them. Even though the men accepted me, I was still a princess. They and I knew it. It kept a certain formality in our relationship.

Later that night in my tent, I withdrew the "dragon book," as I had started to think of it. It fell open to five pages that were stuck together. Chris and I worked through the water-stained writing.

"What do you think this means?" Chris fingered one of the paragraphs. "It looks like the journal of one of the first princesses."

I fear this meeting above all things. What if I am not to his taste?

I frowned. This didn't make sense. One thing I hadn't worried about was that a dragon might not find me flavorful.

Chris verbalized my thoughts. "What if the dragons want you for some other purpose?"

"Perhaps, but what possible use could I be for a dragon?"

The rest of the text was so faded and blurry we couldn't make it out. I put it aside, planning on dedicating time to try to glean hints from it. Chris said she hoped reading the book would convince me to go home. But I knew that I couldn't. Perhaps within this book was some aid, some secret that would help me survive. I remembered my father's last words: "Even a pawn can topple a king." And I was no one's pawn.

On the following morning, Lucinda had healed sufficiently to limp around with a stick for support. Chris ate her breakfast in silence, standing. After two long days of riding, she had little wish to sit. I wondered at her quiet mood, so unlike her normal self. She stirred the morning fire, not looking in my direction.

"I have a paper due and I haven't started writing it." She pulled out the golden card. "I need to go back. I still don't know if all this," she waved her hand around, "is real or a dream. I truly can't tell."

I held my breath; I couldn't bear for her to leave me. Not now, not when we were so close to the dragons.

"I'll be quick. It's just for a few days, no longer."

"Of course," I finally said. "This isn't *your* world, it's merely a *dream* anyway." I bit my tongue. I couldn't believe I had said something so cutting. My only excuse was that we would reach the dragons in under a fortnight so my hold on my emotions was slipping.

Chris looked at me then. "No, I'm not deserting you. I won't. I'll be back, and soon. Make no mistake about it. We're in this together."

I dared not speak. I would say the wrong thing. The last time she left, it was over a fortnight before she returned.

"I have to go back. My mother gets all wiggy if I don't phone her each weekend. Midterms are next week and I have a B plus going in. I can't screw this up." She sounded like she was pleading with me to understand. I didn't.

She sighed then, a small shrug indicating her confusion and discomfort. "My consciousness-raising group says that you're a metaphor for change, for the struggle women are going through. That this kingdom is only a dream representing the patriarchal social structure. The dragons illustrate my fears of being absorbed in a male relationship and I'm trying to put it in perspective, sort of like *Alice in Wonderland* or Dorothy in *The Wizard of Oz*." She scuffed her foot against the trunk of a huge oak. "They say that I'm reaching through to my subconscious and they applaud my imagery." She looked over her eyepieces at me. "I don't think so. I think this is real. Besides," she nodded toward Michael arm-wrestling with Lucinda over who should carry the saddlebags, "this is not how I view the battle for sexual equality.

"I don't care if you're a dream or a figment of my imagination. Whatever. All I know for sure is that you're not going to be eaten by dragons on my watch. You are not going to face this without me. I will be back soon."

I struggled not to sound like I was pleading. "We're to arrive at the cave in twelve days."

Chris nodded. "I'll return before you know it, long before you get there."

I nodded, and a weight lifted from my shoulders as I looked into her eyes, earnest and compelling.

"Okay, now that this is settled, I do need to leave. The paper won't take me any time to write. Midterms will be over in nothing flat after that."

"Yes, I understand." I shook my head. "I don't actually, but I'm trying." I raised my head. "How are you going to go back to your world?"

She drew herself up onto her toes and clicked her heels together.

56

"Click my ruby red slippers together and say: 'There's no place like home.'"

I glanced at her feet. She still had on her brown lace-up boots.

"Oh, not really. I'm just going to 'want' to return." She closed her eyes. I could see her eyelids flutter. "Hmm. Before, I have returned whenever I was startled. Would you pinch me? Maybe that would help."

I reached over and squeezed her wrist. "Harder." I thought about her leaving me and I pinched her, hard. Chris yelped in pain. And she was gone.

Chapter 13

We traveled without much respite the next day and the day after that. Douglas asked when Chris would return. I didn't know. At the top of each hill, at each turn in the road and each night during supper I looked for her, as we edged ever closer to the mountains. From here I could see the jagged silhouette of the great Crystal Mountain, a mountain so high that clouds obscured its snow covered peaks. Nothing good ever came from there. Chilled, I averted my glance, trying to focus elsewhere.

In the evenings I read the dragon book, deciphering lines of faded archaic script. The fragile yellowed pages of vellum cracked beneath my fingers. Nothing seemed helpful to my situation.

I didn't know if it was significant that they only showed up during a ten-year period in each century. Or that the first time the message came from the dragons, there were three princesses chosen, not one. I puzzled over this for a while, not making any sense of it.

Other details didn't seem to apply to me. A family named Mastin was tasked with guiding the princesses through the mountains. It was a job handed down from father to son to grandson. That was not happening in my case: Captain Markus's last name was Clarson, and his mother was a Branneau from the north, not Mastin. There were guidelines for the sacrifices: which of the royal families the princesses could come from, how old the princess was to be and, interestingly, her marital status—uncompromised was the word used. But the book was old and written in many different hands. I wondered what, if anything, was accurate about it, or if it was mostly lore.

I thought of Frederick's comments about deflowered princesses, and wondered if the whole kingdom had somehow gotten wind of this, if it were even true. It did resonate with his tasteless remarks about my... purity.

I worried that I might be a delicacy, something like milk-fed veal or foie gras. I could almost hear the barker calling out: tender female, virginal, royal birthed, gently raised.

I fit the description. I was fast approaching seventeen and unmarried. Sitting as I was in the middle of a forest, cloistered in my tent, I regretted every refused offer of marriage. Now I recalled the fleeting look of fear in my mother's eyes with each refusal. I had wondered why she had wished me to marry early.

I thought about other girls of my age from the nine kingdoms of Gaulen. Why had I been chosen? There were five other princesses near my age. Josephine was sixteen, Marleen was seventeen but long betrothed. Adriana was also sixteen as were Stephanie and Catherine. All were unwed, but, as Mother delicately whispered to me once at a ball, Stephanie had a proclivity for men. Adriana, who looked like the "goddess incarnate", was intellectually challenged, poor dear. Catherine had a face and figure that were stalwart, but fortunately a charming personality. And there I was, the acclaimed catch of nine kingdoms, a matrimonial prize, proud as any noble, dutiful and sure of my place in my world.

It sounded like a macabre country pageant. One that I hadn't entered and didn't wish to win. I didn't even understand the criteria.

This couldn't have been random. Someone must have chosen me. It was not merely bad luck that the token-bearing dove landed in my kingdom. The token bore my name. It meant someone had seen me, selected me. Picked me out from all the princesses of the realms.

Why was I selected? Who watched? Someone who decided to be both judge and executioner. Someone had chosen me, fingered me as the one to sacrifice, the pick of the litter. I wanted to know who. And if by some miracle I lived, I would have their head.

Chapter 14

I thought on this long and hard as we rode through the countryside. Dusk approached and we entered a small town by the name of Last Chance. And, yes, I did note the symbolism.

It was a sad attempt at a town. A three-sided blacksmith shop and an ill-formed inn sided with daub and wattle gripped a squishy toe-hold at the edge of the water-soaked fens. Three badly kept horses were tied out front. A single wagon pulled by two fly-bitten mules lumbered by, laden with slabs of freshly cut peat. At the village inn, Captain Markus was joined by a large burly man of dubious character. There was no doubt of his cleanliness, or rather the lack thereof. He must have weighed sixteen stone. He smelled of animal grease and sweat; and more than dirt, of anger and bile. I shuddered each time he looked my way.

He bowed to me upon leaving. His eyes assessed me as if I were a sweet he was considering. I stared back with as much dignity as I could muster.

I hailed my captain. "Captain Markus, might I speak with you?"

He joined me outside. "About that man," I said, pointing to the rapidly disappearing brown shape. I wasn't sure how to approach this subject. "You're not considering bringing him with us, are you?"

"Tom Mastin? Yes, I am. His family is the bridge between us and the dragons. He's a savvy mountaineer, an excellent woodsman. His family has guided princesses to the dragons' lair for hundreds of years."

Remembering the book, my blood ran cold. One more piece of legend correctly stated. But legend or not, I did not like the man. "I don't trust him," I said flatly.

The captain cocked his head, evaluating my words. I wasn't pleased.

"Begging your pardon, Your Highness, but we need him. His people have first-hand knowledge of the Fandrite Mountains. I have it on good counsel that he's traveled these lands both on foot and by horse."

"That may be, but I don't like the way he looks at me."

Captain Markus nodded, all understanding. "He means no harm

to you. He's just weighing your strength for this trek. He must get us all safely through the fens and into the mountains. He's concerned for you, is all."

In the distance I could see Tom Mastin, could feel myself recoil as he turned toward me. He raised his hand to me in a too familiar salute.

"Captain, I don't want him with us."

He glanced away, clearly annoyed. "I can see why you might be hesitant."

I opened my mouth to inform him that hesitant didn't begin to convey how I felt, but he spoke over me.

"No, hear me out. You're very young and have just had a bad experience. It has made you wary. I apologize for telling you this, but it must be said. The decision is not in your control."

I felt a slow flush of anger rising in my cheeks.

"Still, I wish to reassure you. Tom doesn't have a noble's manner and he is roughly made, but you need to look about you. We're no longer in your father's castle. Courtly manners won't get us to the mountains. This is a hard journey, a rough trip. While I respect your opinion, Your Highness, your father placed this task in my hands. By our good priestess's word, Tom is the only person who knows how to get to the dragons' Crystal Cave."

And so Tom Mastin came with us. I refused to speak with the good captain for two days after that. Tom kept his distance from me, but I could feel his eyes on me, watching.

I did not grow to like Tom, but I couldn't deny that he was competent. We ate better once he was with us. We had boar and grouse, and once he pointed us to a thicket of early berries. He knew where to ford rivers, where to find fresh water and how to locate the safest passes into the mountains. He didn't press me to befriend him, which was just as well. I couldn't get beyond my initial repulsion, not even to question him about his family's part in all this. He would smile at me with a knowing grin, showing his reddened gums and missing teeth, and I would retreat into the image of an unapproachable princess. One whom I hadn't been in weeks.

For all his dirty clothes, his boots and saddle were of well-tooled leather hidden beneath a thick layer of grunge. I could almost feel, not to mention smell, when he was near—and my skin would crawl.

Lucinda watched everyone with equal suspicion, as if I were a perfect blossoming rose that someone might snip before her eyes.

It only added to my feeling of isolation. There was no one to comfort me by placing a hand on mine, no one to distract me from my own plight. I missed my family. My mother and father, my sister Danielle, and my little brothers, Harold and Bartholomew. I would never see them again.

Chris's image came to mind then. She was the only one I could confide in who was willing to speak of what came next. A woman with whom I had nothing in common, a woman from another world.

I sorely felt her absence.

As each day rose with no sign, I feared the worst. Chris was gone, perhaps never to return. I must face the dragons alone.

Chapter 15

Three evenings later we camped at a small copse of larch edging a pond of indigo and turquoise water. A waterfall tumbled down the hillside to spill gloriously into the pond with enough noise to drown out my worry. Lucinda and I left the men to set up camp and walked along the wooded path to the water's edge. The sun was low in the sky and the heat of the day passing, but I was weary of the feel of dirt every time I touched my skin. I removed my gown, shoes and stockings and, clad in my shift, waded waist-deep in the chilly water for a quick wash. I had just turned to come out when the water erupted five yards from me. Amidst splashes and sputtering, Chris's outraged "damn" was unmistakable. Lucinda leapt up, her eyes narrowed suspiciously at the person who floundered near me, until I pantomimed that all was well. She didn't look convinced. Friend or not, Lucinda trusted nothing that even hinted of magic.

Chris barely spared me a glance as she sloshed to dry land, grabbing the eyepieces that threatened to fall from her nose. I was so grateful to see her that I couldn't even muster shock about her clothes. This chemise was a heady mix of bright colors radiating in a spiral with the phrase "Question authority" written across the front. I waded out and dried off as much as I could before pulling my riding dress back over my head.

Chris still didn't acknowledge me, but, muttering invectives, she whipped off her chemise and wrung it out. She was clearly not modest, standing out in the open with only a narrow band of black lace covering her breasts. My eyes lit upon a small blemish on her shoulder marring the white of her skin, a birthmark or the scar of a long-healed wound.

Chris's eyes flashed with alarm and she dropped the chemise, searching her trousers for something. Finally, she held up the gold embossed card. I saw her breathe a sigh of relief.

I could almost dance, I was so happy to see her.

Lucinda walked over and handed her a drying cloth, eyes still wary.

"Lucinda, if you would, go back to camp and get her some warm clothing. She'll catch her death in this chill."

Lucinda was gone but a minute when Tom sauntered out of the wood.

I stopped buttoning my dress. I knew without thinking that he had been watching, waiting for an opportunity, and now Lucinda was gone. Would my men hear me if I screamed?

"Leave now. We're bathing."

He preened at Chris. "Where did you come from? Can't resist a pretty girl needing some attention." He shot me a glance. "Why don't you introduce me to your friend here?" He stood in front of Chris and grinned, displaying his lack of teeth.

Chris continued to adjust her clothing. "Look, I'm not in the mood for fun and games. Okay?"

Quicker than a snake, he reached out and put his arm around her bare waist. "Just my type, naked and sassy."

Chris shoved him away, flinging off his arm. "Listen, asshole, don't touch me again."

Abruptly, he slapped her across the mouth. Chris gasped and recoiled, but Tom held her wrist tightly in his other hand. There was a slight tussle as Chris tried breaking away, but she stayed fixed in place. I reached down and tugged my knife from my leather belt lying tangled on the ground.

Chris gathered herself as I rose and then, amazingly, smiled up at him and giggled. "Oh sir, please ignore my girlish manners. I'm just overwhelmed with your hirsute manliness, your Neanderthal presence, that…" She batted her eyes at him. "How can I say it, that cretin look in your eyes." She trailed a finger down his open shirt. His eyes widened and I could see the delight on his face right before she stepped in close to him and delivered a knee to his privates. He doubled over, grunting in shock as she entwined her hands and slammed them into his nose.

She grabbed the back of his shirt but he recovered, reached up and encircled her throat with one ham-fisted hand. "Think you're clever, do you?" He smiled unpleasantly, blood dripping from both nostrils.

Chris struggled, trying to breathe. One of her hands clawed at his while her other hand pulled something from her trousers. I screamed in fury and distress as I raced toward them. She pointed the object at him, and I heard a hissing noise. He grunted and roared, both hands covering his eyes as he staggered back across the clearing. Gasping obscenities, he pulled a dagger from his waist. Then with a single step, he dropped face forward like a fallen oak. Lucinda stood behind him, holding a small log in both hands.

She wiped the sweat from her face before saying, "Nasty man. No manners."

I ran forward, kicked his dagger away and knelt on the ground beside him, my knife at the nape of his neck. He growled and cursed at me.

"Please, make any move. I would be happy to administer the King's Justice to you for threatening me and my ladies."

Lucinda stood over him holding the log, ready to swing at him again. Captain Markus appeared with five of his men at the edge of the woods. He must have been startled at the scene that spilled out by the water—Chris near naked, me, blood-fury in my face, wet hair streaming across my shoulders and Tom, lying chest down, blood and mucus coursing from his nose, eyes tearing, still gasping for breath. My knife at his throat.

All my attention remained on the man before me, he who had threatened Chris.

"Move, threaten us again. Anything. I beg you, sirrah."

That night was a wonder of deceit and lying. Our stories were trotted out and evaluated, mine, Chris's and Tom's. Captain Markus listened to my tale of attack by Tom, to Chris's sharp, but incomprehensible words about Tom's testosterone problems, whatever those might be, and then to Tom's tale of a man-hungry witch and he, a guileless innocent unable to resist her lure. Tom pointed out that this creature had attacked him by magic, and he was justly afraid for me, the dragons' prize.

I protested, both his version of what happened and his crude attribution of me. Lucinda had come upon the situation late and only seen Tom cursing and holding a knife. She told the captain that she had never trusted him. Markus listened to all. Tom wasn't looking much like a successful assailant. Markus watched while Tom heaved his stomach from the vile power of Chris's magic mist. His nose was broken; there was a huge lump on the back of his head; his eyes were red, swollen and streaming tears. He was a sorry sight. But for the fact that I knew what had happened I might not have believed us either. The fine captain could not accept as true that Chris, unmarked but for a small bruise on her neck, could have unmanned Tom without sorcerous means. She handed the magic bottle to the captain, but it was now drained of power. He looked dubious as Chris explained that the 'mace' was used up.

Once Tom recovered sufficiently, he repeated his story of a woman who had enticed him with her scanty clothes and soft words of encouragement. He was like clay in her hands and he was ashamed of his weakness.

The other men were unsure. I knew they were fond of Chris, of her loyalty and candor, but her manner was too forward, too bold. Undeniably, she was *other*—not of us—something unknown. Her habit of appearing and disappearing unnerved even the most open-minded of them. George and Samuel started to speak up but the captain quelled them with a sharp look.

During all this Captain Markus's face was tight and angry, as I knew mine was. "Whatever happened, it is now over. Tom, you are under orders to stay clear of the women. No matter what the provocation. Your Highness, you are to keep your ladies' conduct," he nodded toward Chris and Lucinda, "above reproach." I opened my mouth to reply and thought better of it as he continued.

"I'll have no other incident like this. This is a difficult, unpleasant job, but I will see it done. There is but one week remaining until we reach the mountain." He stared at each of us. "My watch won't fail because of someone's yearning for a woman. Let there be no misunderstandings about this."

He turned and looked deliberately at Tom, "If I find you within five feet of these women, I'll have you whipped. If you touch one, you'll finish this journey tied and bound." His look pierced each of his men. "As for the rest of you, I expect you to treat these women—all of them—as you would your sister or mother or daughter."

He turned to Lucinda and pointed to Chris, now back in her cheerily colored chemise. "Get her into appropriate clothing, and this time make sure she keeps it on!" He looked around at his men. "Do all of you have nothing to do? If so, I can offer many suggestions. Digging latrines with your fingernails comes to mind." The men scurried away. Captain Markus stared at me for some time and I glared back. Finally, he spun on his heel. He walked to the fire where he sat for most of the evening, cleaning his sword and mending the stitching on his bridle.

I held my ground until he was gone before turning my back. I wished no further exchanges with these two men: Tom because he was a vile, evil man, and the esteemed captain because he refused to damn Tom as the villain he was.

In the following days, I kept a sullen distance from Captain Markus. This was the second time he had taken another's recommendations over mine, dismissing me as if I were an uninformed child. But once when Tom was riding out ahead, I saw Markus' turn toward him, his eyes hot with anger and disgust.

Tom, I refused to acknowledge. Lucinda shrugged and muttered she was keeping a stick near to hand. As we rode, I saw the captain's men, *my men*, exchanging glances. While I knew the men wouldn't confront Tom directly, I suspected that Tom's travels might be rife with accidents. There would be no peace between them. I smiled.

Chris wasn't helping, as she would salute Tom and Captain Markus with her middle finger extended any time either crossed our path. From the look in her eyes, I suspected it wasn't meant politely.

Chapter 16

Our party had just climbed one of the Perpinan hills, when the dark clouds rolled our way. The day was almost ended, the sun low in the western sky. Six miles back was the safety of the Lorne Valley. Surrounding us on this hilltop, strewn in between the granite boulders, were gnarled trees, cracked open by lightning. Down the far side, a mere few hundred yards farther, the forest canopy beckoned, the blue-green of pine and spruce interspersed with the chartreuse of new larch offering a promise of cover and safety. As Captain Markus conferred with the ill-groomed Tom, the light breeze off the mountain became a gust.

The horses reacted before any of us, stamping and kicking at the sound of thunder far to the east, and at some intangible animal sound. I shifted in my saddle and looked back.

Markus and Tom were in a heated conversation. A few of the men gathered around, watching. Lucinda, Chris and I had kept far away from Tom, taking our pleasure from the little "accidents" that befell him each day: his tankard handle breaking, mud clotting his jerkin and, then, a bad case of the trots.

Michael and George had satisfied smirks on their faces after each incident, but none would confess to the deeds. Lucinda acted as if she didn't notice, but I saw her smile as Tom rushed into the bushes multiple times clutching his stomach. And she had handed him his plate that morn.

Thunder rumbled again. We waited anxiously near a narrow fissure in a large gray boulder split in half like an eggshell.

Far above, a flock of birds flew before the brewing storm. I turned in my saddle, my eyes drawn to them. Something about their shape and movement puzzled me. No, they weren't birds, not with tails that streamed out behind and those long sinuous necks. A searing jolt of terror collided against my carefully maintained calm. My heart pounded and I thought wishfully of fainting.

Amidst the distant rumble of thunder came the keening trumpet of an animal, a mixture of hawk shriek and elk bugle. Another cry answered the first. I knew what it was, what it had to be. The pig squealed and tugged at the rope holding her. Winter flung his head and snorted. He quivered beneath my hands as froth sprayed from his mouth. I struggled to hold him. Chris's horse rolled his eyes and sidestepped, nervously giving a little buck. Chris nearly fell. The dragons soared above, heading westward away from the oncoming storm. A cacophony of screeches rained down from the sky.

The other horses erupted, frantic and wild-eyed. Jonathan's horse flung him off as it bucked and shied. Michael's arms bulged as he struggled with two frenzied pack animals. Samuel and George ran for Jonathan and dragged him out from beneath flying hooves. Ethan scrambled toward his tied-down mount. Out of the corner of my eye, I saw Captain Markus spin his horse around and shout to the men as he pointed at me. One of the dragons strayed, circling closer as it struggled against the wind. I could see it clearly, a beast the length of a cottage, with silver and emerald scales glinting in the glare of twilight, a predator's watchful eyes, teeth that could tear and talons that could rend.

The creature uttered another screech as I stared in horror and awe. I sat unmoving, transfixed at its beauty and raw power, frozen like a hare in the shadow of a hawk. Winter bunched his muscles. Again, a screech, louder this time against the fury of the wind now whipping across the mountain. Was it seeking me? Would it pluck me off my mount and carry me away locked in its claws? Bile rose in my throat and flooded my mouth. I wasn't ready.

Somewhere behind me, lightning struck. A tree fractured as thunder cracked almost on top of us. Chris's horse screamed and Chris yelled "Holy shit" right before her horse bolted. Winter took off after him. Captain Markus bellowed for me to pull up but I was too nauseated to do anything but hang on. While I might have been able to bring Winter to a standstill, I couldn't let Chris disappear into the woods by herself. And Janis was bent on disappearing, taking along her unwilling rider. Behind us, more lightning hit, raveling stones and boulders along the path. Winter and Janis surged forward as rocks rained down the mountain. Chris bounced along, glued to Janis's neck like a leech. The horses ran as if chased by demons. I certainly thought we were.

We entered the woods, Janis moving faster than I would have thought possible for a hackneyed horse carrying an unstable rider.

We crashed through brush and dove under trees. Chris was hanging sideways around Janis's neck while I ducked to avoid being swept off by low branches. Janis was laboring, slowing to a fast trot, and I was almost abreast with Chris when Janis veered. Chris tumbled and lay sprawled on the leaf-littered ground.

I hauled Winter to a stop and leapt off. By the time I was at her side, Chris had her legs beneath her and was tugging on an oak branch to pull herself upright.

"Nice riding, huh?" she gasped.

"Are you hurt? Anything broken?"

She did a quick assessment, wriggling her wrists and fingers. "Just sore." She brushed at her hand. "Little thingies embedded in my hands. Scratches, nothing more," she said as I examined them. "Got the wind knocked out of me, but otherwise I'm fine, Genny." She looked about at the tall trees and shrubs. "Where are we? Where are the guys?"

I swung around. The horses had disappeared. The men weren't in sight. I was in a forest with the burn of bile still in my throat. And the dragons, where were they? Had they landed? Were they even now seeking me? I breathed in, afraid to dwell on this.

Chris and I headed back toward the men, or at least that was the direction I thought we took. The light was failing, so it was hard to know. We did manage to find a clearing near a rocky stream. A small waterfall trickled down near a granite wall clotted with moss and ferns. I cleaned up Chris's hands, then washed the acid taste from my mouth. Beside the stream, a cunning little hollow pushed into the hillside. A rocky overhang jutted out, providing protection from the elements. I gave the hollow a quick look for other inhabitants. Chris stood on the creek bank calling until she was hoarse, but no one answered.

"Genny?"

"Yes."

"We're lost, aren't we?"

"So it would seem." I managed to speak without a quaver in my voice.

"And, those were dragons, weren't they?"

I nodded, unable to verbally confirm what we had seen.

Her eyes held mine in understanding. "We need to find your men before we talk about… that." She waved her arms broadly to take in the gloomy clearing. "And this doesn't feel like the best place to dredge up things that go bump in the night."

I nodded and joined her, placing my fears determinedly back in a well-fortified corner, one without dragons. My men would be here any moment, I knew it. I mustn't think of dragons, not here, not now.

I saw movement to our left, across the darkening stream past the shadowy gray boulders. Not dragons. Wolves. Two, no—there were more. Three others slunk out of the brush behind them. I heard a startled squeak from Chris as she turned and saw them.

Chris, please don't disappear. Please don't leave me. I could hear her ragged breathing next to me. My heart raced. I pulled out the knife I'd got from the bard, Trill.

The last of the sunlight slanted across their eyes, cold and calculating, evaluating us and finding easy prey.

Chris whispered to herself over and over, like a litany, "Lions and tigers and bears, oh my."

With my free hand, I tugged her back toward the shelter of the hollow. "Don't turn your back on them. They're wary creatures, but bold if you run. Step back slowly, very slowly."

I held my knife out as I had been taught, an extension of my arm.

"Do you know how to use that?" Chris whispered.

"Some," I replied, my voice shaking. "Our weaponry master often said that holding it in front of one with the pointy end facing out is a start." I backed up another step. "You don't perhaps have any flint upon you, something to start a fire?"

"I've got some matches, I think." She patted her clothes. "Ever the Girl Scout, you know, be prepared and all?" For all the pretense of bravado, we were both trembling.

Whatever matches and girl scouts were, I was fervently in favor of them. The wolves kept their distance at first, watching, assessing, identifying us as harmless before slinking ever closer. Chris continued fumbling at her clothing.

The wolves edged closer, and with each step, my breath caught.

Chris pulled out tiny sticks from her belt pouch, snapping them on a box. She swore as her first strike failed. Then the second failed to spark. We backed up to the hollow and I gained a sense of comfort from the solid rock at my back.

Chris cupped her hands, sheltering the fire starter from the breeze as she muttered incantations. She struck it again and it sparked…and held.

Chris cradled the little flame, nudging it into a handful of dry leaves I lay before her. I risked a glance at the wolves. They hadn't broached the creek yet. My hands shook as I reached for one of the dead branches that littered our retreat. The sky darkened as clouds obscured the moon, releasing the first splattering of raindrops. Chris blew upon the fragile flames. I broke the branch into small pieces and Chris added them one by one. The flame spread as we fed the pile of tinder one twig at a time.

A single wolf lifted his nose as if testing the air. They wouldn't wait long now. Any moment they would be upon us. The fire was too small to deter them.

The sun had just slipped below the horizon when a man leapt between us and the gray snarling shapes that skulked within the night's shadows.

After a startled gasp of "Holy batman, who the hell?" Chris ignored him, focusing her attention on the fire before us.

Cloaked within the dim light, the man's body angled away from us, facing the wolves. From this distance, I couldn't make out his face, but, as Chris cryptically noted, he wasn't anyone we knew. He was slender, but muscles rippled beneath a silver-gray hooded tunic. No sound came from his lips as the wolves continued to creep forward beneath the light of the newly risen moon. His back was to the stream, moonlight glinting off his sword.

Some candlelight of hope flickered. Chris blew again on the flames and another stick caught fire. I added another and then one more.

One of the wolves darted toward the man. He parried the attack with his blade, and we heard the crunch of metal into bone over the yelp of pain. The man stepped backwards into the creek, balancing like a tumbler, one step, then another. The four remaining wolves, heads down, matched his every footfall, waiting for a misstep.

The flame before us grew as we cosseted and coddled it into a sullen but viable fire. Next to me I felt Chris shaking, though it could have been me. My brain focused only on building the fire; nothing else mattered, each twig, each branch that burned meant hope, and every flame that expired, despair.

The wolves separated. Two of them leapt the creek and were upon us before the man could react.

Chris grabbed the end of a burning stick and shoved it at one slavering muzzle. The wolf flinched, snarling as he snapped at it. He feinted away but then darted back to attack again. He lunged past Chris at me, his jaws closing on the folds of my velvet riding skirt. I held the blade with both hands as I stabbed, missing as he twisted away.

The fabric of my skirt ripped. The wolf shook his head, pawing at his mouth to remove the cloth. I stabbed at him again, a glancing blow, but blood covered my hand. He dove toward me, fangs bared as he snapped at my arm. I jerked back, then stabbed again and again, not caring what I struck, until at last he lay unmoving. I stood gasping, staring at the lifeless body. I looked up to see that the man had dispatched the other two wolves and was racing across the creek, water sloshing. Chris screamed and, as I turned, the last wolf leapt straight for her. She threw herself backward and there was a resounding thunk as she hit her head against the rock ledge. Without another sound, she was gone.

The wolf seemed momentarily confused, staring intently at the space where Chris had been one moment ago. The man slew it with a single swipe of his blade. He spun around, but no living wolf remained. We were alone.

My legs gave out beneath me. I'm sure that I didn't faint. I would not have. But I was momentarily confused. Chris was gone, and there was gore covering me. I had killed a creature, I, who hurt nothing. And my riding skirt was ripped.

I searched my brain for something to say but I was so cold and weary and everything seemed unclear. There was a dark stain dripping down the man's leg—blood. Lightning flashed across the sky and four heartbeats later, thunder.

"You're hurt."

He finally spoke in a voice hoarse and soft. "It's nothing. And you, are you harmed, My Lady?"

I looked down at my body, reminded that I had one. Two fingernails were broken and my hair had escaped its net, hanging loose around my shoulders like a tavern girl. "No, I'm not harmed," I said, shoving my hair away from my face. I shook harder and wrapped my arms around my chest. Something sticky glued my fingers to one another, blood, wolf blood. I held my arms out from me as I made my way to the stream to rinse my hands and face in the cold water. I thought things couldn't get any worse but then the sprinkling rain became a torrent.

As I rejoined the stranger, he remained silent. He stepped around me, walked back to the mouth of the hollow and checked the fire that Chris and I had started before dragging in another armful of branches. "And your companion?"

I couldn't think straight. "My companion?"

He blew on the flames before speaking again. "The woman who just disappeared. Where did she go?" The fire snapped and sizzled as he fed it stick after stick, smoke rising from the damp branches.

He pointed to the fire's side, indicating that I should sit. "Your friend?"

Oh, of course! I swayed. He moved a log into place near the warmth of the fire. "Sit."

I took a few steps, before sitting carefully on the log.

"Chris? Away, gone." But now I recalled the sound of her head hitting rock. What if she were dead? Oh Chris. I tried to remember if she had been breathing as she disappeared, but all I could remember was her eyelids closing.

My eyes welled with tears and I turned my face from him. He said nothing more, but continued to feed the flame, though I felt him watching me from the corners of his eyes. He had just saved us, but how did he get here? This was no local woodsman. The fire grew and I came back to myself more and more. Things were not making sense. I tried to pull myself together. Who was this man?

Now I knew that I shouldn't be thinking of such at a time like this, but this was an awkward situation. I was alone with a male—a young, unknown male, at night, with no town within miles—in a space not much larger than my tent. After some of my recent misadventures, perhaps I should have felt more wary, but he didn't elicit that feeling. Quite the contrary.

The rain outside our hollow eased into a steady, sullen patter. The fire grew. Four feet away, he stood with his back to me, dragging in more tree limbs and stacking them in a neat pile. I could almost touch him.

"Thank you."

In the glow of the firelight, I saw him jump at my voice, flinching as though discomforted by my meager words of thanks. He turned part way but didn't lift his face to me. "Anyone would have helped."

"But you did and I am grateful."

He nodded before sitting down and removing his boots and socks, turning them upside down on two sticks he stuck into the ground. I tried to look away from his bare feet.

I had no chaperone, and I didn't even know his rank or where he hailed from. He was disheveled; his leggings were ripped and blood seeped down his knee. For all his protestations, he had been injured while aiding me. But something was wrong. He wasn't questioning what I was doing in this wood. He didn't ask my name. He was surprisingly incurious about finding two women in the middle of nowhere—especially when one of them vanished before his eyes. And what was a fighting man doing in the middle of the forest beyond the Perpinans? Only Tom Mastin knew the way.

He began cleaning his sword, scraping off the blood that covered the blade.

In that moment I grew alert, more so than I had been in weeks. All warm thoughts were pushed to the side as my mind circled and re-circled the discordance here. Many uncomfortable questions leapt into my mind, none of which I could bear to ask the man seated across from me. But even without the wolves, I was positive that I did not wish to be alone. And though his face was bare, masked somewhat by his hood, he felt familiar to me—the turn of his head, the slope of his shoulders, those long, callused fingers, his voice. They all called to something in my memory, something that fostered a sense of comfort, of familiarity. I waved my hand before me to dispel the smoke that rose from the fire, and another scent drifted in the smoke—foreign spice, his scent. I leaned toward him, drinking it in. I'd smelled it before, but where?

He offered me some dried meat, and we chewed in a peculiar camaraderie. While I felt oddly comfortable, given the circumstances, he seemed shy or perhaps on his guard. It was an evening of silence—me, shaken and exhausted; he, obviously ill at ease, retreating into the mundane rituals of cleaning his sword and feeding the fire. Yet he still didn't ask me anything, not my name, not why I was here.

Explanations could wait until the light of day. I could barely keep my eyes open as he shifted things around to arrange a space for me to sleep.

"You're about to fall over. I'll keep watch."

I slept so deeply that I may truly have passed out. I awoke at first light to hear George shouting my name over and over. The fire embers still glowed, the remaining coals carefully banked to keep me warm. I lay between the fire and the radiating stone wall, warm and safe. I sat up, rubbing the sleep from my eyes. My torn snood lay near me, rolling my memory back to the night before. As I was falling asleep, had I felt his finger brush across my face? And heard words spoken softly. "If only. I regret how this must end."

I dismissed my fantasy as I tucked my hair back into the snood and straightened my clothing as best as possible, oddly feeling bereft of his presence and trying not to imagine how I must have looked during the night. My knife lay near me, cleaned.

Lucinda raced to my side, muttering threats about my horse. She and George had found dead wolf bodies, a half-mile away—nowhere near where I was. Markers had been burned into the trees leading the way to my shelter. And Chris's horse and mine tied down nearby.

It wasn't possible for my rescuer to have moved the wolves that far by himself. And, like Chris, he too had disappeared.

Chapter 17

The questions came and I had no answers.

"Where is Chris?" Captain Markus asked.

"Gone." I closed my eyes, praying to the Goddess that Chris lived.

George looked at me quizzically. "Who killed the wolves?"

"A strange man, a warrior."

Lucinda spoke then. "Alone, with a warrior, all night?"

I hesitated, trying to recall the half-remembered caress, was it real? "Yes." And though nothing improper had occurred, part of me wished it might have.

Lucinda must have seen my hesitation as she almost had apoplexy. If I weren't sick with despair, I might have inquired if she would have preferred that I spent the night with the wolves.

No, I didn't see any blazon, no coat of arms. No, I didn't know where he went. Yes, I was fine.

I refused to answer any more questions. My heart was weary. Chris was gone and I didn't know if she still lived. Nothing more mattered.

George looked as if he wished to ask me something more but reconsidered, falling back on saying, "There's a brave girl." I wanted to stamp my foot and say I wasn't brave. That I wished there were no dragons, that my only challenge was managing my entourage. I longed for the comforts of my castle room with its soft bed and thick carpets, but I was too tired, too exhausted to make a fuss.

I could sense them looking at me, looking at my scratched arms and broken fingernails, sure that something must have happened, something I wasn't willing to mention. My hair broke loose from my snood as I turned away, strands of the frayed netting hanging limp against my neck. I pulled the ragged remains of the net from my nape, feeling my hair fall in a tangle down my back. Though nothing untoward had occurred, how could they think otherwise?

My mind went back to the man from last night. Did he truly say something about *my end* or was that a dream?

The captain barked out orders to his men to search for my rescuer. Though he spent half the morning, the man wasn't found. Neither was our pig. Eventually, we had to leave and continue our journey. I forced myself not to search the sky for emerald scales and wings, not to listen for that bugling trumpet or the leathery whoosh of wings. Nor look for a sword-wielding stranger.

The next day, the land changed and we slowed to a crawl. I had almost recovered from the night before, but was always worrying about Chris and mulling over the man who protected me. I could still see in my mind's eye the flash of his sword. My thoughts kept circling back to it, round and round, something I should have noted. I was sure it would come to me once I had a restful night's sleep.

We traveled that day through pines and thick shrubby brush into low marsh lands, the fens. Each of us followed single file on a narrow elusive pathway, walking our horses carefully so as not to disappear into the water with its sinkholes and snakes. It was a land so covered with midges and small flying insects that the ground seemed to vibrate if stared at too long.

There were many things of beauty. The fens had a splendor of its own. Through mists that covered the ground, one could see trailing moss hanging from the few straggling trees that clung on low earthen mounds. There were birds, large wading birds—herons, ibis and storks, some that I had only read about—stalking about in the low water or standing like statues waiting for careless fish to come their way. In the occasional clump of brush, I heard the grunting of stoat and the accompanying squeal of piglets. Once, cloaked within the reeds, I spied a fox carrying a small water bird in its mouth.

After inhaling one too many small insects, I put a veil of netting across my face. The whine as they hovered around my head was almost intolerable. The horses had it worst of all, constantly harried by the creatures. I wiped off little flecks of blood from Winter's neck. He fidgeted beneath me, rippling his withers and swishing his tail, as we slogged across the spongy ground.

Tom grunted, speaking over my head to the captain. "We'll be out from this by late afternoon. It's only twenty miles at this crossing. Once we head up into the mountain pass, we leave the midges behind."

Our cart creaked along in front of me, bumping over uneven ground as it was dutifully pulled by a pack horse. It rumbled over a ditch, landing on the other side with a crunch, then lumbered on like a drunkard, tipping precariously side to side. Something was wrong. I opened my mouth to speak when Jonathan swore. "Captain, the cart looks like it's not going to make it."

The axle was broken.

I could hear Captain Markus telling me that all the cart really did, now that the pig was gone, was hold my chair. His mouth moved but I refused to hear him. They unstrapped the chair, abandoning it on the side of the path. Spikes of despair combed through my brain as I watched water lap its base.

I dismounted and walked over to it. My courage abandoned me.

The chair had empowered me, a thread of stability that led back to home and family and self. It had given me a sense of hope and held me to who I was. A symbol of all that was and would never be again—and there it lay, discarded like an old piece of clothing that no longer held its splendor. Lucinda came up behind me and hugged me to her ample bosom. I lay my head on her shoulder for a moment before turning and preparing to remount.

George awkwardly patted my back as if I were a horse to be quieted. Lucinda offered to brush my hair into the elaborate swirls I had worn since I was turned out at sixteen, but I refused. I couldn't bring myself to care.

I longed for Chris, yearned for her presence. I knew she would return if it were possible. But what if she was dead? Once again I remembered the crack as she hit the rock. I started listing the princesses again: Teresa, Anisette, Ophelia, Isabelle,
Nicolette, Chantal, Alexandra, Penelope,
Sophia, Elsbeth,
Rosalind, Willa,
Lynette, Victoria.
I paused, then named, Genevieve.
And, lastly, I named Chris, wondering if she too were lost.

Chapter 18

Late that evening, after I said my goodnights to everyone, I lay awake in my tent. It seemed that as my remaining days and nights dwindled, my questions multiplied like court petitioners. Where did the dragons come from? Who was the man from the previous night? Where had I seen him before? Would I be able to meet my fate with courage and honor? Was there not a possible way out? Where, oh where was Chris? Was she hurt? Even alive?

The men were quiet. Since the wolves, the captain had increased the night sentries. All the men looked worn. The captain's face was drawn, Michael had bags under his eyes that could hold water. As the silence of the evening settled, I heard tree frogs and cicadas, and the various noises of sleeping men. Round and round my mind circled with questions.

Nearby I heard lowered voices, but they rang clear for me. Captain Markus's low bass pounded though my thin tent wall, "What do you think you're doing? You know what's going to happen. This isn't a simple ride in the country."

I couldn't hear George's response, a whispered answer, too low to catch.

"Your coddling her is not doing her any favors."

George raised his voice a notch. "She's but a young girl, the same age as my Molly. There's no need to make this journey any rougher than it already is. She's never complained, not once. Each morning I see her arise, her face pale as my arse, with that *look* in her eyes. Can't you see the terror? She knows. She's not stupid. How can you deny her the least bit of kindness?"

"It isn't being kind to her that I worry about. It's you. We are going to have to leave her in three days. To a fate that none of us can bear to think about, much less mention. You saw the beasts flying above us the other day. Not one of us is going to come out of this unscathed. Do you really believe that you can cavort with her all these days and then calmly walk away after leaving her to the dragons? I can't. I know that. I'll keep my distance and…" there was a pause "—I strongly recommend that you do, too."

I lay unmoving for the next hour. Ice pulsing, dams breaking in my veins. Sleep was not possible. Finally, I got up and went to sit at the fire. George was there staring into the night. He looked up as I approached.

"Couldn't sleep?" he asked.

I smiled. "I needed to talk with you." I prodded another log into the fire. "I overheard you and the captain."

He watched me for some moments before responding. "Tonight?"

"Yes."

He blew out a sigh. "Hard enough to know, isn't it, without hearing us creeping around arguing about it."

"True. Still, it's a good thing for me to acknowledge." I leaned my elbows on my knees and turned my head toward him. "You've been wonderful to me and made this trip endurable. You, and the others. I can appreciate the captain's feelings on this, but I've had an opportunity that few royals have. And I want you to know that I am very grateful."

He sat silent, attending me, still as the night.

I drew a breath. "But he is right. I hadn't thought how hard this would be for you and the men. You must carry no guilt back, no remorse." I hesitated, swallowing, beating down a sob. "You have all done a service to me and I am charging you with making them understand, after…." I stopped as my voice started to waver. I waited until I could speak once again. "Thank them, and thank you, for befriending me."

Chapter 19

A single day remained, one last sunset and sunrise. Tomorrow we would be at the dragons' hold, and Chris had not returned. I had no doubt that if she lived, she would be here.

We climbed a trail that clung to the mountain much like a burr upon the hem of my gown. The slightest misstep sent rocks raveling down the mountain path, merging with trickles of silver waterfalls that appeared and disappeared as we rounded corners. Fern crouching in crevices stuck their fronds up through the mosses and bracken that blanketed the path. We stopped often now, letting the horses breathe. Winter hung his head as he walked, blowing through his nose.

Captain Markus called a halt at an outcrop of rock where we pressed away from the mountain's edge. Here he directed the men to unload all supplies not needed for the last steep push over the mountain's crest, for the next day, my last day, and cache them for when they returned. The captain spoke to Malcolm, and he shot a quick startled look at me before dismounting and hobbling Janis.

I walked over to him, "No, that's Chris's horse. She'll need something to ride."

He looked at me with sympathy. "We all need to accept the fact that she is not coming back." After staring at him for too long, I spun and walked away. Above, three buzzards circled. I turned my head to the stone wall and willed myself not to cry. I didn't offer my help as my men pulled out food for our midday meal.

Once we had eaten our cold luncheon of cheese and dry hard tack, the captain determined the horses were sufficiently rested. He seemed anxious to put this rocky promontory behind us, as was I. The ground dropped into the open space below us into the mists that hugged the land. Keeping my head turned from the edge, I mounted, urging Winter forward.

The air whirled. Winter reared. Dust rose, rocks scattered. A figure tumbled near me. It was Chris, sliding off the path, down the mountain.

She screamed, grabbing for a small scrubby black pine that clung to the cliff's edge. Captain Markus was nearest. He leapt off his horse, tying a rope from his waist to his saddle as he moved, then flung himself face down at the cliff's edge and wrapped his hand around Chris's wrist. Her hand slipped from the tree and another scream echoed across the mountain. Markus slid forward, now dangling off the edge, holding tight to one wrist while reaching for Chris's other hand. "Back, back, Pumpkin." The big roan dug his feet in the ground and stepped back. Stones sprayed as the horse fought for purchase. Markus cursed, fingers stretching for Chris's other hand as she hung out over the precipice. Michael and Lawrence dismounted and stood on either side of the captain's horse, steadying him. "Forward one more step and I'll have her." The horse took a careful step, then dug his heels into the stone and dirt as the captain launched himself downward, latching onto Chris's arm. "Now back, damn it! Back!"

I hadn't noticed that I had dismounted, nor had I felt Lucinda's hands on my shoulders. I shook her off, racing to their side, overcoming my fear of the abyss, as Markus pulled Chris over the canyon's rim to safety. Markus looked shaken and white beneath his normal stony facade.

"Thank you for saving her," I whispered.

Lawrence gently led Chris to safer ground as the captain undid the rope from his waist. Chris bent over, palms on her knees, breathing deep gulps of air. She stood and faced Captain Markus, holding out her hand. He clasped it; the lines on his face seemed etched even deeper than they had been.

"Thank you, thank you." They both seemed uncomfortable with any further conversation.

The captain insisted that we leave immediately. The day was passing and we had to be over this ridge by evening. George unhobbled and saddled Janis before I had steadied myself. Lucinda hastily shoved Chris into a large sack-like jacket and skirt, covering her chemise that stated in bold lettering, "Hell, no. We won't go."

Tom watched Chris with a sullen look on his face, but never spoke.

We were mounted and moving before I had a moment of privacy with Chris.

As we single filed up the trail, I closed the distance between us. "Are you well?"

A funny expression crossed her face. "Well, enough. It's been pretty exciting over in Berkeley also."

"What happened after you disappeared?"

"Ah, well…my friends heard me groaning in my dorm. They called the campus nurse. I had a mild concussion, or so they insisted. Then my dorm roommate called my mother. Big mistake. I'd been telling people that I had gone home to Fresno when I was here." Her nose wrinkled as she said, "It was getting very complicated over there. Now my mom thinks I'm involved with some radical group and got the concussion during a protest in Berkeley. Mom wanted to call the newspapers to register a police brutality complaint. My friends don't know what to think."

Perhaps it was frayed nerves or perhaps it was the rush from her fall as she rattled on to me about her adventures, with nary a breath between her words. I couldn't understand a single piece of what she said, but I was so grateful she was back.

I gave her what I hoped was my most sympathetic expression. She went on, throwing up her hands. "I'm not a good liar, Genny. Dissembling and redirecting is getting more and more difficult, but the truth would get me locked up in some padded ward, pumped up with drugs." She arched her eyebrow at me. "Not how I want to spend my winter break."

She swept her hands out at my questioning look. "No matter, I'm caught between two worlds and not quite sure how to deal with it."

I opened my mouth to ask a question when Chris got an odd light in her eyes and spoke yet again, spilling forth words in what seemed an attempt to ease her discomfort.

She looked down at her hand as if inspecting her nails. "In some odd ways it has been very useful. I wrote a paper about this place for my Women's Studies class a week ago. I got an A plus on it for creativity and the use of metaphors. It was titled 'Fantasy World Images to Explicate Sexual Politics.' But this is more like something out of *The Hobbit*." She frowned over at the men as if re-assessing. "Only there's no Gandalf and no hobbits either." She jerked her head over toward Tom with an evil grin, "Well, maybe there's a goblin."

I let her continue, trying to imagine, but not succeeding, what it must be like living as she was between two worlds.

"I don't know if you are real or some bizarre section of my brain going walkabout, but when I came to myself in my dorm, I smelled of dirt, saddle leather and sweaty horse. This last time I also had blisters on my butt from riding and a very large bump on the back of my head. I was so covered in horsehair that my friends asked me if I had been wrestling with a dog."

Chris let out an unladylike snort as her hand rose to touch her head. She winced. "But," Chris's voice dropped and I leaned sideways in my saddle to hear her. "I saw them too—those things in the sky—right before we got lost in the woods." She shivered and was quiet. "Bottom line, you're not going to be dragon fodder. Not if there is anything I can do to change this."

At last, something I did understand.

Chapter 20

After two hours of hard climbing, we arrived at a false summit—the penultimate summit of my journey. The shadow of the final peak of the Crystal Mountain touched the tops of scraggly pines that were huddled together as if in fear.

At the edge of these, Chris was now hemmed in by the captain's men. Lucinda stood nearby, her hands clasped in front of her as if she were in mourning. George and Malcolm shifted uncertainly.

I glared at Captain Markus. "Release Chris, immediately!"

The captain pursed his lips before speaking. "Your Highness, the time is here. You now go to your final destination." He looked me directly in the eye. "She can't go. She won't accept what will happen, and so she *must* be restrained, but only until you're away.

"Tom says that you must be at the cave entrance before dusk."

He looked over at the sun, assessing. It was still shining brightly, but low in the sky. Darkness came quickly in these mountains. Tom stood a little way off, holding three of the horses: his own, the captain's, and mine.

Markus spoke to me again as he poured a mixture into a cup. "We have to leave, your Highness. I'm doing what I can to help you. Take this and you will sleep."

He moved toward me, his hand outstretched, and I retreated a half-step, jerking away from him. "Don't you dare tell me how it is to be. I have my own plans about how this will end. Don't touch me! I know my duty." I was terrified and spitting mad.

He held a cup out to me. "This will calm you, and then we must be gone."

I felt myself baring my teeth at him. "I said, no!"

He pointed again to the cup and I instinctively stepped back.

"Your Highness, please, don't make this more difficult. Drink. Once it is done, we will release your lady. She is overwrought. Lucinda will watch her until I return from the cave. Now, drink." He looked at me beseechingly, desperation in his eyes.

I backed up farther as the sweet syrupy smell of poppies hit my nose. "No, I will go to the dragons on my own power, with all my wits about me, not as a staked-out goat. Father wouldn't want this. He didn't."

"Your father, your father!" Distance from the palace had made Markus bold. "Where is he now! These are dragons, fire-breathing dragons. You saw them. They can destroy the lives and livelihood of our whole world. I have no stomach for this, but it is my duty and I will see it properly done. No matter the cost to you." He took a breath. "Or to me."

"Tom says each princess has always been left outside the Crystal Cave and tied to a stone pillar." His voice wavered. "You must meet your end alone, but I'll not leave you there fearful and aware." He gruffly pressed the cup into my hands. "You will at least sleep and have no knowledge of what will come. It is the best I can do for you."

Before he could react, I dashed the potion onto the ground and glared back at him.

Captain Markus looked at the liquid seeping into the ground and then lifted his eyes to meet mine. I could hear the men grumbling even from here. Chris was cursing, saying every vile thing she could think of, and she was not known for her restraint. The captain would have to concede that I was a princess and he, merely my father's hired help. I raised my chin, defying him.

The Captain looked suddenly very tired. "Shall I describe what is going to happen? Must I do this? Speak to you of entrails and pain, remind you of your screams that will come as the dragons attack you with claws and tear you apart?"

He faltered here, trembling and white. I raised my chin higher.

"Please, Your Highness, I beg you." His voice cracked with emotion as he spoke. "Please! Do this for me, for my men. They revere you. They would die for you if it would help."

He was right. In that moment, I knew it. How simple-minded I must seem to him, thinking I could change what was going to happen, what must happen, for my land to be saved.

From this distance, we could both see the men watching, tension rippling through them. If I just said one word they would come, revolt right then and there. And for what? I still had to die. And they would die also for defying their commander. Their families left bereft so I could pretend that my ending would be different. I couldn't.

"Your Highness," the captain implored, "none of us can bear this. Must I beg?" He looked at me then and started to kneel. "It will give them, me some comfort knowing that you are…unaware, when you are taken."

All my careful plans with Chris: the chair, the pig. All my unspoken hopes that somehow I might escape this, gone. I held out my hand. "No, no more." I hadn't thought this through. I felt as if I were being ripped apart already.

Behind me I a heard a grunt from one of my men as Chris must have tried to escape. "You will release Chris?" I asked.

He pulled out his sword, pressing the hilt into my hand. "Upon my honor, as soon as my task is done, she will be released. No one will harm her."

I watched his eyes. All I saw was fear. Fear of what would occur if he failed in this task and fear for me. "If you have more," I turned my hand toward the empty cup, "I will drink it."

Markus leapt up and returned with a flask, stirring in a white powder before refilling the cup. "I promise. You will rest. Nothing will mar your sleep."

I heard another grunt and then a yell. "Goddamn it, Genny, don't listen to him!"

I resisted her plea.

"I'll stay by you until the potion takes hold."

"No, leave me." And so saying, I turned my back on him, walked into the privacy of my tent and drank deeply.

Lucinda joined me, silently removing my sweat-soaked clothing and changing me into something appropriate for my last journey, my shroud. Brushing out my hair, wiping my face and hands clean. In a small felted bag, she placed my treasures: my knife, the pawn my father handed me, tying the cord around my wrist, preparing the body for death, though I still lived.

I let her, not wishing to cause anyone more grief and trouble. I took another sip.

Once she was finished, I sat, settling the half-empty cup in my lap as I looked out to the mountain. It was almost over. This long trek now was at an end. One more princess delivered to the beasts. Soon, my thoughts started wandering and my eyelids grew heavy. Strong arms held me upright. Lucinda sat beside me, tears streaming down her face. I tried to be brave for all of us.

As I lifted the cup to my mouth, I recalled the man who had saved me from the wolves. I could see him cleaning his sword beside the fire, see the designs embossed into the bone handle.

Sleep was drifting upon me when I remembered the delicate interlocking pattern that overlaid the sword hilt. I hesitated, pushing the cup away. Half the potion was gone. My mind danced, a slow stately pavane, and I saw first the sword, then the pattern rimming Chris's card, and then the pattern on my knife hilt that the bard had given me. I held them in my mind's eye and slowly reviewed them again. The patterns were identical.

I met Lucinda's tear-stained eyes, as I realized my mistake. Carefully, I poured the remainder of the cup onto the ground, and then my eyes closed.

Chapter 21

I knew I should struggle back from this dream-like state, but I couldn't convince myself that it mattered. I would be eaten anyway—what could possibly make a difference? Perhaps this was better; I might not feel the pain as much. A nagging thought kept trying to insinuate itself forward, something I should remember, something relevant. It skittered away and I let it. Everything seemed so unimportant; sleep was nearby, beckoning like a lost friend. My head dropped onto my chest, too weighty a burden to lift. A voice shouted, muffled and unintelligible as if heard through water. I thought my mother called to me. My hands, no longer tied, fell to my sides, but they were so heavy. I must have slipped sideways as my head bumped the ground. Something was forced into my mouth and I gagged. I bit down and a woman yelped. Once again fingers were inserted and I roused enough to retch.

As I heaved over and over, I heard Chris's desperate voice. "That's it, empty your gut. Come on, wake up. Oh, gross. How much of it did you drink anyway?"

I lifted my head and stared into Chris's frantic face.

"We've got to get out of here," she insisted.

I closed my eyes.

"No, don't go back to sleep." I felt her shaking my shoulders. "Oh, for friggin' sake." She tugged me upright.

I opened my eyes again as she pulled me away from a single post set against a swirling sapphire and crimson sky.

"Can you walk?"

I nodded, admiring the panoramic view.

"Will you focus! Move your feet. God, you weigh a ton."

I tottered along with her. Something crept low along my brain, something important. Something about a weapon. I couldn't remember. My head ached and I reached one hand up to hold it atop my neck.

"Come on, only another little step. Move, move." Chris shoved me toward the mountain face. A dozen holes gaped like mouths and I resisted her, struggling.

"Stop it! They're just caves, Genny. This mountain is riddled with them. We have to hide." I felt her stop tugging on me and stiffen. I breathed and looked around. We were on a high plateau. I smiled. I could see forever here. In the distance, far away, birds flew.

"Oh my god! Here they come!" She snapped me forward and shoved me into the maw of a low black hole.

Chris lit her magic sticks as I sat whimpering in the dark. I was coming out of my daze and didn't like what I saw, a dark cold space smelling of what must be bat dung. I kept my hands on my lap.

"Listen to me. We're safe here. No dragon can squeeze into this small a cave. They'd have to tear the whole mountain apart."

Unlit torches were set in the walls every few feet; I weakly pointed to one. Chris's gaze followed my hand. She grabbed the torch, lit it and placed it back in its sconce. "Who put these here, do you think?"

I couldn't respond—too tired. In the dim light, all my fuzzy thoughts swirled around like uncatchable fireflies.

Outside, the trumpeting screech of dragons echoed across the mountain. The earth rumbled and the walls of the cave reverberated as they landed heavily on the ground.

I could see the whites of her eyes as Chris looked over at me. "I think they noticed you're gone. Too bad we lost the pig; it could be real useful about now."

Fear and shock are heady attention-getters. My mind was coalescing quicker than a company of men bracing for battle. I stood up shakily. And then I remembered: the etchings on the sword.

"…may I shee…" I couldn't get my mouth to work quite right, but my mind raced faster and faster. "Might I see your card?" In the torchlight, Chris looked totally disheveled, her long hair disordered, sticking out every which way. I touched my hair, checking for my last intact snood. It was missing, my hair trailed loose, my face must be smudged with dirt.

Chris was back in her blue trousers and a chemise of yellow with writing again, "The more I see the less I know for sure." I agreed. Impatiently, she reached into the folds of her trousers and pulled out the card. "Good idea, should we try to both use the card to leave?"

I groaned as my stomach lurched.

"Okay, maybe not right this minute." She looked at me again. "Do you have any idea how you're decked out? Tom insisted Lucinda do you up before they packed you off. Some fluffy gold dress and your hair all brushed out into ringlets almost to your waist. You looked like some movie starlet about to be delivered to King Kong. Lucinda was outraged, but the captain said Tom's word was law on this."

I looked down. Even in the low light, I could see my wrist covered in white lace with satin-padded buttons marching up my arm into golden sleeves; my skirt was golden with white gussets. This wasn't a funeral shroud. Why was I dressed in such finery, almost like a bride? When Lucinda had brought me the dress to put on and fussed with my hair, I was too despondent to even notice. But now it did seem strange. More than strange—perverse.

I tried not to think back to the tears my castle retainers must have shed sewing those tiny stitches, piecing this gown together, envisioning it being shredded at the end, my end.

Out on the mountain, the noise changed. A man yelled, "Where is she?" There was silence. "You don't think she fell or jumped, do you?"

"She's not here. I'll check the base of the mountain."

Another responded, a baritone. "Not her, too proud and too clever. She hasn't gone into a swoon. If I were her, I would have taken refuge in the caves."

"I told you we should not do it this way," another voice inserted.

A deep voice responded, "This is how it has always been done. They are always left here, at the carved stone post."

"And what did Grandmama say about that? You know what was said about her mother."

The deep voice growled, "We're all aware of that story. There's no need for you to bring it up again."

"Well, I just thought maybe…"

"Enough."

"At the very least, we should have brought your sister. Our princess might have been comforted seeing another lady."

"It's a little late to think about that. And our princess didn't wait around long enough to be introduced, did she?"

A tenor spoke up. "Look, this is not an auspicious start. Now we're going to have to track the princess down."

"And how do you figure we do that?"

No one answered, and I felt a surge of hope. Maybe this was it.

They would give up and go back to wherever they came from.

Another voice echoed up to us: "Poor little thing, probably somewhere in those caves, afraid and lost."

The baritone spoke again with a surety that raised bumps on my arms. "Not this one. She's no one's fool. She'll come out of her own accord. And, my brothers, when she does, we had better be prepared."

I tried to place that voice, a voice I couldn't possibly know, but did.

The voices trailed away. I knew that baritone. Where had I heard him before? I scrabbled over to Chris and looked at the border on her metal card. Even in the shadowed light, I could see those weren't flying birds engraved into the background. They were dragons. And the pattern, it was the same as was on my knife, the one given to me by Trill, our sweet-voiced traveling bard. And—oh yes—the *nice* man who had rescued me from the wolves; his sword also had the same pattern engraved upon it. I dug my fingernails into the palm of my hand as the realization came to me. All the pieces tied together. I knew why he had barely spoken, why he kept his head down.

I would know him. They were one and the same.

What game was this that these men were playing? I was not here to be eaten by dragons, but for what? What possible explanation could there be for this deception?

My thoughts still spun from the potion and my head pounded. I needed rest and time to think this through. Then I would face the men and the dragons.

Chapter 22

It had been a long, unpleasant night. I spent too much time sobbing both from relief and from the fear of what was to come with the morning. I was stripped of my defenses, my barriers broken and demolished. My head pounded from the lingering effects of the potion.

Finally, we had fallen into a restless sleep with Chris curled next to me; both of us shivered with the cold, and I was still nauseated from the tonic I had been given.

The flurry of bat wings announced the morning, awakening us to the grim reality of cold stone. The men hadn't returned.

"How did you find me?" I asked Chris. "Did the captain let you loose?"

Chris hissed, an almost sibilant sound. "You missed quite the little soap opera after you passed out. Tom had almost chortled when Markus paid him his nine pieces of gold. Then while Markus was busy guilt tripping you to drink the potion, Tom, that, that—" here her language became vulgar. I didn't recognize all of the words but the ones I did were quite rude. She took a breath. "He took George aside and made him an offer. He'd give one of those gold pieces back, if he could have me thrown in. Just tie me up somewhere close and tell the good captain I escaped. He'd come back for me later.

"Or... they might find leaving the Fandrite mountains to be... difficult."

I shivered at her words. "Oh, Chris." I reached out and grabbed her hand.

Chris grinned then, a slightly feral smile. "It's okay, nothing like a little stress to bring out the best in people. Once they rode off with you packaged like some bizarre birthday present, I pulled out my magic card and tried to leave. I couldn't. George knew what I was trying to do. He walked over, winked and slapped me." She wriggled her jaw as if remembering. "That did it, just as he knew it would. I was back in Berkeley with a reddened face."

"Oh, my."

Chris said, "Wished I could have seen the captain's face when he returned."

I nodded, stating the obvious, "George knew you would find me. He was giving you a chance, giving both of us a chance. Thank you. I owe you much. Upon my honor, I had no idea that you'd be at risk."

Chris shrugged. "No big thing. You would have done the same for me if I were being attacked by dragons or pod people or blood-sucking creatures from Mars."

I held out my hand as to an equal, and she grasped it. No matter how alien her words, no matter where she was from, Chris was my friend, my ally.

We both jumped at the sounds of scraping and thumping on a ledge of rock not far away. I made out a faint silhouette rimmed with a fiery glow as a rank odor reached my nose. Chris and I shrank back into a stone hollow until the noise shuffled off.

Chris whispered in my ear. "What was that?" We both listened.

I picked myself up, shuddering. "Please, no more dangers. Whatever it is, it stinks. I don't wish to meet up with it in a cave. Quickly, we need to move in case it returns."

We set off to explore the dark labyrinth-like caves, crouching over as we inched through a narrow corridor, never going too far for fear of getting lost. We stumbled around in the flickering light carrying a single torch, following the rushing sound of water until we found a glorious stream that pooled in a rock cleft. Chris pulled out a coarsely woven cloth bag embroidered with letters spelling out "Northface" and sat cross-legged beside me. From within the bag she drew forth supplies brought from her world of Berkeley: foodstuffs, more of her odd clothing and— blessedly—a hair brush. We drank and tidied ourselves up as best as we could, debating how to approach the situation. As I braided my hair into a single thick plait, Chris railed against the strictures of dragons and men and power, all that she guessed was tied up in this.

Below, dragon bugles bounced from floor to cavern ceilings, causing rocks to ravel down unexpectedly. They were here with us inside the dark bowels of this mountain. We had to face this: find the dragons, the men with them and unveil the secrets that brought us here.

With those few hours of sleep and no longer nauseous, I felt more in control.

Chris and I stumbled out onto a ledge where we could hear the dragons lumbering below us, trumpeting. Still the men hadn't returned. It wasn't comforting. I believed they weren't here to harm me, but what if I was wrong? Each time I prepared to descend, the deep rock-shattering noises of the dragons shook my resolve.

Earlier that day Chris had agreed with me, saying, "Making a bad decision is better than making no decision at all. We can't stay here forever." But now that we were closer, hearing the dragons, feeling the reverberations through the rock as they stomped below, and smelling the sulfur fumes from their breath, she reconsidered. "Except when it comes with the possibility of being eaten by large fire-breathing monsters that should be imaginary." She closed her eyes, reopening them rapidly as a loud trumpeting call seemed to scale the walls.

My gaze rested on a flight of steps carved into the stone that led down to what looked like an open cavern, part of the ceiling broken out to sky. Two torches, now beginning to sputter and smoke, lit the way. Chris shook her head at my look. "Don't go down the stairs. You know, like in the movies when the heroine hears all the weird noises in the basement and she opens the basement door and starts down. Then the scary music starts." Chris grinned at me, "Okay, maybe you don't know, but trust me, no one in *my* world would go down there."

"I'm not of your world. I want answers and that's where they are. You heard the dragons. I'll not return home and have these creatures terrorizing the countryside. And where are the men we heard?" For all my brave words, my heart was pounding, thumping against my bodice as I spoke. Each dragon's call that I heard and felt through the rocks made my heart clench in fear.

From somewhere below, the dragons' bugling slammed again against the cave walls. Their fire blasted across the cave, scorching the walls and spraying them with red and orange flames. We both cringed and shrank back.

I whispered, "They're right below us. Right down these stairs."

Chris grabbed my arm, whispering, "Look, we can turn back. I'll create a diversion and you can be gone."

"Be gone where?" I objected, whispering back.

"Away, anywhere away. You know, like not here, surrounded by dark and stone with lizards crawling around below us. Very large flying lizards," she amended, "that are annoyed and hunting us."

"They don't know where we are." I waved my hand at the lowly lit cavern. "These caves seem enormous, probably larger then my family's whole castle, with tunnels spilling out everywhere. Noise is hard to locate and we're quiet." The dragons called out again, spewing flames. "They sound so agitated."

"Maybe they're hungry. After all, they missed a meal," Chris said.

At my shocked expression, she retracted her words. "Sorry, bad joke."

I started to bite my lip and then quickly caught myself. "Perhaps we *should* wait for those men to return. Once outside of the caves we'd be like rabbits to a hawk. I'm not leaving until I understand what this is about. We heard men last night, and now they are gone. I'm certain they will return."

Chris peered out into the cacophony of noise. "Maybe the dragons are like horses, trained to be ridden, like in that Anne McCaffrey book. Maybe that's why the men were here."

I nodded, swallowing a catch in my throat as I tried to hide my fear. "Perhaps." I rubbed my forehead with my thumbs. "I'm not eager to rush down among those animals either. But I need to understand what awaits me."

My stomach rumbled and I was momentarily distracted. "Do you have any more of those little round sweet things?"

Chris rummaged through her pocket, pulling out an assortment of coins and crinkled papers. "I think we ate all the M&M's last night."

We sat companionably in the low light, pretending that all was well.

Below us, the dragons bellowed and trumpeted. Chris crept to the edge of the wall and flattened herself on the cave floor, trying to get a better view into the cavern below. I sat nearby, unwilling to prostrate myself. We peered between the rocks again. The noise got louder with the banging, stomping and the whooshing sound of huge wings. They moved into view, first one and then more. Huge monsters, the same as I had seen in the sky but a few weeks before. But so much closer.

One shifted, snaking his head upward and unfurling his wings in the huge cavern below. Another turned, reaching high to rake his claws upon the stone wall. As I watched stones ravel down and closed my eyes against the sight. I felt my heart pound against my ribcage.

Chris shook her head. "I'm definitely not going down there."

...

Evening came. Chris and I shivered as we watched from our hiding place. Below us, the air spun about the dragons, shiny specks of light amidst a massive swirl of colors. Scales obscured, their dragon bodies hidden within a cloak of colored dust. As the air resolved itself, five men appeared, their skin shimmering with the change. Five men with the glow of scales and the sparkle of light surrounding them as the dust settled beneath their feet. Five naked men who stretched and shrugged in their changed bodies as they donned leather tunics and breeches. I drew in a breath, unable to comprehend what I had just seen; trying to make sense of the broad expanses of chest and muscled legs that seemed to appear and disappear within the dust and light. Humans: men who could change into dragons and back again. I was afraid to blink, or to turn my head, that they might vanish before me. Here I was, staring while naked men dressed, and I was too startled to be embarrassed.

Next to me, Chris breathed out what sounded like a prayer. "Oh! My! God!" I could feel her body shaking as she reached for my equally trembling hand. Her breath caught as she whispered in my ear. "This is too weird."

Chapter 23

The smell of cooked food and the hot, smudgy odor of burning oil from tapers hit my nose. The men sat clustered around a rough-hewn table, their voices raised in argument. In the quiet of the cave, my name carried clearly up to me, echoing off the stone walls. Below, one man paced and three others stood in a toe-to-toe discussion, red-faced with anger or frustration. One sat with his head bowed in his hands. Before him was what looked to be a meat stew. My stomach growled.

I watched them; those men who were and were not men. Strange creatures for whom I had been brought all this way—across forest, fen and mountains, believing that my death was the end. I fingered the golden lace under my hands, a bridal dress. Oh yes, I was prepared to face them.

I picked up a hefty rock, turning it in my hands as I looked down at these creatures. These vile beasts that had deceived my father, my land and me. I levered myself up, took aim and heaved the stone down onto these…these…whatever they were. It clattered and thumped down into the lower cavern, bouncing along until it rolled to a stop in front of one of them.

Chris handed me another large stone. "You missed." Her voice echoed. Below was sudden silence.

The men looked up then, scanning the rocks where Chris and I hid.

The enormity of what I had done hit me. I could hide no longer.

I rose, and as my feet found the stairs, Chris carefully followed in my wake like the perfect lady-in-waiting.

Never had I made an entrance like this, bruises on my arms, my hair in a single braid, grime beneath my nails, and my dress stained and wrinkled. I raised my chin high, taking each step as if a room full of admirers awaited me, and not the monsters below. They were clearly unsettled. I had to assume I wasn't supposed to know they were men who could turn into dragons. Or perhaps they weren't accustomed to having rocks thrown at them.

One of them cleared his throat and the noise echoed. My breath caught. Too many of them, all large, hair the shades of fallen leaves, sleeked neatly back, looking like court nobles and not the beasts I had just seen. Five sets of eyes followed my descent more intently than at any arrival to a formal ball. Chris clung close behind, whispering something I couldn't make out.

I took another step. We were cold and famished. They had a fire. The scent of roasted food emboldened me, and the trickery, the months of infuriating trickery, enraged me.

My eyes locked onto each man. Standing forward was a tall, well-muscled man with dark intense eyes; alongside him was a bull of a man, with broad shoulders and a determined chin. A slender youth sat at a crude wooden table, his leg jiggling nervously. Another man, with a thin mustache, perhaps twelve years my senior, leaned whispering in his ear.

There would be one more. I knew that *he* was there, the man who'd rescued me from the wolves, the bard who wrote and sang a ballad to my name before I'd left my home.

Trill.

As we stood high above them, I could hear them speaking softly among themselves. Still I questioned, what was this, a ruse, some further deception? But underneath my questions, I knew why I was brought here.

Our echoing steps announced our arrival. I refused to drop my calm, my facade of control. No longer did I believe that I would be fed to the dragons. I would live. All my tears, my nights of terror were for naught. I'd been played for a fool. With my every footfall I grew angrier, my fears pushed to the background in the face of this hoax. I scanned the men; yes, there were five of them. Five men with tawny skin, loitered about the cave floor, replacing five jewel-colored dragons.

Four more steps to the bottom of the stairs, and then four more to stand facing them. Surrounding them, decorating the caves like silent sentinels, were columns of stone, several rising up from the ground, and others hanging like icicles from the ceiling.

There, standing somewhat back, I saw him, the same man who *found* me in the wood not but a week ago. The bard, Trill, the man who gave me the knife and the ever-so-cryptic sendoff. They were one and the same. Two of the others I recognized also, the youth and large bull-shouldered man. The clever minstrels who had performed that night so many months ago, a lifetime it seemed, singing and playing, while

I prepared for my death. Now they stood here looking as if there had been some slight misunderstanding, a mere oversight about my true fate. Trill, at least, had the decency to appear anguished and on edge. My eyes narrowed as I looked them over. Whatever they were planning, I wanted these men, if such they were, to end up sorry they had played it at my expense.

One of them, the tall imposing man with dark eyes, stepped forward, offering me his hand. "Welcome, Princess Genevieve, and—" he glanced around to Trill as if to confirm something "—of course, the Lady Chris."

Yes, Trill knew Chris's name, remembered her from our *tete-a-tete* among the wolves.

I slapped his hand down. They all jumped.

"How dare you think to touch me."

Next to me, Chris whispered, "Oh shit."

Though his eyebrows drew down in anger, he raised his hands in sublimation. "You have much to be...confused about, but—"

"But naught. Only a knave would bring me here. I'm a Princess and you are but a—"

The tall man regained his composure, putting on an impressive facade. "King," he finished for me.

My eyes narrowed at this new information. "In my realm, no noble would behave so ignobly, but then my father set a high standard of chivalry." Chris, standing behind me, grabbed my bodice sleeve. Over and over, she whispered, "This is a test, this is only a test. If this had been a real emergency..."

Though his face grew hard, he ignored my outburst, as if dealing with a child. "This has not been the best reception for you, I fear, but we are eager to make it up to you." He smiled, though it was a meager thing. "Please, sit, eat. We will explain."

I stood where I was, unsmiling. Chris fidgeted at my side.

One of them grabbed two trenchers laden with what smelled like venison stew and offered them to us.

Trill spoke low. "Please."

Chris and I walked past our dark-eyed host. I pulled my skirts to the side as I passed Trill and sat on a stone seat. It was hard not to wolf the food down. I was well aware how I looked, donned in a now-crinkled gown of gold and white, my hair bedraggled. I mentally dared anyone to speak of it. I took my knife out to eat, the knife Trill had given me a lifetime ago. It was all I could do not to stick it in his arm.

Once I gathered control over my voice, I spoke. "Very well, feel free to clarify this situation. I have journeyed long to hear this. No one could be more fervent to understand than I." I brought the wooden spoon up to my mouth and began to eat. They relaxed, and two of them even had the effrontery to make as if to sit also.

"I did not give you permission to sit in my presence."

After a moment's quiet, I reconsidered. I must deal with these… men. "You have the advantage of me," I started. "Perhaps we should begin with introductions. You know my name and why I am here." My voice held an edge.

The dark-eyed man glued his smile back on, pointing to each man in turn. "Let us remedy that immediately. I am Hugh Buchan, King of Pritorous, and these are my brothers, Tristan and Piers." Tristan avoided my eyes, and Piers, the youngest, went back to jiggling his leg. "And," Hugh continued as if nothing had happened, "my cousins, Dukes Rauf and James."

As he introduced them, the large shouldered man bowed, as did the mustachioed man.

Tristan, not Trill. He had even lied about his name.

Hugh spoke, breaking through the tension in the air. "We wish to apologize for the inconvenience to you. I know this has been very trying and…" Here he hesitated. My eyebrows rose in disbelief. Apparently, he thought he could just brazen through this with some pat speech.

At my look, he started again. "We regret any distress you might have experienced." Beside me, Chris almost snorted her food through her nose. I ignored her. She would never make a lady-in-waiting—not enough personal restraint.

"Certainly, we wish to make clear that we offer you no harm, and will take every effort to make you comfortable from here on in our journey."

"I beg your pardon?" I curved my lips into a smile, but I'm sure it looked as if I were baring my teeth. "What did you say?"

"You are in no danger," he said, as if thinking to reassure me.

"No," I said, slowing my speech to make sure he would understand. "It is the second part of your statement that I am questioning." Every fiber of my body hung in stillness, a bell waiting for the clapper to strike.

"That we need to leave soon? The weather can be tricky if we get early winter storms."

My hand hovered over my trencher, frozen as I listened for the answer. "And what is that to me, might I ask?"

He glanced over at his kinsmen. I could see them shifting nervously in the torch light.

In the silence that followed, I waited, biting my cheek to remain quiet, forcing them to answer.

He looked less than pleased to have to tell me this. "You are the chosen bride."

Chapter 24

I stabbed my knife into my plate, where it stuck fast. All the men jumped. Chris's trencher clattered onto the cave floor. The echo went on forever.

The youngest, Piers, I believe, whispered, "I told you we should have listened to Grandmother."

It was some moments until I was finally able to speak civilly. "So this was all a ruse, a plot to snare a royal princess." My throat ached with the urge to scream at him.

"No, no," he said, "not a plot. Part of a negotiated agreement, a compact we have with your people."

My jaw hardened. "Are you saying that my father lied to me? Let me believe I was to die?"

Tristan finally spoke. "None of the monarchs were…privy to the minutiae of this agreement. We only spoke with the church leaders—in your kingdom, her name was Mother Morigan."

I allowed myself a quick look at the bard, Trill—no, Tristan—and the two other musicians from months ago. Tristan stared intently at the ground while Piers and Rauf, their eyes wide and mouths gaping, seemed quite captivated by the discussion. So this was a hidden agreement tightly controlled by the priestesses, circumventing the kings entirely?

"And how do yon musical merrymakers fit into this?" I jerked my chin toward the three men.

"Someone had to find the perfect princess, someone to deliver the bride-price to the church." Hugh smiled now, nodding. "Otherwise, how would we know whom to choose?"

I stared at him in disbelief. I couldn't think of anything to say that would be in the least diplomatic.

He shuffled his feet unobtrusively. "Perhaps we should start at the beginning." He looked as if he was treading carefully. "We are from far away, across these mountains.

"Your presence here is the fruition of a compact, one between your people and ours for the last eight hundred years. The treaty allows us to choose a princess, a bride, to become queen." Hugh smiled at me.

I pointed my finger at him. "Why?"

Hugh bowed. "Your lands have long been known for their charming women."

I could see Tristan wince. Beside me, Chris muttered, "Give it a break."

"As yours is for secretive, deceiving men?" I snapped, not allowing myself the liberty of glaring at Tristan.

I was too angry to say more.

Chris addressed Hugh. "So why? What do you get out of this besides a female? Surely you have those in your land. It seems a bizarre way to select a partner."

"Yes, why did you seek a woman, charming or otherwise, from my country?" I added, not bothering to remove the snarl from my voice.

I didn't believe that my parents would have applauded either Chris's or my diplomacy, but I was angry and tired; and Chris, well, she was Chris.

"Long ago, we sought a land willing to trade a royal bride. But at first we were refused."

I waited.

Hugh seemed to come to a decision. "There was discomfort about our abilities. We're an old race, a strong race." Here he flexed his muscles and almost preened. "But our talents made your people uneasy." He looked out over his men, then shrugged in dismissal. "People fear what they don't understand."

"Ah, yes, your talents. I couldn't help but notice that you are not always so—manly. Was that the discomfort you speak of?" I wiggled my knife free.

He breathed out before speaking again, "Yes, that is true. We had hoped to bring this information to you slowly. We are a race able to transform into dragons, to breathe fire, to command the skies."

"Is that why you cower here, rather than approaching my father directly for my hand?"

The temperature rose in the hall. Some of the men seemed to glow. Chris scooted closer to me. No one spoke for the passing of many breaths. I didn't care. I wouldn't concede again because of fear.

"You question our bravery, My Lady?" I could see glints like embers swimming in his eyes. His hands clinched into fists before him as he struggled for control.

I looked up at him calmly and then said the words slowly, one at a time. "No, I question your honesty!" Behind me Chris trembled, her fingernails digging into my arm.

Hugh's upper lip curled into a snarl and three men moved to his side. Tristan stood then, stepping forward.

I seethed.

"Oh yes, the good bard. Here to tell me a story," I taunted.

"Peace." He held up his hand. "Bide, and hear my words."

"Please go ahead." I sniffed in disdain. "I love a good tale."

"Eleven hundred years ago during the reign of our King Kester IV, a pass over the mountains collapsed, closing down the annual caravan route. Some voiced concern, but, though few, we are an insular people. Our land is plentiful: many animals to hunt, lakes teeming with life, our mountains rich with raw ores. Our people are skilled craftsmen. We were content; none saw it as a problem. But then, several hundred years later, some were no longer able to change between dragon to human at their wish."

The one with the thin straight mustache, James, interrupted. "Actually, it was only the nobles. Before then, we'd wed the occasional outsider."

Tristan nodded in agreement before continuing. "Some called it a curse. Since the pass closed, we married only within our royal families."

Chris chewed on her lip, then added, "You were too inbred."

Tristan nodded. "The Court Physicians confirmed our best guess, we needed to marry outsiders. Those without dragon blood."

James cleared his throat, rambling forth. "It was Denston's son, the fourth Denston, who was locked in his dragon form for a year. The histories say it shook Denston III to his golden core. Nothing could be done. To break the curse, the royals realized they must look elsewhere for mates."

Rauf added, "But none of the royals could leave. Our people would never leave."

Piers spoke then. "Except for our last princess, Victoria."

James corrected him, "That was much later, and she wasn't a Pritorian. She just married one."

"You're right. She was the last chosen princess…" Piers looked at me. "Until Genevieve."

I held myself still, barely managing not to react at hearing of my Great Aunt Victoria. Would they tell me what happened to her? What was her fate?

Hugh turned toward them, angry with the interruptions and with the clear intention of blood-letting. The others backed down.

He went on. "Our royal family needed human wives to survive. Finally, a decision was made. Three human princesses were chosen to marry the three sons of the king in Pritorous. Chosen and carried back."

First truth, I thought.

Chris figured it out immediately, whispering, "They kidnapped them. Just like Romans with the Sabine women."

Tristan spoke, continuing his tale. "There was war, ten years of it. Your people marched on the Fandrite mountains. Thousands of men died, from disease and cold as much as from fire and claw. Dragons, too, were killed. We flew into Gaulen, burned the land, razed towns and villages. Ten years of dying, lands burned, towns destroyed—I'm not defending what our ancestors did. It was a long time ago, part of our mutual history."

Chris spoke out. "So how did it end?"

Hugh interrupted here, taking back the story as his own. "Your country lost much, a generation of its best men, lands withered, towns reduced to ash, trade eliminated. But we died too."

Second truth. I remembered reading of the destruction that ensued from an ancient war. It was a time of chaos, almost a millennium ago, and few documents survived. I nodded my head for him to continue.

"Realizing the failure of war, a coterie of your kings sent ambassadors, ten of your most able men. Only three survived the journey through the Fandrites to appear before our kings, two church leaders and the mountaineer who led them, called Bill Mastin.

"Those men came to understand that they could protect your kingdoms from the scourge of dragonfire by ensuring the regular influx of new blood into our royal line. A princess would be given to us. And we would retain our humanity."

Piers said, "A princess that we choose—based on careful deliberations of her strengths and suitability." He gave me a nod as if I should be flattered.

Hugh added, "We would compensate the family for their loss, as per the pact."

Chris whispered in my ear, something about mail order brides. I couldn't listen to her now; this was too important. Everything they said made sense. This had been negotiated exclusively through the church and the Mastin family. They fed only the barest information to the kings, only that the dragons required a princess.

"And the kidnapped girls?" Chris asked.

Tristan nodded at her question. "They negotiated the peace treaty. It was named for them, The Princess Pact."

"Just like that, huh, kidnapped women now bartering for more kidnapping."

Tristan leveled his eyes at her. "Ten years had passed. They had settled into their marriages and families—our histories say they were even happy. In any event, they understood the needs of both and the risks of war."

Chris snorted., "Stockholm syndrome, nothing more. And everyone lived happily ever after, right?"

James spoke up. "There were difficulties. Peace came, time passed, and young men forgot the war, the fires, the bloodshed. They sought us out. Some wanted to prove their valor by slaying a dragon, and some sought dragon blood for arcane rites." Here he paused, distress painted across his face. "The way to our land is fraught with peril: ice storms, avalanches and fierce winds that chill to the bone. Many died."

Hugh's eyes shone fiercely. "Finally, two Pritorians were killed while flying low over the mountains. Killed by your people." The planes of his face turned taut and white. "Those men were hunted down and brought to justice."

Piers turned to me to interject again, but he closed his mouth as Tristan took up the tale once more.

"We realized that in order to keep the treaty, we must disappear. Snares were laid and traps set at the borders. We travelled through your lands telling tales and singing songs to inspire fear of these mountains."

"But still you seek to marry outside of your own people," I said.

"We must." Tristan's teeth clenched. "Some of us…some of us still find ourselves locked in dragon form for longer than we wish."

An unsettling quiet seemed to pervade the cave-room and some unspoken words passed me by. Some hint of sorrow or distress directed at Tristan. I couldn't tell. Nor did I care. Tristan continued with no expression upon his face. "In isolation, we fear the loss of our humanity, not in this century or the next, but eventually."

Chris spoke. "Okay, I can see that fire-breathing dragons wouldn't be best as neighbors. So why didn't you track down more human women—not that I'm encouraging you to, you might note."

Hugh looked down his nose at her. "We are honorable. We still hold to the treaty, as do you. It can be a hardship for us, but one just manageable."

I continued tapping my knife against the stone as I evaluated his words, wondering if there was some further message that he wasn't saying.

Still, it made sense, I thought. I'd heard these stories and songs myself.

Third truth.

"So you sought a princess every hundred years…" I started.

The men looked at each other. Piers spoke. "Not truly. We seek a princess whenever we have royalty who agrees to marry a human. The pact allows for up to two in a hundred year period."

James added, "Certainly in recent centuries, it may have been fewer but it isn't because we don't look other times. We seek out a good match, but sometimes we don't find anyone suitable. Sometimes we've chosen one of our own. Or perhaps a princess is in line to rule. Back then no one thought to ask for a prince."

Rauf nodded, agreeing. "This search happened to be a good fit."

Piers gave me a merry smile. "Yes, we were particularly pleased with you."

There must have been fire in my eyes as Chris muttered in my ear, "Oh wow. Lucky you. Aren't you just too special."

Chapter 25

It took me a full minute to rearrange my thoughts, absorbing what I just heard. I ventured another question, an important one.

"Should I agree to this, which of your party seeks my hand?" It must be Tristan, I knew it must be him.

Chris whipped around, her mouth open.

Hugh moved a step closer, ignoring my growing anger. I watched in surprise as he dropped to one knee reaching for my hand, eyes bright with the glow of self-confidence. "As king, the honor is mine to accept your hand in troth and make you my queen."

A quick glance showed Tristan, his face neutral, his fingers pressed against the table. I started tapping my knife again to cover my embarrassment. Tristan wasn't interested in me for himself, merely picking out a prize for his brother.

Hugh looked up at me, perplexed that I hadn't responded. "We've kept our promise. Everything has been done according to the rules. A High Priestess, your Mother Morigan, was contacted, a bride-price delivered. We then sent a message to your king, a golden token identifying you as chosen. And, lastly, a Mastin contacted to guide you."

My head snapped up. They had mentioned this before and finally it hit me. *Money! Money had been paid for my delivery? So is that yet another reason why the church held this information so close?*

"The alliance is ratified when the bride is brought to us. You are here, are you not? You were chosen." He seemed surprised by my continued silence. "This is an honor for you. Our queens are revered, heeded, not shuttled off as decoration, as are some in your land." Hugh was frowning now, looking nowhere near as pleasant as he had before.

I should have guessed. Mother Morigan and Tom Mastin knew, but the treaty details forgotten, overlaid with centuries of myth and fear. Only the secrecy kept—and the money. If I ever returned home, I would tear that edifice to shreds with my bare hands. If I could but get back.

I put my anger aside and returned to the matter at hand.

"Perhaps you forget. You had me drugged and tied to a post, a distinct misunderstanding of the word 'agreement.' By my assessment that is not a particularly good start for marriage."

They were silent then. I could feel their discomfort. I wasn't grateful or honored. Neither was I so deliriously happy not to be destined for the dinner plate that I was eager to marry one of these things.

They also failed to see that this conversation was over. I needed time to think, to lick my hurt feelings and to decide how to deal with these men who weren't men.

Hugh's mouth twitched in annoyance, but he continued. "It was necessary. We didn't want you to harm yourself, but the Pact must remain secret." He set his shoulders before he spoke again. "This is no different than any other politically arranged marriage."

He was right. This really was no different from what my parents had prepared me for all my life. I was born and bred to be married to a powerful ruler. Married off to acquire land or strengthen ties between kingdoms. My hands gripped my fine silk skirt, now covered with dirt and grime. But *never* had I been treated like this, never pulled as a puppet by invisible strings, nor had I ever expected to wed a beast.

Hugh continued. "It's simple. This serves the needs of both our countries. We have spent a great deal of time and effort selecting you. Look at this from a practical view; because we remain part human, your country is safe and fruitful. This is a good alliance, a good match."

He walked back and forth, his hands behind his back. "I'm here and think you lovely and charming. You're here and, I hope, see me in a similar light. Anything else can be discussed after our return home."

Chris interrupted him. "Why the rush?"

Hugh looked like he might ignore her, but then spoke. "The winter storms are due. Wind, hail and lightning that make flying difficult." He nodded. "So perhaps you should collect your things and say your goodbyes to your friend." He jerked his head at Chris.

"Or perhaps not," I responded.

I put my knife away and beckoned to Chris. "While I appreciate all the effort to which you have gone, I shall not make such a momentous decision without somber reflection." As I spoke, Hugh's mouth turned down and he shook his head. Perhaps he wasn't used to being opposed. "Your *offer* will receive every consideration." I sat my now empty trencher down and rose to my feet, taking care not to acknowledge Tristan in any way.

"It has been instructive meeting you and your relatives. I appreciate you taking the time to present me with these specifics. Unfortunately, I am still recovering from the ill effects of my journey here…and from the potion that I was given before our meeting."

He stood there tongue-tied, clearly displeased.

"Was that part of the treaty also? The sleeping potion?" I inquired politely. I didn't need to wait for a response. I needed to leave before I behaved inappropriately. "I shall retire now and think on your proposal."

He jumped to his feet, reaching out his hand as if to grab my arm. "You can't leave!"

I looked at his hand as if it were a worm.

I drew myself up to my full five foot two and turned the force of my righteous anger on him. "Are you saying that I am a prisoner? Did I misunderstand your intent?" I snapped.

"No, but for your safety…" he began.

"Did you bring me to a place where I am not safe? Or are you saying that you and yours are not safe?" I countered.

"No, no. Nothing like that, but…"

"In that case, we shall retire." I stood, glancing around at the food cooking over the fire. "Until further notice, we will take our meals in our—accommodations." My eyes scanned the area, taking in the diverse expressions of shock.

"I believe that this conversation is concluded. Any further discussion should be relayed through my—" I nudged Chris.

She jerked to attention. "Lawyer."

"Counsel," I amended. I turned and started back up the stone steps. Chris trotted after me looking slightly befuddled.

One of the men, James, the one who had a very detailed memory of history, stepped forward, handing Chris a satchel and couple of blankets as she brushed by. "It's cold."

Chris shrugged him off, but took the blankets and the satchel.

Chapter 26

When we returned to our cave room, Chris tugged at my sleeve. "Okay, now we know this was all a scam. Let's leave. I don't believe these guys will try to force you to go with them. They're not going to stop you from returning to your family. We can walk out of here and be back to your people in, oh...." Her voice trailed off as if she realized what she was suggesting. "Four or five weeks?"

As the afterglow of my temper wore off, I realized what I had done: defied dragons. Five of them, to be precise. I hid my trembling hands at my side and shook my head at her. Chris was opposed to my staying here and engaging with them; there was no need to let her know how frightened I really was of these creatures. Or how I had longed for one of their company to comfort me.

I investigated the contents of the satchel that James had pressed on Chris. "Lovely, just a cheery stroll through wolf-infested lands. No food, no horses. Or perhaps you see us flying high above, clutched protectively in the dragons' talons."

Chris didn't respond.

"And then after we return from this casual walk through the wilderness..." I put my finger on my chin.

"Yes, I can see myself going before my parents now. No, they were not going to eat me; there never was any danger. And, yes, it would have made an excellent alliance. Yes, I was willing to go to my death for duty, but not to marry. I walked away."

I had to stop speaking or I would cry. I remembered my mother's last hug, her face white as she gripped me as if she would never let me go.

I covered my silence by pretending interest in unpacking the contents of the satchel while I gained control of my tears.

I pulled out a simple divided gown, made for riding, and some small-clothes. There was also a cloak made of short brown fur and a pair of sturdy boots; all seemed to be my size. I cringed inwardly, realizing these creatures were so knowing of my person. They had planned everything carefully, every detail considered.

"I need to think on this. I need information and time."

Chris threw her hands up in disgust. "What is there to think about? They are talking about an agreement from eight hundred years ago! That's like forever."

I shook my head at her again. "No, it isn't. Many treaties are that old or older." My hands clenched and unclenched. I struggled to relax. "It isn't much different to what was always my destiny—a negotiated marriage to some royalty in a far-off kingdom. It's merely taken a different form than I anticipated." I willed myself to face the thought of marriage to Hugh—a dragon. A monster.

Chris started pacing. "You can't be taking this seriously." She looked around our quarters as if searching for a solution among the roughly crenelated stone walls. "Maybe I can take you back to Berkeley with the card. I'll tell them…I don't know, we'll think of something."

I sat down, trying to calm myself, to think. "What about the Pact? It is an agreement between my land and theirs. It can't be dismissed out of hand."

Chris walked back to me. "But you've never seen it, it's just their say-so. And, even if it exists, it's just a piece of paper that some men—sort of men," she amended, "who are dead—long dead, I might note—cooked up a zillion years ago. Let it go." She waved her hands through the air.

"But it's a compact that is keeping my country, my people, my land from destruction. This is about duty. Father would say that it should be honored."

Chris tilted her head up to the stone ceiling in exasperation. "Why are you accepting their story? Your father doesn't even know about this Pact. You told me. He thinks you're a dragon snack by now—delivered by Tom the Troll."

I wished she weren't so vulgar.

"My father may not know the specifics, but he knew enough to send me, to not refuse them. If I invalidate the agreement, what harm am I inflicting on my country?"

"Well, whatever, you can't just hand yourself over to some guy because he says so. This is blackmail, coercion. It's…it's paternalistic!" She looked at me as if assessing my understanding.

I glared her down. "I'm a princess. Royal marriages are part of our alliances. An important part of our lives. As I've told you dozens of times, this is how my world is, how it is run: on treaties, alliances, and balance."

Chris started pacing again. "These so-called men are the enemy. They're using you. You're playing the role of willing sacrifice for your family and they're not even here to applaud." She stamped her foot and stared at me then, and I stared back.

"You're a wuss! After all we've been through, are you going to roll over and play dead?"

"This is how royal families arrange marriages. Not even my brothers can marry for love." I could feel the tension roiling through me, my shoulders tightening.

She shook her head. "This is wrong. You're going to trail after these lizard-men like a lamb with a pink ribbon around its neck. You're surrendering. You're giving your life to these…these hybrids to be a broodmare, a dragonette carrier."

"I am not surrendering!" I screeched. We were both surprised at my outburst. I took another breath, trying to compose myself.

It would seem that there was no middle ground for Chris and me on this subject. We were loud enough that the stone walls bounced our voices back, sounding like a mob of people. It was undignified. I lowered my voice. "I need time. Time to figure out what is best for Verdcux, and what is best for me."

"Fine!" Chris took in a deep breath and started in again at a whisper. "Okay, let's look at it from another perspective. Let's assume, temporarily, that this Pact keeps these 'creatures' from devolving into real dragons and overrunning your world, like locust or kudzu or Nixon." She trailed off. "Why do you have to marry him? What about a friendly handshake and we part as friends? Or you could change places with some nice girl from your town who wants to raise dragon babies. So they don't get the prom queen this time. They really only need a female who is willing to breed with a half-dragon." Her voice was rising up in volume again and I put my finger to my lips to remind her that we might be heard.

I stood up tall and addressed her. "I *am* special. I'm a princess."

Chris threw up her hands and stomped back across the floor.

A hollow feeling grew as I contemplated my new fate. A fearful image of my marriage bed leapt into my mind. I resisted putting my face into my hands and sobbing.

Chris tromped back, obviously preparing another verbal tactic.

She leaned over, whispering, "Yuck. Think about it. You're to marry Hugh, a lifetime with 'mister I-am-your-lord-and-master,' just because his name is embossed on a piece of paper. Sure, he's pretty, in an over-muscled, Errol Flynn kind of way, but he's a prick. He's too full of himself. I mean, we're talking serious testosterone poisoning here."

"Wait, what did you say?"

"That he's a prick?"

"No, not that." I thought about my father's council, the papers they pored over before agreeing to a new compact, that I had read myself as part of my training. "I need to see the contract. I need to know what the boundaries are concerning my obligations to these people."

I pulled out the pawn my father had given me and sat down on the cold stone. I smiled. It was my move.

Chapter 27

I held out my hand. "I would like to see the compact, please."

Hugh looked startled. "Compact?" He blinked. I pressed my back against the hard rock wall, trying to look regal and confident. It was difficult; I could not forget that dragons surrounded me.

"The agreement. I want to see the Princess Pact."

He frowned.

"Is there some difficulty with this request? I have never seen one, nor, I am certain, had my father. Why should I believe your legendary tale?" I asked. He stood stony-faced across from me. This was a contest of wills, and no one who knew me ever doubted my will.

"There is a written agreement, is there not?" I arched one eyebrow. Be they dragons or wolves or men too full of themselves, I would not flinch. I held his eyes.

"The contract, please."

He blinked again and a small furrow of confusion crossed his face. He flicked a glance at Chris standing at my side in her sunshine yellow chemise that read, "A woman without a man is like a fish without a bicycle." I could almost see inside his head as he struggled with several emotions.

He snorted at me, indignation writ on his face. "You think we carry it around like a stick?" Somewhere behind us, I heard a rustle.

James coughed, then cleared his throat. "Actually, we do. A copy is stored here, that is. It is one of the original conditions for the transfer."

Hugh did not look pleased, but seemed satisfied with glowering at his cousin, a promise of later consequences possibly. I didn't care. I was determined to see the document. What agreements had been made and how was it worded? Perhaps there was a missing signature or an ambiguous turn of phrase, anything I could use to turn to my advantage.

James rummaged through a leather bag tucked beneath a ledge and pulled out an oilskin-covered packet. Hugh stepped over and snatched it from him. He held it out to me, almost disdainfully. "Would you like me to help you read it?"

I lifted the cover, extracted a packet of folded documents, and met his eyes with equal disdain. "I believe that we can manage, but if we need any help, I certainly know who to ask."

As I turned to leave, I chanced a look at Tristan. A single eyebrow lifted.

Back in our quarters, I sat reading page after page of tiny archaic script. I recognized the seal of Gaulen on each page. The language was formal and pedantic, laden with legal terms and conditions. I sighed, struggling with the curly script and thanking my tutors for forcing me to read scroll after scroll of ancient text. I would not compromise myself by asking the men for assistance. I would figure it out. Nearby, Chris fussed with her pack and hummed to herself.

"What day is it?"

I didn't look up. "I don't know. Does it matter?"

Chris turned toward me with a silly grin on her face. "It's the sixteenth of October." A ridiculous sliver of a candlestick was lit, and as she carried it over to me, she sang a little ditty, repetitive, but sweet. I had never heard a birthday song before.

I bowed my head in acknowledgement and clapped my hands as she concluded. "You remembered."

"Yep. Make a wish and blow it out."

I closed my eyes and thought of my home and my family and all that I loved. And I wished them safe. I blew until the stick no longer burned. I wondered if my wish would come true. It seemed likely that I would never know.

Chapter 28

Hugh and the other four men stood gathered before me. I took in a hasty breath, hoping they wouldn't notice my nervousness.

I held the contract in one hand. "I thank you for providing me with this." The men stared at me, as if any moment they might change into what they were—dragons. I resisted shivering at the palpable smell of sulfur that engulfed me. "It's been so illuminating." I stood planted, swallowing any fear that might undermine my words. Beside me, Chris squeezed my hand in encouragement.

"This has provided me with a more complete understanding of what the first princesses negotiated, and why, those many years ago." I looked directly at Hugh. "I also see that it is my choice whom I marry. One of the reasons that several nobles are traditionally sent, is it not?" At his expression of outrage, I quickly looked down at the document, paraphrasing, "Five men are needed to bring a princess safely through the high pass between your lands and mine." I trailed my finger across the wording. "Hale and healthy men of honor for her to choose from." I looked up at them. "So that puts a very different turn on this. The contract is valid as long as I marry into the royal family." I chanced a look at the other men through my lashes. "I may select any one of you and meet the conditions of this treaty." The room was so silent you could hear the click of an errant bat flapping around in the uppermost climes of the cave.

Hugh stepped forward. "No, this is not possible."

I smiled brightly at him and, with my fingertip, underscored the wording in question. He wasn't looking happy.

"Each of you will be evaluated to see if any one of you meets my standards—as I was evaluated by yon three envoys there." I allowed myself a flash of annoyance toward Tristan. "A contest is reasonable." I looked out at each of them in turn. "Perhaps three, to give careful deliberations of your strengths and suitability," I finished, throwing their wording back at them.

Hugh had the most interesting scowl, but I stuck to my speech.

"While I'm sure you are all truly wonderful, we don't know each other and, given the circumstances," I reminded them, "my father has not been afforded the opportunity to select one of you."

They looked at one another in disbelief and then at Hugh, who sputtered, "It has always been the eldest son of the king."

"Chantal." James nodded as if pleased with the memory. "After the First Princesses, she's the only one who didn't. She married Clement, the youngest of old King Allard's sons. All the rest married first sons, as has become tradition."

Hugh jumped on that. "There must have been some reason, some pressing reason not to follow tradition, not to marry the king. He was ill or deformed…"

"The language here is that they were 'hale, healthy and of honor.' Do you doubt this?" I waved the papers.

"This was agreed upon by your high consul and by our advisors, then ratified by our Kings." I stared at them for the full space of a breath, letting it sink in. "Are you saying these men weren't learned enough to define the scope of a treaty?"

No one spoke.

"Or should I be asking if all of you are 'hale, healthy and of honor'?" I looked at the strong male bodies across from me. Tristan's face paled but I didn't give him the pleasure of my curiosity. "If that is not the case, I will be happy to return to my home."

I scanned their faces. Disbelief, anger, interest, reflection and yearning crossed different countenances.

"Certainly, I wish to comply with the Princess Pact. As you said, you chose me based on careful deliberations. I propose a series of challenges for me to select an appropriate groom. As I said, three seems a reasonable number." I smiled again, hoping I could outmaneuver them.

"What kind of challenges?" Hugh spat. I thought I saw the hint of flame in his mouth and my stomach clenched.

"If you accept my decision, I agree to return with you," I said, ignoring a kick from Chris. "But it would be my choice, my decision, which of you I wed. These challenges will show me who you are, your strengths and your skills. And show, by your own behavior, who my choice should be."

Hugh rallied, staring down each of his kin. "No. This is not possible. You were chosen for me." He reached out as if to grab me. Chris insinuated herself between the two of us.

"Don't even think about it," she said slowly. They both froze, eyes locked, staring one another down. Something flashed between them, something I couldn't read.

I intervened before it escalated into something more. "You took time to choose me for your kingdom, to form an alliance that will maintain the compact. I also need time. This is too important a decision to rush, to close my eyes and randomly pick. I would know you, each of you."

I looked at Hugh seething in front of me. "Perhaps you are the one I will choose. But first we will have the contests," I reminded him.

A muscle in his face twitched. "We cannot wait here for you to playact a game, a farce. The storms will come. This can be addressed later after we return home."

I raised my head and stuck out my chin. "No, I will decide here. You think I don't know what will happen once I'm in your lands? There, you are king. No other men would dare offer for me. I'd be herded into marriage with you like a lone calf by wolves. No, I will decide here."

A vein pulsed in his forehead. The others imperceptibly drew away from him. "You are here alone without counsel."

I waved my hand at Chris, pointing out his oversight.

His eyes landed on her. He gave a dismissive jerk of his head. "She's a stranger from a place far-off. This is not a decision that a mere chit should help make, one that could affect both our lands." He spoke in a tone calculated to reduce my argument to that of a willful child.

My face flushed. I could feel my temper rising also. "I see. I'm good enough to be your queen and bedmate, but not good enough to choose my own counsel, nor make a decision this important to my life and welfare." I sensed the others stirring restlessly.

"I repeat: I do wish to adhere to this compact, but you also are bound by it. The Princess Pact is clear. You choose the princess, but I choose my husband." I dismissed him and his posturing.

He started to speak but I was tired of it, tired of being agreeable, tired of smiling as I was going to my death, and very tired of others controlling my fate. "You may decide not to enter these contests; that is entirely up to you." I moved a step closer, projecting my voice. "But I will do the selecting of my husband!"

Chapter 29

There was a subtle change in the room as each of the other man-dragons seemed to consider the possibilities. It was obvious that not one of them had read the contract closely; I wondered how its original dictum had been lost, when it was so clearly spelled out.

Hugh smiled as if he had one last move to make. "Do you truly understand the consequences, My Lady? If you chose another, you won't be queen. You're a proud woman, bred to rule. Would you remain a princess, sitting powerless in a foreign land? My cousins and brothers are good men, but I am king, not them."

I frowned. From a princess to a morsel, to queen, and back to princess, my status ricocheted.

Chris looked incensed. "You're such a jerk. You devalue all women with that statement, not just Genny. Like that's all women think about in marrying, not love or friendship but only status and money."

Hugh was right and Chris was wrong. Money was important and status more so. How could it not be? Love was but a word in a troubadour's ballad. And friendship…I wasn't a dreamer. But I wasn't about to give Hugh any more leverage than he already had.

I smiled. "My decision stands. As we have seen from the documents, you are merely my suitor, one of several." I waved my hand at the other men.

Rauf spoke then so quietly that I almost missed his words. "She might marry any one of us? Who of us wouldn't wish for that?"

Hugh's face had turned a dark purple at Chris's comment, darker after mine and black after Rauf's. I held my ground, watching Hugh glower. I wouldn't be led about by the nose for a coronet.

One of the men called Hugh's name as a glazed look in his eyes smoldered and burned. He turned to them and roared. I stood, not breathing, my head up, my eyes unwavering. How could such a sound come from a human throat? Was he changing? I felt a trickle of sweat between my breasts, a frisson of fear that I had pushed him too far. But I could not back down. Not now, not here.

Rauf spoke, as if reassessing. "There is power and status in marrying a human."

Hugh spun towards him. His eyes darkened, his pupils enlarged. Wisps of smoke seeped out of his nose. Suddenly the cave, large as it was, seemed small. Chris tugged at my arm as the air around him wavered. The other men realigned, moved quickly into a small semi-circle between us and Hugh.

Piers, who was barely my age and looked as if he had only recently started to shave, grabbed Chris's arm and mine and dragged us behind a large rocky formation. "Um, your proposal comes as a slight surprise. I, ah…believe that Hugh needs a bit of time to consider it fully."

Before our eyes, Hugh transformed into a dragon. A tail, thick as a tree trunk, writhed and swept the floor but a few dozen spans from my feet. The gold and coral scales upon his back glinted in the torchlight, each as large as a child's hand, hundreds of them. And beyond that, a head the full height of a man, with teeth. I couldn't move. I shut my eyes, knowing I would die here in a dark echoing cave. Chris bumped against me and I snapped my eyes opened. Two others changed, Tristan, with scales of silver and emerald, and Rauf, bronze and turquoise, kaleidoscopes of color.

Hugh roared again and steam poured from his mouth, flickers of flame snaking out. His tail swiped across a quartz outcropping, sending shards of stone across the cave. Red dust exploded into the cavern and everything appeared as through a rosy haze. Piers waded into the fray, changing as he moved. Steam pulsed and all were lost to my sight in the depths of the shadowed cave. Chris's eyes were huge and I shook so hard that the ancient papers rattled in my hands.

"I believe he is not used to being gainsaid," I whispered.

Chris nodded, her fingers trembling on my arm.

"As my great-grandmamma used to say, 'Do not meddle in the affairs of dragons, because you are crunchy and taste good with ketchup,'" Chris whispered back from behind our stone shield.

My teeth chattered as I replied. "It isn't as if I have much of a choice." Her words repeated in my mind. "I thought you didn't have dragons in your world."

"We don't. It's just a saying."

Some debris thumped the stone wall to our side and bounced

off. Within the haze, I couldn't make out individual bodies as they vied against one another.

Her hands dug into my wrist. "They seem…distracted. It may be a good time to leave."

I whispered back through my clenched teeth. "I won't be intimidated by a puffed-up male. If I back down now, I forfeit any power I have over my future."

She looked at me, eyes bright with fear. "I take back everything I said about your being a wuss." Beyond us, the long necks and tails of four dragons flailed, breaking rock formations into shards.

James, still in human form, stood between us and his dragon kinsmen. We all ducked as a spat of flame whipped by us. It finally seemed to register to James that Chris and I might not be accustomed to such a display.

He turned to us and bowed, then checked behind him before speaking. "This may take a wee bit longer to resolve. It is just a misunderstanding—a minor dispute among family. Hugh is a great fellow, but we've all been tense with this trip and everything. With a little more time, you will be able to see that Hugh has the utmost respect for you, that he's a fine leader and has a good head on his shoulders. But, right now…." He ducked as a rock sailed by. "Right now," he repeated, "I think it best that you retire while we sort this out."

Chris and I looked at each other and then at the flying rocks, bared teeth and claws beyond us. I nodded and we scooted away with as much dignity as we could muster.

Chapter 30

Back in our cavern "room" we discussed our situation again—and again, and again.

"You're still considering this? After what we just saw?" Chris shouted. "What do you need to convince yourself that this is crazy? They are monsters. You saw them. You're planning a white-veil marriage to a thirty-foot-long, scaly creature with eight-inch claws and teeth. If you have the littlest marital spat you could end up like a toasted marshmallow." She stopped, waiting to see if I had changed my mind. I was working my way through her bizarre language.

"And, oh yeah, he would be so sorry, so contrite!" Chris rummaged through her bags and pulled out some clothing and a much-needed hair brush. We were both coated heavily with debris from the dragons' "discussion."

I carefully removed my dust-covered dress and waited for Chris to help me with it. Of course she didn't. She paced. I abandoned any hope of her coming to my aid and started donning the pieces of clothing she handed me.

Her voice became muffled as she tugged a clean chemise over her head. "You can't marry one of them. You don't know them. You don't know where they live. You don't even know if their human wives survive birthing a dragon! What if you lay an egg or something?"

As she continued her diatribe, some of her more creative images gave me pause. I pushed past the horrific visions that came to mind, interrupting her description of one particularly unlikely mating. "You heard, it's been done before many times. This is a political marriage, just as he said, for the good of both lands. And stop yelling at me," I added, nearly yelling myself. I caught myself and spoke softly, more like hissing now. "Lower your voice. We can be heard throughout the cavern," I admonished. Anyone in my entourage would have quieted at my tone.

Chris only got louder. "They're having a knock-down, drag-out fight below and you worry about us yelling? You are totally and absolutely crazy! Deluded!" She stood with her nose inches from mine.

I felt my own temper rise. I had tolerated her insults and disrespect for too long. How dare she treat me like a demented old aunt.

I turned my back on her and stalked to the opposite end of the cave. Chris followed, one step behind.

She was worse than the Duke of Montreau's rat terrier. "You're being used as a status symbol, like a trophy wife, no different. Or maybe more like cattle raiding in Scotland, a prize. Why can't you see this?" she continued with her foreign allusions.

I whirled toward her. "What I see is that you have no understanding of duty."

Chris's gray eyes darkened, her skin flushed and shimmered, reminding me of the dragons as they shifted. It must be an illusion from the torchlight in the caves. We glared at one another.

I couldn't believe we had come to this. I took a breath, reaching for a calm, rational tone. "This solution has promise, both for me and for my land. My father would be pleased, my lands safe from war with dragon fire. Think on it. I could choose my future husband out of five eligible men." Sort of men, I amended to myself. "And if I choose Hugh, I will be queen."

"If we aren't flattened like pancakes or burnt to cinders during the prenuptial arrangements," Chris added, flailing her arms.

Pushing my fears down once more, I continued, ignoring her comments. "I'm going to negotiate a reasonable settlement and get it in writing—before I leave this place." I looked at the documents again and shook my head. "We should go through these papers again. I want to make sure I didn't miss anything."

Chris shook her head, open-mouthed in astonishment. "Didn't you notice? They're dragons, huge scaly monsters with teeth and talons and fire!"

"At least none of them is fifty and bald with a huge paunch. That was certainly a possibility for an alliance at home after King Charles' wife died; someone is going to have to marry him."

Chris closed her eyes. "Either way, this is wrong. Don't you see? You were tricked. They aren't going to change 'cause you shake your royal finger at them. It's like my nana used to say: 'Neither systems, nor people, nor dragons change without significant need.'

"They will do this again, century after century, like they're doing here. And the next princess may not be as plucky as you. She might end her life rather than go or capitulate to the first dragon that offers her his—claw."

I frowned at that. "What you say has merit. But that doesn't change what I must do. I'm staying."

Chris shook her head at me again, then went to peer down to where the dragons thrashed about. "You are pigheaded," she called over her shoulder, "but as my nana said, 'even pigheads crack 'neath a dragon's jaw.'" I joined her and we watched the walls glow with fire. There was a certain sparkle about it that caught the eye.

"Chris, why would your great-grandmother speak of dragons? You've said she was neither a seer nor a witch, so why? Was there anything notable about her?"

She looked up, shaking off the mesmeric effects of the flames reflected on the wall. "No, nothing. It was sort of a joke. She was a fanciful old lady." Chris's brow knotted. "I can't think of anything abnormal about her. She was so much the proper lady. And always certain that people would jump when she said 'frog.' We used to call her Queen Ria behind her back."

I shook my head. "No, there must be something. She gave you the card, did she not? You've quoted her a number of times speaking of dragons, yet you've told me over and over, dragons don't exist in your world."

Chris frowned and spoke as if reminiscing. "I guess there were a few odd things. She came over from the Scottish Highlands at the turn of the last century. She arrived at Ellis Island by herself, pregnant and alone. Her husband had died during their journey to America. I never knew of what. She was always a bit reticent about it. I often wondered if she left to hide an illicit pregnancy. You know, that she wasn't actually married and got caught."

Chris's face flushed. "I need to get some air. I can't think in this place." We both jumped as the glow of flames spattered against the stone-step walls. "Wow, talk about your challenging relationships. I've heard my friends talk about boyfriends breathing fire, but this is the first time I've ever seen it. So is this going to be one of your tests? I hold a candle out at arm's length and see which one can light it without setting me on fire?"

"I don't believe that will be necessary," I demurred.

Chris raised one incredulous eyebrow and walked out of our cave room.

Chapter 31

Chris had been gone for what seemed like hours. Now that I had time for reflection, the reality of my delicate position sprayed over me like an icy stream. I was frightened.

My initial outrage and indignation had seeped out, leaving only fear and horror. In the shadowed light, the silence stretched me to the ends of myself. For all my bravado, I didn't know how much longer I could keep up the illusion of strength, for them or for myself. Once Chris left, I felt drained. The massive weight of the stone cave pressed against me, making it difficult to think clearly. I was tired of trying to be brave, of trying to be rational, of trying to disguise my fear.

Objectively, my situation had vastly improved. I lived, though I would never see my siblings grow into adults, nor my parents age. Instead they would live, year after year, with the guilt of my supposed death.

But now a future lay before me, ambiguous, one where I had to walk a careful path. A misstep, a careless word, would carve in stone the rest of my life. A marriage in a strange land to a half man, half dragon. My thoughts veered to one particular man-dragon—one that I wished would step forward and…

I shook myself; this was no time to be the fanciful miss dreaming of illusions. They were not human.

Only honor and duty forced me to consider their offer. I reminded myself of my father's whispered advice after taking my rook with his knight during my ninth year: "Consider the war, not the battle. Most important: never, ever concede."

But, for all my bluster, I was at their mercy. I had no coin to play. No one was coming to my rescue. They thought me dead.

And there was the treaty. I must marry one of them or else…or else what? I didn't know.

Perhaps Chris was right; maybe there was another way to protect my home. Mayhap they exaggerated the danger. It wouldn't be the first time, nor would it be the last, that people twisted the truth to leverage an agreement to benefit themselves.

My mind circled back to Chris. It seemed peculiar that precisely when I needed her, she appeared from a distant world. Something slipped across my mind like a feather, something she had said. Something odd, some passing comment about her great-grandmother. What was it that didn't make sense?

I heard the crunch of steps as someone approached and then hesitated. I ran forward, eager to see Chris again, to make amends and start anew. My face fell, but my tell-tale heart beat faster. Tristan, the erstwhile bard, and Piers, the youngest of the man-dragons, crooked their heads around the corner, bearing steaming bowls of stew. Every time Tristan appeared, I felt a pull, one that I struggled to contain.

Tristan cleared his throat. "If there is anything we can do to make this easier…" I turned away from him. I knew my countenance must show the flush that rose to my face.

"Aside from returning me to my life and my family?" I said, slapping a bitter edge in my voice to disguise my reactions. "No. Nothing."

Piers's eyes grew large and he backed out quickly. Tristan paused before speaking. "Please, believe me. You won't come to harm at our hands. Even though our comforts here are meager." He turned toward the small pile of goods in the corner. "What little we have we extend to you."

Finally, one more missing piece slid into place.

"It was you, wasn't it? You were there at gatherings and dances, playing music, singing. You're who marked me as chosen."

His face closed up. "You know I was among those who picked you. The three of us, Piers, Rauf, and I, were sent to find a princess."

"Might I ask, why me? Did I draw the short straw?"

He sighed. "We were obviously looking for a princess. Someone worthy of a king. We wanted someone with backbone and strength." He laughed deprecatingly as a slow flush crawled up his neck. "Someone I… we could envision marrying. And there you were, bright, courageous, well-spoken and beautiful. We congratulated ourselves when we found you. We were so sure."

Here with him alone, my breathing quickened. I ground my teeth to hold myself aloof. "You mean you, not we. *You* were sure."

He was quiet and then acknowledged, "Yes, me."

My heart betrayed me again, beating faster and faster. How could I feel so deceived and yet simultaneously feel this yearning?

He shifted our conversation then. "I didn't consider the cost of keeping our purpose known only to your Priestess. I tried to convince myself that it was not my concern. It was an understanding between your spiritual advisors and my kingdom. However, as the days went on, I found myself increasingly uncomfortable. I returned and tried to get an audience with the Priestess. Four times I went. She was unavailable and the doors barred.

"And then that night, I watched you at supper and saw the toll that this was taking on you. Piers, Rauf and I talked that night, back and forth, debating our need to protect our kingdom, against our responsibility to our future princess, you. We were conflicted. It was too unkind, too severe a condemnation for anyone to endure, much less a gently-raised lady."

There it was again, another reminder that he had caused all of this to happen. My temper flared.

"And this is where you've taken me, a 'gently-raised lady'?" I parroted. "To wed a dragon?" I lobbed a low comment, "Perhaps marrying a half-beast is only slightly better to me than being eaten by one."

He flinched.

He looked hard at me then, met my eyes and held them. I struggled not to lose my bearings in the otherness there, not to drown in the sea of wildness and warmth. Tristan seemed lost within himself, then gave a little shake, continuing as if I had not spoken.

He looked past me, speaking with careful precision. "I know this can't be easy for you, presented with a suitor from a foreign land. A people unlike your own. All of us are under much strain, but my brothers and cousins are good men. Men you'd want to have at your back."

He avoided my eyes as he spoke next. "I understand you not wanting to marry one who is not wholly human. I've thought much on this."

What was this about, some new gambit?

Now that I was close to him, I marveled at the foreignness in his eyes. His pupils were more oval than round, and within their depths I could see power and a strange wildness. Beyond that I saw hints of compassion and sadness. And something more—longing?

I almost snorted at my imaginings. No matter how human he looked now, he was a dragon. And one with his own agenda.

But as we stood so close, I breathed in his scent. Longing coursed across my body, flooding my thoughts. The distance between us seemed to fade. Did he lean closer, or did I? I wanted—I didn't want.

I couldn't.

I braced myself and stared straight into those strange blue eyes. "You lied to me."

He met my eyes briefly, before leaning against the door, looking beyond me at the wall. "No, never."

I thought back. "Perhaps not in so many words. But you knew what was to happen and you let me believe that I was to die. Is that honest? Do you consider that fair and honorable?" He stood unmoving as if now part of the stone wall.

He turned to leave. As he disappeared from my view, I heard him speak, "Not particularly, My Lady."

It felt like any hope I might have had disappeared with him.

Chapter 32

I refused any discourse with the man-dragons the remainder of that day and the next afternoon. Meals were delivered by one or another of them. Chris received them, silencing any discussion from our captors. By that second evening, I had a plan. I started down the cold stone stairs, back to where they milled around awaiting my presence. Chris joined me before I was halfway there. We finished descending the stairs in silence.

"I'm ready for us to move forward."

Five heads spun toward me and five chins lifted with interest. Since I had refused to return with them, the man-dragons had seemed conflicted about how to proceed. My stand had spread discord among them; I could see bruises on Hugh's right cheek and Rauf's lip was puffed. The walls were scorched from the aftermath of dragon fire. Factions were forming, then fissuring. Piers, James and even Tristan seemed sympathetic to my situation, as if they too were ill at ease. Hugh and Rauf I couldn't read.

As though putting a foot in an icy stream, I edged into my discourse, one toe at a time, my smile hiding both my anxiety and my fury.

I lowered my voice and peered up through my lashes at them. "I've selected the challenges for you." When logic and force failed, honey, as my mother had said, could be a powerful draw.

I attempted to project a look that was both girlish and regal. "It will help me make a well-formed decision as to whom I shall marry."

My apprehension I hid beneath a coquettish smile. It wouldn't do to approach this forcefully; I needed to win them over, so they would want to oblige me. I wished for a fan to hide any doubt that might show on my face.

I caught Tristan watching me and shaking his head. After our last encounter, he must think me a shrew. I turned my head to cover my blush and noticed Hugh watching Chris, or rather Chris's chest. Perhaps he was evaluating the tantalizing words written across today's chemise front,

"Warning: I have an attitude, and I *do* know how to use it." The chemise was a bit revealing. Well, more than a bit.

Gathering my courage, I forged ahead. "Let us begin anew. This situation is not of your making. Perhaps you also have some discontent with how this came to be." I fluttered my eyelashes, enough to let the men feel manly.

"You're overdoing it." Chris leaned toward me and whispered. "Hugh is looking at you like a wolf at a tethered goat."

I kept my eyes from him. What would Chris know of such things? But I focused on the others and adjusted my lines of persuasion.

"Not that I agree with what's been done," I amended. "But can't we move forward, create a resolution—one in which each of us is satisfied?" They looked at one another, their tension radiating from some unspoken decision. A chill jabbed at my heart. Something was up. My pretense was failing, my push to cheery assurance slipping like water through my hands. I unlocked my fingers and forced my arms to my sides in an effort to appear relaxed.

"We need to begin, as you have indicated, as quickly as possible." At their blank looks, I started again, trying to assert control. "One of you must wed a human princess, and I agree to this. But there is a caveat. *I* will choose which one." I took in a breath, then continued. "I've decided how best to gather information. One, we will have a sword display so I can see you fight. Two, each of you will play chess—against me. And three, each of you will be asked to bring me the perfect gift."

Hugh's sardonic voice interfered with my declaration. "And if we choose not to *play* but simply take you back to our kingdom as the treaty allows? Or do you prefer that we break our part of the treaty?"

Fear flashed in my chest. Would my world then be at risk?

Check.

I was losing control. I revised my tactics, to spin it on its axis.

I lifted my chin. "No, we both keep our ends of the treaty. But with my rules. Otherwise, though you have a princess, you have one who seeks to undermine you the rest of your life. Is that *your* wish? Or do you want someone who will support you, raise your children and stand by your side?" I strained to keep my face composed.

They furrowed their brows in the face of the changes in my demeanor. Tristan and James flashed a short look between them before studiously staring at the floor. Rauf looked contemplative. I felt my blood chill.

Hugh lowered his eyes before looking back at me with a wolfish grin. "Perhaps it makes no great difference to us." There it was. They had talked, made a decision. My options had dwindled.

Check again.

The other four men were now at attention, their gaze flicking back and forth between Hugh and me. I stared ahead while searching for the right thing to say. I could think of nothing. I swallowed. All my hopes of succeeding with reason, flattery and winsome looks sank like a stone, without a single bubble to mark their departure.

I was losing. My ears roared with noise. I couldn't think.

From somewhere I heard James say, "Don't push her."

Hugh shrugged, "We're leaving today, Genevieve. You need to concede at least to this, for your own good and the good of our worlds. We've waited, hoping that you would take a rational approach to your destiny." He smiled at me. "It's over. The game is ended. We leave within the hour—with you."

His last words rang in my head like a funeral bell.

This was not a game of honor, but one where I embodied the spoils of war, the carrion-crow pickings after a battle. I stood there in shock. Tristan continued staring at the floor, as if unwilling to acknowledge what was happening. Rauf and Piers flanked the far wall like ship scavengers waiting for the plunder to wash up with the tide.

They had been planning this, watching me, amused and sly. No power, no choice. Chris was right; they saw me as a broodmare, not a princess. The imprisoning weight of the caves closed in on me, leaching my thoughts, my strength.

I had but one move left. I pulled my knife free, Tristan's knife, and pushed it against my wrist, ignoring the sharp intake of breath around me. "I'll not be taken this way, as a trophy, a prized catch. That will not happen."

Behind me, Chris gasped, "Oh my god."

Hugh started forward as if to grab me and, in my panic, I pressed the knife in sharply. Pain flared at my wrist and blood oozed across my hand. "Don't come closer." I spoke slowly, trying to keep my voice from wavering. "I was willing to die for my land, willing to marry for my land. But know you, I will choose death before the dishonor of being taken by force."

I watched Hugh while keeping a rocky ledge between us. All eyes were on me. No one moved. I didn't wish to die. I wanted to live, to marry. But not this way, not in a union with no honor. My head throbbed in beat to the sharp pain in my wrist. Could I do this? I didn't know. I had to make them believe that I would, and the only way I could do so was to believe it myself.

When I next spoke, it was with the despondency, despair, and anger that had accumulated for the past two months. After all I had gone through, it was over. I might die here in this echoing cave by my own hand.

My breath caught in my throat as I struggled to make my stand clear. "Perhaps you could stop me now, wrest this from my hand before I do too much damage to myself—or perhaps not." My body trembled, and I steeled myself, tightening my grip on the knife. "I will not be dragged off as anyone's foray plunder. Eventually, I will end this." There was silence for many heartbeats. Chris didn't move. Even her energy was stilled during this standoff.

No one breathed. Must I sacrifice the queen to win the game? Or would they bend to my wish? Death had no appeal for me, but life as a pawn had less.

James whispered then, "Just like Penelope."

Hugh spoke, his voice just above a whisper. "Be quiet, James. She's bluffing." He took a half step toward me. "Come, give it up. Don't damage your pretty arm to make a point." But his lips were white against his skin.

I pushed again, steeling myself against the pain, against my own regret. Blood dripped to the ground. "Stand away. Remember, because of your actions, I've already faced my death. No. Here is where I stand. No more, no more." Hugh took another careful step. I pushed the knife deeper into the tender inside of my wrist. Warm blood pulsed across my hand. My eyes glazed with the pain and the men looked like statues 'neath the rock that surrounded us.

"Do you truly wish me dead? Are you so arrogant that you will take that risk? Accept it as a truth, I won't go with you as your trophy." My hand felt like ice.

Please, please, don't push me to this, I don't wish to die here. Please, I don't know if I can do this, but I will not be dishonored. Not be taken captive by men for whom honor is but a word.

My fingers were locked around the hilt of the knife. My breath caught in my throat; my blood pounded at my wrist and throat. The drip became a trickle that I heard as it fell on stone.

From across the room, Tristan spoke. "Peace," he said. Hugh's head snapped up, turning at Tristan's word. A look, a world of information, passed between those two, a slash of something that I couldn't read. Tristan eyes flamed and Hugh's face changed from rage to something akin to grudging acceptance before it solidified into a mask of ice.

"My brother, we can't lose her this way." My breath came in gasps as Tristan continued to speak. "A few days, one handful, we can still safely return by foot. If we have to fly her out, we will. Let that be the consequence. She is to be wife to one of us, possibly our queen. Let us start now respecting her word."

Hugh gave a single nod.

Then, as if nothing had happened, as if he and I were the only ones who existed, Tristan slowly stepped toward me, locking his eyes with mine and holding out his hand as if to ward off my death. "No one is going to force you, Princess. Release the knife. No one here wishes you harm. It will be as you say. We will abide by your rules." He stopped motionless about four body lengths from me, his eyes holding mine, tying me to the earth, to life.

Through my pain and fear, I saw the others bow their heads in agreement. Hugh said nothing, then he, too, nodded in agreement. "As the storms hold, we will wait."

My voice quavered. "Then I may choose?" I felt my head getting light.

Tristan nodded. He crossed to my side, gently extracting the knife from my clenched fingers as he wrapped his other hand over my wrist to staunch the flow of blood.

And then I did faint.

Chapter 33

When I came back to myself, the evening was well advanced.

Chris and I were outside under a sky lit with stars that dazzled. Coals banked against the mountainside reflected heat onto my face. Our eyes met and I saw tears welling in hers.

She brushed them aside. "What did you think you were doing? Killing yourself isn't an answer. I mean, then you're dead."

She fixed me with her gaze. "Would you truly have done it, killed yourself?"

I remained silent for some time, looking inward for the truth. "I don't know. I truly don't."

Chris pressed her hands against her forehead as if in pain. "Just when I think I understand where you're coming from, you do something else to confuse me. That was an incredibly stupid trick." She peeked through her fingers. "I can't believe you did that! What if they hadn't agreed?"

My wrist burned beneath the wrap that bound it. Bile churned in me as I remembered the blood. I wasn't sure what I had intended when I threw down that gauntlet other than to prevent them from going forward with their plans for me.

"I believe myself honorable, one who does her duty no matter how distasteful. It's how I was reared, why I came here as the sacrifice. There is no honor in men dragging me away to a marriage. For what would my sacrifice be?" I pushed myself up until I was facing the moon, letting its soft glow caress my skin. "For me, my obligation was met once I was tied to that post."

I held out my hand, palm upward.

"My mother taught me that power was not a favor to be snatched away by a greedy hand." I looked her in the eye. "The treaty allows me to select a spouse. I couldn't let these men callously decide my fate."

Chris stared back. "Wow. I guess all families are the same. My nana used to harp on something like that, obligation, duty, and personal power." Tossing and catching a rock over and over, she opened her mouth to speak and then seemed to reconsider. A single lost cloud crossed above and hid the moon, changing the light from the warmth of silver to the gold of the reflected embers.

With a shake, Chris roused herself from her reverie.

"So now what? We go home?" she asked with a wistful smile.

I shook my head and held out my hand. "Now I choose a husband."

The following day was a reprieve. In order to stay, we needed supplies. Two of the men hunted for game. The other three set to make our lodging more comfortable, collecting wood and building up a large fire for warmth.

All of them watched the sky as if anticipating storms, but the horizon remained clear. Unless the weather changed, I was safe. They conceded six days, five for me to select a mate. But upon the sixth I must choose.

At our morning meal, Hugh made one last attempt to persuade me. "We already know who is the best with a sword," he said. "We can save you the trouble."

I politely restated my intent to see it through. He bowed and moved back to stoking the fire, perhaps unwilling to face Chris glowering by my side.

I remained ill at ease, unable to settle. Their presence reminded me of what I had gone through, of Tom Mastin's threats to Chris, of the long frightening journey here and of my first sight of the five dragons flying overhead. I shivered uncontrollably before I recovered myself.

Nevertheless, I moved forward with my plan. To wed a dragon, a beast.

Tristan stayed far from me, first off hunting with Rauf and then engaged in conversations with James and Piers. In fact, since he had staunched my wound, he seldom spoke to me. Perhaps he was catering to Hugh's authority. Or maybe he simply didn't like me. A handful of tears fell. I brushed them away. I couldn't linger on this. It wasn't helpful.

The sun's arc had passed its zenith. Chris and I sat on a stone seat beneath a blue and white sky, watching the men.

Now that the boundaries were clearly defined, they treated both Chris and me with gallant deference, standing up when either of us entered their presence, waiting to eat until we were seated, drawing us into polite conversations. Nothing happened that I could point to and say, *dragon*.

But in the back of my mind, and locked in tightly, I knew what they were and that they had tricked me.

I took a breath in and tried to release my anger, to hold myself to the same standards I expected of them. I wasn't sure I could quite yet.

James, stammering with embarrassment, drew me aside and spoke of his love back home. A lady dragon from a nearby town had stolen his heart. He begged my forgiveness but declared he could not compete for my hand.

How interesting, marrying for love. I wondered what his parents thought of this. I couldn't but wish him well. "Thank you for your honesty. While I regret your decision, I wish you and your lady every happiness."

He looked so relieved that I almost didn't register his next words. "Sadly, this leaves you only three to vie for your hand."

"Three?"

"I doubt Tristan will enter the contests. He wouldn't want to saddle any woman with his affliction, especially not a human bride."

My voice trembled. "What affliction?"

He shrugged. "Since the age of twelve, Tristan turns pure dragon in the winter months, for as long as the snow falls. That's why he led the search for you this summer. He knows how important it is to marry outside our people."

I felt my face pale. Tristan. That was why he was avoiding me.

Tristan sought me out before the moon eclipsed the lower hills. He held himself tall and straight. His face set in the way I'd come to understand indicated discomfort. "My Lady."

My face felt set also. I knew what he was going to say. He would refuse to offer for me. I lifted my chin so he didn't think I was some chit whose emotions ruled her.

"James said he told you."

"Yes."

He looked away for a moment, then faced me again. "I'm sorry you had to hear it that way. I wished to tell you myself."

"No matter."

He seemed about to say something else, perhaps to explain, but my pride could take no more.

 I nodded my head in dismissal and walked away.

Chapter 34

That night I lingered in that misty space between wakefulness and sleep, replaying the day's events, evaluating each of the men, trying, unsuccessfully, not to think of Tristan, when I stiffened at a sound.

Scritch, scritch.

I had almost fallen back asleep when something rancid wafted across my nose, the smell of vermin or decay. I was questioning my own hygiene when the noise came again, a soft snuffling noise and the scratch of claws against a hard surface. I raised my head, listening.

These caves were never silent; water dripped and flowed, and any noise at all reverberated, echoing off hard stone surfaces. In the early mornings, nesting bats chittered to their young. The man-dragons clomped across the stone corridors, the empty spaces repeating their footfalls and voices as they called back and forth, infiltrating my dreams with their racket. All these I had heard before.

This was new. Not a noise to which I was accustomed.

I almost convinced myself that I was making an acorn into an oak when I heard raspy breathing. Chris stirred restlessly in her sleep, flinging out an arm. The noise stopped. I strained, listening into the black of the cave, holding my breath. Was something there?

Under the cover of my blanket, I searched for my knife. Tristan's knife. At least he hadn't asked to have it returned. Another scurrying sound and the stink of fetid meat and rot grew stronger. My finger wrapped around the knife's handle. Then I recalled I had smelled this before, when Chris and I first came into the caves. I struggled to keep my breath steady even as I inched my other hand out from my blanket, feeling for Chris's magic fire sticks. I heard a low guttural sound and the click of nails to my right. Something was in the cave room with us.

I struck the fire starter once, holding it with unsteady fingers as I lit the lantern by my side.

Chris rolled over, wincing at the sharp light. "Good grief, what is that smell?" I scanned the cave, hoping nothing was there.

I heard it again, sounding close, just beyond Chris in the shadows. I raised the lantern higher.

"Oh my god!" Chris exclaimed.

There, backed against a wall, not a body's length from us, I saw a wide black snout, little beady eyes and teeth—too many teeth in a mouth that snarled and sprayed yellowed spittle. As we stared, it lunged at us, hissing, fangs bared. Inside its mouth, I saw the glow of an orange-red ball of roiling liquid.

Chris screeched as it spat and a flame hissed by. Chris grabbed a rock and flung it at the beast. There was a distinct thunk and the creature squealed. It retreated, scuttled back into the depths of our quarters on four porcine-like hooves, a myriad of barbed spines across its back clacking against one another.

From outside our quarters, voices rang out, "What's happening?"

"The women! One of them screamed."

Into our sleeping quarters rushed Tristan, Hugh, Rauf and James, swords out, silent but for the low growls that came from deep within their chests.

I pointed a finger toward the dark shadows that cloaked the rock walls. "It went that way."

The men took their torches and disappeared.

Piers poked his head around the corner. The soft fuzz on his cheeks made him look even younger in this light. "May I come in?"

Chris seemed ready to embrace him. He stayed by our side, three or four measured steps away, trying, but not succeeding, to ignore our state of undress. Every so often he would look our way and then quickly duck his head.

I had grabbed a blanket around me, holding it snug. Chris was practically naked, her shift hanging down mid-hip, with loosely woven short trousers below that.

"I most humbly beg your pardon. This was my watch." His voice trailed away.

He looked at Chris again as if transfixed, no longer making an effort to disguise his interest. As the light glinted across her chest the writing on her night shift stated, "Come on baby, light my fire."

Piers shook himself and seemed possessed by an impulse to bolt. Amusement steadied my nerves.

From the outer caverns, one of the men called out. Three other voices joined him, swords clanking as they moved quickly through the echoing rooms. A high pitched scream reverberated through the caves and I cringed.

Within a short time, Rauf and James returned, bearing a limp carcass between them. Hugh led the way, with anger, Tristan close behind, his face closed and tight.

Piers flinched before their gaze. Hugh spoke, first looking at me, then at Chris. "Are you hurt?" We both shook our heads and the tension drained from Hugh. "We promised you safety. If you had been harmed…"

Piers opened his mouth to defend himself. "I stepped away for only a minute, maybe two. I don't know how a fire boar could have gotten by me."

Anger, and something else, maybe disappointment, roiled from Hugh's shoulders. "There are no excuses. You were to protect them."

Tristan placed his hand on Piers' shoulder. "Their safety was entrusted to you." He looked over at Hugh. "Perhaps it's too great a responsibility for one his age. He's younger than our princess."

Hugh pressed his lips together. "Think what could have happened. Boars are nasty-tempered beasts. Not only do they breathe fire, their spines are poisonous."

James and the others nodded.

Hugh squared his shoulders, ill at ease. "It is upon me to mete out his punishment." Chris quietly stepped up behind him, resplendent in her chemise.

Hugh looked miserable, his sword grasped in his hand. He raised it without thinking, "Piers…"

Chris squeaked, "No," and reached out to stop Hugh. He recoiled, startled by her touch, and his elbow drew back, catching her off balance. She fell with a sudden "Oof" and I heard a familiar thunk as her head hit the floor. But she did not disappear.

Hugh spun, his face ashen. I shot a murderous look at him as I helped her stand, slowly, carefully, as she was obviously in pain.

"I, I didn't know you were there. I would never," he stammered, holding his free hand out to make amends.

Chris stood level with Hugh, hauled back her arm and punched his shoulder. She yelped in surprise, cradling her knuckles. He didn't flinch. It must have hurt her, as she gasped, bending forward and holding her arm close to her torso.

After a final rub to her fist, she lifted her head, dismissing his apology. "We're even now. And stop lording it over Piers. He's just a boy, for heaven's sake." Chris cradled her hand against her body.

Hugh regained his composure, covering his discomfort with a stiff back and stiffer language. He sheathed his sword. "No, I should have been more cautious. Please, forgive me, Lady." His eyes almost crossed as he fought to ignore her sheer chemise with its curious writing. "I have harmed you."

"Oh stop it, you're forgiven already. I'll be better in a minute, soon as the room stops spinning." Her face was white and drawn even in the low light. "You're making too much of a fuss over this."

"No, this is my error. I…"

"Stop. Okay?" Chris snapped. "I just need to lie down for a second." She swayed slightly.

Hugh caught her, as it seemed she might fall. Indecision crossed his face as he slowly and gently picked her up, and carried her to our bedding. Chris, after a moment of panic, ceased struggling. She seemed bemused, like a child watching a magician for the first time.

Chapter 35

Bathed in the early morning light, I stood upon the plateau of the mountain looking across the void, where not so long ago I was drugged and tied.

Behind me, the men, the same I feared as dragons, warmed up muscles and tendons swinging their swords. So much had changed since then, it felt a lifetime distant. Now we conversed as companions.

Observing them spar, I could see that they were skilled fighters, with the expertise of many years of training—more than I would have thought necessary for men who could transform themselves into dragons.

Even with all that rode on these tests, my mind couldn't settle. I felt spikes of questions rolling around my head: questions about Chris, the other princesses, Tristan—my future.

Chris and Hugh exited the cave then, far enough apart to the eye, but they moved as if an invisible rod were attached betwixt, opposing and yet connecting them.

As I caught Chris's eyes, she shook herself almost as if she were ridding herself of some elusive emotion. When she came to my side, lines of sadness wreathed her smile, as if caught between conflicting desires.

Hugh joined the others, drawing lines in the dirt to define the fencing area. Piers, as per his youthful exuberance, objected. "Why can't we fight in the sky as dragons?"

Hugh looked up from pacing off the square space. He lifted his head towards the north as if smelling the winds, then seeming satisfied, spoke. "We've agreed to meet Genevieve's dictates. She specified swords. This is to show our expertise as humans, not dragons."

I nodded, pleased that Hugh was truly respecting my word.

Rauf brushed away Piers's suggestion, "This is not an opportunity for you to show off your aerial acrobatics, Piers."

James nodded, waving his hand in my direction. "She couldn't see you that high up."

"It's just a sparring match," Piers protested. "We could tell her who won."

"Piers, leave off. We do this as she wishes," Tristan said.

Piers looked over to me as if hoping I would change my mind. It was hard to resist the plea in his eyes.

I smiled at him, trying to soften my words. "Hugh is correct, my decision stands."

Hugh and Tristan both inspected the newly-defined contest grounds. As they passed one another, an unseen wall seemed to push them apart. I wondered if they had a row after Tristan intervened on my behalf. The other men sensed it also, and there was silence for longer than felt comfortable.

Rauf, Piers, and James, removing stones and the occasional branch, ignored the disunity between their kinsmen.

Tristan's smile eased the ripple of tension. "So what next, my brother?"

Hugh met his eyes. "We settle on which of us is to pair off for the first round. And then, we fight."

It was a simple decision, which they resolved by the draw of sticks.

Within minutes after, Rauf and Hugh stepped inside the small ash-bordered ground, saluted one another and waited for my signal to begin. To the far right, the sunlight caught on the crystals that clung to the entrance of the cave, causing rainbows to shimmer upon the ground.

I gestured for the men to start. Rauf and Hugh began circling carefully around each other.

Rauf lunged forward two steps, sword extended, but Hugh danced out of reach, each of his steps precisely placed.

I turned to Chris to seek her advice. She seemed distracted by the crystals. I sighed inwardly. I needed her counsel. Perhaps she had some thoughts on the men's swordsmanship. But before I could speak, she wrinkled her brow in consternation, saying. "Remember what I said about a mystery?"

The men engaged again, and I whispered a quick "shhh" to Chris. Hugh took the offensive, his sword barely moving as he took three quick steps in.

Chris imposed again, placing her hand on mine. "I'm not sure if I should even mention this to you. I mean we're already beyond rational thought. And it doesn't really have anything to do with this." She jerked her chin toward the men. "Here we are with dragons and all. They are

146

real. And caves, the *crystal* caves." I divided my attention between Chris and the duel, giving neither its due.

She looked at me as if checking that I understood. "You asked if there was anything relevant to this about my nana. I said no, but now when I look back…" She twitched one shoulder. "You know what they say, once is happenstance, twice coincidence, but three times, three is enemy action." She stared at me.

I heard a noise and turned. Rauf was pressing Hugh back to the field's edge. My hands clasped together. Rauf held the upper hand now, but this looked far from over. Hugh's stance appeared relaxed and focused.

Chris whispered in my ear. "There's my name. Chris is short for Crystal. It caused a spat between my parents. I have this funny little birthmark that looks sort of like a crystal." She tugged her sleeve off her shoulder to show me the small cluster of shiny triangles that marred her skin. "When Nana saw it, she insisted that I be named Crystal. Maybe they looked like gemstones to her."

I had seen it before; but now close up, the birthmark looked to me more like a cluster of tiny scales. The men stepped back and forth across the ring. Tic, tic, tic. I listened to Chris with half an ear.

"Nana said it was a mark of her long-lost husband's family. She had a hissy fit, all over a name." Chris cocked her head. "Nana said that of all her great-grandchildren, I was the one who deserved that name, and she immediately threatened to pull her money, money my parents needed for a down payment on a house. My parents joked she didn't have to go that far. They actually liked the name. So okay, maybe it is just coincidence: Nana was just a difficult, opinionated old woman. Here we are in the Crystal Caves, but it's only a name. Right?"

Out of the corner of my eyes, I could see her looking directly at me, raising her eyebrows. "I mean it's nothing really, just an odd coincidence. That's all, right?"

My frown must have registered as she resumed watching the duel.

Tic, tic, tic, tic, slash. The men engaged each other and then withdrew, circling once again. I could see each of their personalities written in the steel they wielded. Rauf's moves were formidable but he lacked Hugh's precision. As I watched him, I could easily believe Hugh had been born with a sword in his hand.

Intrigued by her words, I asked, "Is Crystal an unusual name in your world? Is that what you are trying to tell me?" I had never heard of such a name, but…

"Not super common."

I frowned. "Perhaps we're both reaching too hard for a rational explanation." The men were now about two body lengths apart, swords out. I risked another look at Chris. She stared across the grounds, not focusing. "What about your golden card? Didn't you tell me she bequeathed it to…."

I stopped mid-speech as the fighting stopped, Hugh's sword at Rauf's throat. Hugh's glance flashed to Chris before it landed on me. I nodded to Hugh, acknowledging the win. Chris didn't move.

Both men joined us as we prepared our luncheon. I could tell that Chris wished to speak more, but further talk would have to wait until we were alone. I wondered if there were other questions that needed to be asked. I just wasn't sure where to start.

Try as I might to forget Tristan's words, they niggled at me. Neither did I mention his decision to Chris. I didn't wish to discuss it. Three suitors should be plenty for any lady.

Chris didn't notice my distraction as she behaved like a child on a swing, oscillating between two points: one, trying to convince me the men were demon spawn; and two, defending them. A number of times during the day she seemed to catch herself mid-speak as she leapt to their defense. She would then flush, uncharacteristically, before turning away with a confused frown.

Beyond, I could hear the men's swords clashing as they practiced in another area of the cave. Chris had gone in to watch them, or knowing her character, perhaps join in the swordplay. After our luncheon, with fire boar as the main and only course, James and I discussed politics at the edge of the cavern stream. I felt Tristan's presence before he spoke.

"How do you fare, My Lady?" His face fixed in a pleasant expression as if he were determined to prove he was in good spirits. Mayhap he was.

I brushed back the loose strands that escaped my braid. "Well, thank you." My hand grasped my plait of hair.

Chris, Hugh, Piers, and Rauf trotted in, engrossed in trading stories and jokes. Chris, her angst from the morning blown away like the clouds, nudged me as she dropped to my side. "Yuck. I hope to never see a flaming pig again, dead or alive."

"Fire boar," Tristan corrected.

She grimaced. "Whatever. Now that I've eaten one, I think I might prefer it live." After a moment's thought, she amended, "Only from a great distance."

Tristan's smile didn't reach his eyes. "I take it that roast fire boar isn't to your taste, My Lady?"

"It's Chris, just Chris," she corrected. "I'm not complaining, not really. The food is filling, and I'm grateful to have it. But," she ran her tongue across her teeth. "It's like there's a film that sticks to the teeth. A texture that's a cross between liver and lard."

Tristan nodded. "It's somewhat of a delicacy in my land. After a long winter, many look eagerly to the heavily fatted meat. When I was little, I always hated it. My brothers and I would hide it in our laps, hoping our mother didn't see, before handing it off to our dogs waiting impatiently beneath the table. The nursemaids must have known, though I don't think they ever told on us. Our clothes were greasy from the meat, and late evenings would find us in the kitchen begging the cook for bread and cheese."

"But," Chris said, "you're dragons. Don't you normally live a more, uh, natural life?"

Tristan grew quiet.

Piers was the first to respond. "Dad would flail us if we turned dragon within the castle." He looked over at his brothers, Hugh and Tristan. "Remember when you both flew into the dining hall with the elk?"

Tristan nodded at me, the sadness in his eyes contradicting the beginnings of a true smile on his lips at this memory. "We were so pleased with our first dragon catch that we soared in the open doors, dropping our catch into the midst of a banquet with visiting nobles all donned in their best formal wear."

Hugh said. "Dad's face looked as hard as stone, he was so mad." He turned to Piers. "You don't really remember that, do you? You were only, what, three, four?"

"Oh, I remember all right. I was fully four. Anne was eight. You and Tristan were almost grown in our eyes, thirteen and twelve. Anne and I were awed."

Tristan snorted. "What I remember is Mom's look of dismay."

Piers looked at Chris. "They were so puffed up with themselves.

The carcass was charred with fire, still dripping blood and gore."

"Hugh and I worked so hard to fly it home, both of us struggling midair with this beast. We were sure we would be praised."

Hugh sighed. "It was a rough couple of days after."

The tension between him and Tristan dissipated then, blown away by the shared memory.

Piers leaned forward. "I remember it being freezing cold. Snow coming down like layer upon layer of white fabric."

James added, "Wasn't that the first winter Tristan was locked into his dragon body?"

Rauf and Hugh looked everywhere but at Tristan. James's mouth clamped tight as if worried that he would say something else hurtful.

Piers, not noticing the sadness in Tristan's face, said, "Anne cried when he wasn't allowed inside."

"Remember, Tristan? Every evening for weeks, she would weep when you weren't there to read her a bedtime story. Many nights I found her outside curled beneath your wing, reading to you before Hugh carried her back to her bed."

No one spoke for a time. Tristan refused to acknowledge this discussion. In the distance, I could hear the small brown bats as they returned from feeding.

Chris broke the silence, reaching over and giving Tristan's shoulder a squeeze. "I'm sure that both you and Hugh were extraordinarily resourceful and daring. I hope someone was appropriately appreciative."

"Anne was." Tristan shook his head as if trying to shed something. "She clapped her hands like we had brought it just for her."

He looked eager to change the subject. "Tell us something about yourself, My Lady. All we know about you is that you're a loyal friend to our princess. And from a far-away land. Do you have siblings?"

Chris rolled her eyes. "Nope. Mom said I was such a hellion as a toddler she refused to contemplate two of me."

"What about your lands. How is your court life?" James asked, squinting at her.

"Oh, there's no court, just school, classes, tests. Sometimes we get together and party. Maybe go out and dance to a local dance band." She looked so wistful as she spoke. She glanced at me then and said quickly. "Not that I wouldn't rather be here, of course."

Guilt coursed through me, a black wave of self-reproach. She should leave. I needed to bid her farewell and let her return to the world of Berkeley.

Piers suddenly brightened. "The lady wants music? Allow me." He settled near my feet, strumming his lute, the water adding a gentle percussion to his tune. Since the boar incident, he had trailed behind like a supplicant, convinced his duty was to entertain Chris and me at every opportunity.

Tristan spoke again, his voice pitched low, gently riding over the melody. I could hear concern in his voice. "Princess, how *do* you fare? Is this to your taste?" His eyes searched mine, and I wondered what he was truly asking.

Piers hummed along, finishing one tune and starting another. Before I could respond, Tristan tensed and faced Piers, shaking his head at him. A muscle twitched below his eye. A smell, the whiff of smoke. Tristan's eyes hardened. In that moment, I thought he might transform into a dragon.

It was a haunting melody. I stammered, trying to diffuse the tension. "That's lovely, Piers. Does it have words?"

Piers had a mischievous look on his face. "Tristan, sing your song. She wants to hear it."

Tristan ignored him. A flare of panic crossed his face. Piers grinned and started singing,

"Lady with sea-green eyes and dragon-fire hair
Captured in the twilight of my mind,
Standing lost beside the weeping trees,
Far away from all, fair and lovely,
Lost to all, lost to me."

Blood pulsed in my neck, flaming into my cheeks as I listened. This was the song that Frederick, the unpleasant viscount, must have heard. The song about me. Piers continued to sing and my face grew hot.

Hugh growled and the music stopped abruptly.

Tristan, red-faced also, stumbled over his words, apologizing. "Please forgive us. This song was not meant to tease. It was never meant for your ears."

I couldn't breathe, couldn't respond.

Tristan gritted his teeth. "It's only a song. I must have been melancholy that day, to write something so maudlin." He raised both hands as if in offering, then tightened his lips and snapped, "Piers, come with me. We have something to discuss."

Piers resisted, eyes wide with trepidation, but Tristan's hand on his shoulder allowed no argument as he was marched out of earshot. Rauf followed, grinning as if looking forward to some earthy amusement.

James grumbled to Hugh, "This isn't entirely Piers's fault. We should have told him immediately when Tristan said he wasn't competing." He turned and followed the others.

Hugh nodded as if distracted. As he moved to join his kin, he paused, looking over toward Chris and me, his face both thoughtful and distant. "It was just a song." Then he strode away.

The cave was silent but for the trickle of water flowing and the sound of distant footsteps.

Engulfed as I was with thoughts of Tristan and songs of love, it was hard for me to think in a rational way. This was not something to pursue. He wouldn't be competing. He wasn't even as human as the other man-dragons. Moreover, Tristan had written this before he really knew me, when I was but a *chosen* princess, chosen for Hugh to be his queen.

Chris watched, obviously waiting for me to speak. I examined my nails, willing my skin to return to its normal color.

"Chris, you should leave. Go back to your home where you will be comfortable and safe." I struggled to keep the misery from my voice.

"What? Where did that come from? I'm not going anywhere until this is over."

I moved to sit next to her, grasping her hands in mine. "You have done your part, more than anyone could have ever expected. You saved me, helped hold me together during this trial and stood by my side through all manner of disasters. There is no more you can do. I'm fine. You cannot stay here forever. You have your own life to attend to."

She looked out into the deep shadows of the cave where the soft yellow glow of the lantern's light didn't reach. "You're wrong, you know. I'm not staying just for you anymore."

I raised my eyebrows in disbelief.

"Sure, in the beginning that's how it started, a curiosity, then a challenge. But now it's become more of a mystery—my being here, I mean. Why me? There are many questions. Too many. I'm not leaving until I figure them out."

Tears welled up in my eyes, threatening to overflow.

Chris shifted, and a grin crept across her face. "So what did you think about all that?"

"About you staying?" I asked, hoping that was what she was referring to. "I'm very grateful. More than you can know." Guilt twisted my stomach.

Chris said, "Oh, come off it. The song, silly. I saw you look at him. Just a bit in love, are you?"

"No, not at all. I was caught unaware and I felt uncomfortable. Nothing more."

"Admit it," she said, almost laughing at me. "You have a crush on him."

"No." While I didn't understand her exact phrase, I knew what she was implying.

Chris tilted her head. "You play with your hair whenever he is around."

"I do not!" I replied. I was a better master of myself than *that*.

Chris grinned with a smug cat-that-caught-the-finch look. "Oh, but you do."

I dashed that look with my next words. "He's not entering the contests."

"What? Why? I thought, I mean…"

I lowered my head, unwilling to look her in the eyes. "Tristan isn't offering for my hand."

"But why?"

"He's afflicted. He gets trapped for months in his dragon form, much like his ancestors."

Chris was silent for a long time. "But he likes you and you like him. I know you do."

"He isn't human. None of them are, but Tristan is truly a dragon for months. Not even able to speak. I would be isolated for months each and every year."

Chris seemed to consider that. "Lots of women marry guys who travel part of the year. It's the same thing."

"As the only human in a land of dragons, it would be like being cloistered."

"But you like him," she repeated.

My voice came out harsher than I had planned. "Leave off. He's not competing for me. He can't be reliably human."

There was an edge that crawled across her voice. "Isn't that like not being white enough? Or do you think it is more like a disability?"

"Obviously, it is a disadvantage. You, yourself, have made that point over and over these last days. What if he never changed back to human? He would be a dragon, not sometimes a dragon, but a dragon forever."

"What are you afraid of? That's what this is about, isn't it? You're scared."

"Yes, I'm scared. What if his mind becomes that of a beast, what then? I would be wed forever to a…" I couldn't say it.

She ignored my comment, fixating on the one thing I didn't wish to pursue. "You're not afraid of Tristan. You're afraid of his difference. You're discounting him without even a thought just because he's a little different.

"You don't think he's good enough for you! Not proper for a royal princess."

I refused to respond to that. I reminded her, "*He* has refused to enter the contest. I didn't decide for him."

"But you have. You've let him."

And she walked away.

Chapter 36

Not long after, Chris and I sat out in the afternoon sun, basking in its warmth. We both pretended nothing had happened between us. I was relieved; I couldn't bear to lose her friendship.

She wriggled her fingers. "Doesn't Hugh's hair just make you want to touch it? That one curl that sneaks over his ear."

My mind made a quick leap from Hugh's russet hair to Tristan's unruly chestnut thatch. I blushed, shook my head, and banished that image yet again.

The man-dragons were never far from us, one of them inevitably standing guard nearby. And again they appeared just as I was hoping to ask more about Chris's gold card.

Hugh and Rauf strode toward us, and Chris tensed up like a hound catching the scent of a fox, with that alert look of interest and expectancy.

They bowed. "May we sit with you?" Hugh asked.

I nodded my assent, although I was discomforted dressed in one of Chris's shirts over a satin chemise and a dusty skirt. Rauf flopped beside me but Hugh looked at Chris, waiting.

"Oh sure," she finally said.

Hugh placed himself a body's width from Chris.

I smiled, trying to make amends for her curtness. "How nice of you to join us."

"My pleasure, My Lady."

Chris ignored him, looking out to the west as if she could see trouble coming.

Hugh sighed, looking as uncomfortable as I had ever seen him. "I wish to beg a favor."

My body tensed. Had they changed their minds again?

"Though I had hoped to proceed with the next sword challenge, I request that tomorrow would be kinder to those who fight."

I breathed carefully, not wanting him to know I had doubted his word. "Certainly. Is there some reason?"

Hugh hesitated. Rauf laughed aloud. "Piers's mouth ran him afoul of trouble. His left eye is swollen shut."

Chris eyebrows came down in a vee. "What happened?"

Rauf's belly laugh echoed. "Brothers! He walked into Tris's hand—suddenly."

Chris winced. "Is he okay? Is Tristan okay?"

Hugh responded. "They are both a little battered, but nothing that won't be better with a night of rest. If my skill is to be tested, I'd rather it not be said I fought from an unfair advantage."

I shut my brain from thoughts of Tristan and filled the void with polite chatter. Hugh tilted his head, listening carefully, adding a pleasantry or two and including Chris in our conversation. His manners were impeccable. Even here, removed from court and trappings, his presence was confident and kingly. I was finding it hard to remember why I had been so opposed to him.

Rauf gently teased me about my oddly combined clothing, eager to put himself forward. "We're delighted to see you looking so bonny. How might a dragon please a human princess?" he asked. "Is there anything that I might do to make your time here more pleasant?"

"No, thank you. I'm quite settled now." I looked down too quickly. How could I be happy this isolated from my family?

"Ah, but you mustn't be so sad." Rauf had seen through my words. "You know we are not ogres, merely dragons, and only the nicest, as you can see."

I grinned at his attempt to amuse me.

Chris crossed her legs and tugged at her wrinkled chemise on which was written the interesting adage, "If you can't take the heat, don't tickle the dragon." Hugh looked over to see how I was taking Rauf's flirting and then went back to talking with Chris.

Rauf was persistent. "A woman like you, as beautiful as a summer's day, deserves to be treated like fine porcelain. While we're lacking in that in these caves, I believe once we return to our land you will find many things to complement your beauty, as well as many things to love. Certainly, if you chose me I will make that so." He winked.

I smiled, but was cautious with my response. I wasn't so easily bought or flattered. "How kind of you. All of you are being lovely. It's difficult to select one from such admirable suitors."

He mistook my reserve as a challenge, as something to be won over.

"It must be hard to leave your previous life behind. What do you miss most?"

That was an easy question to answer. "Family and friends. My little brother, Harold. He is such a scamp, but I love him dearly."

A smile burst across his face as if I had handed him a key to a puzzle. And then it was gone before I could figure out what had happened.

"Yes, I would feel the same way," he nodded. "My brothers and cousins are with me much of each year. I can only imagine how great a loss it must be for you."

He left after that, with a chaste kiss on my hand, but something in his voice gave me pause.

Chapter 37

With every hour that passed, the Pritorians and I settled into gentler dealings with one another. Piers, Rauf, and Hugh all tried to charm us. James watched as if cataloging this for future generations. Tristan stood apart.

Even though Tristan had withdrawn from the challenges, there remained some discomfort between him and Hugh. A feeling in the air whenever they were together, small roughnesses that would surface and then slough off, leaving behind a residue of tension. Perhaps as brothers so close in age, they had always been competitive.

With every interaction, I gained insight into the man-dragons and their culture. A firm hand had shaped their manners. There was an ease, a relaxed banter that drew me in as my father's guard had.

This night, Hugh, Rauf and James performed an impromptu ballad for us, a break between the tensions of these days. The other man-dragons sat apart, seemingly unconcerned, though Piers appeared chastened and Tristan's face looked stiff.

For all their gallantry, they were no different from my brothers with their occasional squabbling. Tristan and Piers, both sporting swollen eyes, seemed to have worked through their difficulties as Tristan accompanied Piers's lute with a mandolin. Doubtless, the men were attempting to be pleasant, trying to amuse Chris and me. I found my fears drifting away like dry leaves blown before the wind.

Standing there, I watched them. Rauf, big and burly, a wink and a smile when he caught me looking his way. Piers, exuberant and funny. And Hugh. There were many reasons to choose him. He was the king, a man comfortable with his place in society. He was forceful, determined and smart. Yes, he could be over-bearing, but that might temper with age. His word was good and the men respected him. I smiled, watching him, envisioning myself as his queen. I could be influential in renewing relations with my country—perhaps instrumental in reopening trade. The pleasure I felt surprised me, as I had never yearned for power.

James and Piers persuaded Chris to learn the steps to one of their country's jigs. I was surprised that she, a commoner after all, moved so well, though the lesson ended abruptly when she pirouetted, tripped and fell forward onto Hugh. Both of them hesitated, and it seemed to me that Hugh's hands lingered on her arms before they separated.

I shook my head and sat down, dismissing my chary thoughts. That was how it was with Chris. Somehow, something always happened to her: she'd hit her head, or fall down a cliff or a branch would leap out and smite her, always something.

Rauf attached himself to my side, bending my ear with his adventures. I enjoyed his company, his bear-like strength hidden beneath a warm grin.

Chris rejoined us, legs interlocked in her usual immodest posture.

As James began playing a haunting melody on a small wooden flute, Chris leaned over and nudged me with her elbow.

I jumped as Rauf shouted out a request for a new song. He grabbed a drum and hurried to join his brother.

Chris placed a hand at my waist, calling me back to her. "Remember what I was telling you? Here's another odd bit. It's silly, but when I was little, Nana told me stories, wonderful tales of magical lands, of princes and princesses and dragons. I think that's why I was so struck when I first heard about you and the dragons.

"It miffed Nana that I identified with the dragons and not the princesses."

Again, I thought, *yet another mention of dragons, from Chris's world, a place where they didn't exist.*

"I would rush about with a cape for wings pretending I was a dragon, flapping my arms and growling. Once, in a sugar-driven frenzy of confidence, I leapt off our upstairs deck."

At my incredulous look, she shrugged and grinned.

"I was sure I could fly. I spent the next month with my arm in a cast. Mother blamed Nana and her stories; but Nana looked at me from beneath those heavily-lidded eyes of hers and proclaimed, 'One can't make an eagle into a dove.'"

"What happened to her?"

"She went into a nursing home soon after, where she terrorized the staff with her imperious ways. Still, Nana was a grand old lady. I was devastated when she died last spring."

Both of us started as the men's voices ended their song with a rousing shout. A short time later, Rauf and Piers leapt up, enacting what looked like a particularly silly folk tale from their land—something to do with a flameless dragon and sheep. Before Chris could continue, Rauf came over. "Genevieve, come, we need a pretty lady to assist us."

I demurred, but he persuaded Chris to join him and Piers, to play a clever, but lonely, dragon-maiden in their skit.

Hugh, James and I laughed as they paraded before us, their silly antics designed to amuse. Tristan sat off to the right. Our eyes met and neither of us blinked.

Later, long past when the moon was at her height, Chris and I fell into our beds and lost the chance to talk.

I awoke to whispers outside my door. A look at Chris's tangled pallet showed she was gone, her sandals missing. Something was disquieting her. I wished again that we had had the opportunity to finish our conversation.

The whispers became louder, resolving into a heated discussion between Rauf and Tristan.

"Why is this so important to you, Rauf? Really, why are you pursuing Genevieve?"

"She's pretty and smart enough not to be a burden. Hugh has power and the crown. Piers has years to prove himself. You're the one everyone has looked to for greatness: gallant, smart and politically savvy. The perfect 'spare.' No one ever expected much from me. This is my chance."

"Rauf, you're a duke, you have lands to rule, as we all do."

Rauf gave a low laugh. "My lands are small and mountainous. A human princess could make winters much warmer. I wouldn't have the worry that my children would have your unfortunate dragon problem."

No sound came from outside my doorway except a low rumbling growl, though my heart was beating so loudly I was afraid they must hear.

"Tristan. I didn't mean to say that." Rauf sounded genuinely remorseful. "I'm helping to make it a fair contest, no more than that."

Tristan voice dropped even quieter. "She's alone here, with only Chris to stand for her. You're muddying her decision."

Rauf chuckled. "Jealous?"

My body was still in anticipation of his answer.

160

Tristan didn't respond to the bait, saying instead, "Every time I see you, you're standing at her shoulder, pushing yourself forward."

"Come now, Cousin, I've watched how you look at her. You aim high; you're not usually willing to sit upon a lower mountain."

Silence again.

"Well, she asked for choices." Rauf's voice grew defiant. "I'm a choice, and I'm happy to push myself forward."

"You always are, Rauf."

"Can't you be pleased for me? I have a good chance of winning."

I could hear the frown in Tristan's voice. "How are you going to win? Hugh bested you with swords and none of us can beat him at chess."

Rauf's voice lowered then. "There is the last contest. I have a trump card up my sleeve."

"Rauf, don't do anything rash."

In the quiet that followed, I heard boots scuffle as if one of them had moved closer.

I heard Tristan's voice, barely—he was speaking so softly. "Perhaps I should reconsider entering. To even things out."

"Not because you have affection for her?"

Though I strained forward, I couldn't hear what Tristan replied. Rauf left then in a clatter of footsteps. I knew Tristan was still there. He wouldn't leave his post. That wasn't who he was.

After a seemly amount of time, I faked waking, making noises as if I were stretching, got to my feet, pulled a blanket about my shoulders and stepped out to where Tristan remained on guard.

"Where is Chris?" I asked, my face carefully composed. He didn't answer for a heartbeat. I guessed he wasn't eager to parley with me.

"She wanted to go outside. Hugh's attending her." We stood there like a socially backward couple, neither of us willing to make a move.

I was unsure how to broach the subject of the contests without seeming brazen. "What happened to Denston IV? The one whose problem started all of this? I never heard the end of that tale."

Tristan tilted his head like he was trying to see inside me. "You heard. He was locked each year into dragon form, from the first snowfall to the last snowfall before spring—same as I am."

"What happened? He spent his years alone and isolated?"

"No, he ruled. He was known as Denston the Determined. He was one of the first three dragons who married a human princess."

I searched his face, waiting for the answer. "You said they were all happily married."

"So I did."

"And his children?"

He stared at me, saying it slowly. "Four healthy boys."

I couldn't stop myself. "And are you less than he?"

He started forward and then caught himself. "I'm less than no one."

Tristan looked away. "Perhaps you heard Rauf and me speaking. Is that what has brought about these questions?"

I stared at him, neither acknowledging nor denying.

He spoke carefully as if every word needed to be perfect. "All of us want your happiness. You deserve to be queen."

I gave a derisive snort. "You say this as if you know me well. Perhaps I don't see it so. Perhaps I see your meddling as yet another example of how you are restricting my choices."

Tristan acted like I had thrown water at him, but I continued, my voice rising. "What you're protecting me from is the ability to make my own decisions."

He stepped forward, grabbing my shoulders. He held himself very still, as if undecided whether to shake me, let me go or fold me into an embrace.

My face flushed. Which did I want? Slowly, he released me, dragging his hands gently down my arms before putting some distance between us. I quivered, still feeling the heat from his fingers on my arms.

Uncertain, I retreated into my quarters, lobbing a parting shot. "Remember, I did not disqualify you from the contests—you did that yourself."

Chapter 38

It was the morning of the third day since my reprieve. The sun had been up for hours when I finally awoke. Chris lay sprawled next to me, deep asleep. I hadn't heard her return.

I quietly dressed and walked outside into the clearing, leaving Chris to her dreams and leaving mine behind. I'd done everything but throw myself at Tristan last night and my dreams woke me with the intensity of longing.

I sat outside in a flat, sheltered coppice beyond the cave entrance, where gray cliffs mottled with green lichens stretched up to the sky.

Tristan walked out, gave me a single unreadable look and started warming up as if for the duel.

My world spun. I looked to James standing at my left, as I tried to understand what was happening.

He shrugged, whispering, "Tristan changed his mind. He spoke with our kinsmen soon after dawn." He blinked twice before he spoke again. "Hugh is annoyed, Rauf looks disgruntled and Piers is anxious as he must face Tristan in the ring. But this is as it should be. I told Tristan not to withdraw."

Something fluttered inside me. This had to be about last night. I recalled the conversation. Maybe I was fooling myself. Maybe he wasn't really contending for me, but making a point to Rauf.

Maybe…Chris slid in beside me, her eyes shadowed with dark circles, and I tried to separate myself from those thoughts.

Before I could speak to her, Piers came over and greeted us. He left just as quickly to talk with Hugh and James.

"Chris, are you unwell? We've been waiting for you before resuming the contests," I asked, grabbing her hand to comfort her. Or perhaps it was for my comfort, so tense was I at Tristan's change of heart.

"Sorry," Chris muttered. "I slept badly last night."

As did I, I thought.

Piers and Tristan faced off in the small flat space, within the rough area that had been marked off with ash. The two men sidled around facing each other, swords drawn, waiting for the other to make his move. As in the first contest, the remaining man-dragons stood around the periphery. I caught Hugh's eyes on me. James focused on the fight, calling out encouragement. Rauf watched with undisguised disappointment.

Tristan had all the advantage in this contest, longer reach and greater skill. It was over almost before it began. Piers leapt forward into a lunge that Tristan easily sidestepped. Tristan feinted to his left and followed through with an impressive swing of his blade. It slammed against Piers's sword arm, dislodging his sword. The sword was flung to the ground and the match ended.

Impulsive and fast as he was, Piers hadn't stood a chance against Tristan's fluid skill and strength. He crouched on the ground, clutching his wrist. Tristan moved aside, awaiting my verdict. I nodded. Tristan bowed and then helped Piers up, carefully examining his arm.

Hugh strode over. "How is he?"

"Only a bruise," Tristan said, releasing Piers's arm.

Hugh frowned as he bent to retrieve Piers's sword. "How many times have I told you not to rush your lunge?"

Piers's protest was hidden beneath the others' voices.

My body trembled. I no longer listened to their discussion. My mind was wrapped around Tristan. Why had he entered? Duty, pride or love? Or something else entirely.

And why should I care, when I had every expectation of being Hugh's queen? Or had that now changed?

Chris poked me in the side—there was no training the woman. The trial was barely over, and she was unable to concentrate. My head turned of itself toward Tristan. Our eyes met and both of us quickly looked away. Ah yes, she wasn't the only one who was distracted.

"Remember what I was saying yesterday?" Chris asked, pushing the glass ovals up on her nose. "Here's the crazy part. I don't know if this is just my imagination or something real. But I feel odd in this place, like something is about to happen. That something is all out of whack. My insides feel weird."

I wrenched my thoughts away from Tristan and studied her face again; she did look flushed.

She dragged a stick in the ground, tracing little circles, not looking at me. "Maybe it's just the power of suggestion. You know, like I'm starting to believe that this place has magic or something."

Chris's eye-pieces stood out from the white of her skin as she continued. "There's one more thing."

I sat, trying to listen.

"Last winter I visited Nana in the nursing home. She was pretty much out of it by then; her mind couldn't hold on to much. Her eyes were closed, but the nurses encouraged me to talk to her as she rested. I was rambling on about a demonstration on women's rights I had helped organize.

"Nana rallied and snorted, 'You wouldn't understand choice. You young folks now think you understand politics and bravery in the face of overwhelming odds. There were choices that I had to make, hard choices. I've often wondered if I made the right one.' She drifted off again and I thought she had fallen asleep."

I put my hand over Chris's, hoping to make her pause. Nothing she was saying made sense. But Chris soldiered on.

"She mumbled to herself then, something about centuries. About 'some unfortunate girl…'

"Then Nana's eyes snapped open and she leaned forward, stronger than I had seen her in months. 'You want to be part of a demonstration? To make a difference to women? If you want to prove your point, my dear, you should try to demonstrate to dragons. Remind me sometime.'

"She stared deep into my eyes. 'Then we shall see who you are. If you have the backbone to stand by your words when there is true need for change.'

"She sank back down, exhausted. 'You're so much like my husband, your great-grandfather, same hair, same intensity and fire, even the same birthmark. Reminding me, always reminding me…'"

I felt my eyebrows come together and a chill ran through me. The birthmark that looked like scales.

"Nana's voice had quavered. 'I'd like to know, does your blood run more to my family or his? Perhaps…we shall see.' And then she fell asleep and didn't say another word."

Chris continued, "I didn't understand. She died the next month. And this golden card was tucked into that enamel box, with a note saying it was for me alone.

"And here I am. Whisked to your side each time I use it like Tonto to the Lone Ranger. It has to be connected with her, to this place. But why? What is the tie?"

My mind whirled. This seemed important, yet the concepts again were beyond me. Chris was from another world; there was no reasonable connection to these caves. I decided to venture a question, to see if I could better understand.

"So who are Tonto and the single ranger? And what is a demonstration?"

Chris tilted her head toward me, rolling her eyes in exasperation. "It isn't important, just two people who were pals in my world. And demonstration, well, it's a peaceful way of standing up to those in power for something important."

I narrowed my eyes, trying to imagine a demonstration before my father.

Chapter 39

By midafternoon gray clouds glided over us, combining and recombining in darker and darker bundles, heavy with rain. Rauf and James had "changed" and flown into them, returning to say it was only a light rain coming, nothing more.

Hugh and Tristan walked across the ground, each ignoring the other, the air so thick between them that one could almost see it.

They stepped into the circle and faced each other. At a signal from James, they drew their swords and saluted each other, their eyes never wavering. The two men circled, step by wary step. Chris and I leaned against each other. No one breathed, or so it seemed, in the silence that encapsulated this match.

They tested each other, swords conversing, meeting with a metallic tic. Neither was willing to commit to a blow. Cautiously, they each slid sun-wise, step by step around. Tic, tic, tic, again and again the swords tapped. Hugh, confident; Tristan, watching for opportunity.

Hugh leapt forward, his sword thrusting. Tristan danced a breath away even as his sword whipped into action, a quick parry before retreating. The fighting began in earnest; Tristan darted in like a snake with a snap of his sword on Hugh's. Then Hugh parried, but was pushed back by Tristan's advance—two steps, then three, though Tristan failed to penetrate Hugh's guard.

Again they circled, leaping forward with the power and force of long-horned sheep. The resulting clash of steel filled the air. Tristan and Hugh engaged shoulder to shoulder, as if in an embrace, their swords pressing together over their heads, both of them trembling with effort. They pushed apart and the swords were once more free, silver metal pulsing. The whisk of swords clashing so near their heads caused me to shrink away. I heard myself gasp.

Hugh stepped back, and they faced each other, eyes intent. Hugh attacked, advancing so fast that I was unable to discern each thrust, riposte and counterthrust. But Tristan gave no quarter. The silver of their swords flashed over and over. I could see no change until a thin line of blood splotched Hugh's shirt.

Chris grabbed my hand, whispering, "I think he's hurt. Did he just get hurt?"

She asked after Hugh, not Tristan. I couldn't take my eyes off the match to question this. I couldn't look away. Whose blood was it? Why didn't they stop? They should have stopped at first blood.

They circled again, leaping back into the fight, parrying and feinting back and forth across the bounded circle, edge to edge. Tic, tic, slash. They separated and with renewed zeal leapt forward again. Tic, tic, slash. And again. Tic, tic, slash.

How long had I been watching? Their movements now slowed, straining with the effort to meet clash with clash.

Both men looked exhausted, the only noise their ragged breathing. Blood now stained both their clothes. I thought there was a small cut on Tristan's forearm and another on Hugh's shoulder, but they never were still enough for me to be sure. Hugh attacked, his stance no longer quite as precise. Tristan retreated, his movement fluid still. He's watching, I thought. Watching and waiting, wearing him down.

James and the others had grown silent as this struggle continued.

Sweat beaded on the warriors' foreheads, hesitating at their eyebrows before dripping down across their eyes. Blood trickled down both of their arms from the myriad nicks and scratches.

This was unlike any of the other fights, like no tournament I had ever seen. Certainly not like anything at my father's court. The other men were silent, none of the cheering and joking that had accompanied the previous contests. I should call it off, end this now before one of them was seriously hurt. But I feared any distraction might cause one or the other to be harmed.

They clashed again, close and tight, Hugh grappling against Tristan, swords unable to move. They fell apart, staggered back from one another. Tristan's shirt slipped downward and a flash of something small, dark and shiny, lay upon his collarbone before it vanished beneath his shirt...a birthmark, a scar? I looked to Chris, but she must not have noticed, her eyes centered on Hugh.

Once more they came together, blades meeting with a jar and sliding off as they recovered. Hugh lunged forward with a powerful thrust, which slid past the guard of Tristan's sword, and missed piercing

Tristan's side by but a hair's breadth.

Sweat stuck their shirts to their bodies. Hugh's sleeve hung loose, ripped above the elbow, Tristan's shirt torn about the cuff. All around them nothing sounded but their footfalls, the harsh intake of controlled breath and the ever-present snick of metal. Shadows of both dragon and man interwove as they circled, their strength flagging. Eyes burning, smoke slithering out from nostrils, they slowed, each sword parry arduous, their movements labored. Step by step, both men drank in gulps of air, waiting for a break, an unchecked moment when they could leap again, like two dogs fighting for dominance.

As the fight proceeded, the shadows of their dragon shapes grew more substantive, surrounding each. I watched, awed and frightened.

Piers, his voice in a whisper, said, "I've never seen anything like this. They both risk losing control. They can't go much longer. No one could."

Tristan turned, exposing his flank to Hugh's blade. But just as Hugh stretched forward with his sword pressing hard, his body slightly off balance, Tristan advanced, and with a backstroke from the flat of his blade, swung, connecting solidly against his brother's hip. Hugh tried to step away, but his hip seemed unable to bear the weight. He caught himself, but too late. Tristan stood, his sword point at Hugh's neck, as Hugh, arms down, gulped in deep breaths of air. Hugh's head lifted as he looked my way, his eyes sliding over to Chris. She held my arm as if to keep herself from rushing forward.

Tristan turned to me, saluted, and then moved to help Hugh off the arena. My heart pounded as if I too had been in that ring.

Chapter 40

After a spate of fitful rain, I walked outside, breathing in the moisture-laden air as I stared off to the west where my family was. I longed to see them again and to comfort them with the knowledge that I was still alive. Puddles of rainwater dotted the ground. The trees drooped with moisture not yet removed by the sun or wind. I too felt laden.

I missed my companions from our journey here—Lucinda, Michael and all my father's men. I wondered how they were. The burden of guilt undoubtedly rode them.

I must have been lost in my thoughts as I didn't hear Chris join me; she wasn't known for her silence.

She sat quietly, throwing stones into the puddles, watching them splash before they sank. "So now that the first contest is over, has anyone risen to the top of your list?"

Her eyebrows scrunched down. "Tristan's first with the sword. Is that what you hoped for, or are you still opposed to him?"

I deflected her question. "It will take more than skill with weaponry for me to choose a husband."

She continued with the roster of names. "So Hugh, Rauf and Piers are still in the race?"

I heard her linger as she spoke Hugh's name and I couldn't quite make my eyes meet hers. "It's not only about who wins. It's never been about that."

Chris's mouth twisted in disbelief.

"At first, it was a way to take back control, to take back my life."

"And now?"

"It came from a conversation with my parents. Father said he could tell more about men within a few minutes on a battlefield than months of watching them in court, how they fight, how they strategize."

"My mother added, 'And how they treat their loved ones.' The contests are also about how they respond, not solely who wins. It is about how they behave toward each other and to us. So yes, the contests count.

But so does every time we speak with them."

Chris grunted, clearly not impressed with my logic. Something else must have been on her mind.

She continued flipping stones. "Do you think Hugh is okay with this? I mean, he came here planning to marry and all."

Ah, so that was it—Hugh. I asked the question wanting to see where the wind was blowing. "Are you inclined toward Hugh?"

Chris was silent, staring at a stone that lay quiet in her hand. I felt a tension that stretched out into the desolate landscape below. "No, don't be silly. I can't live in a fantasy world forever. My life is in Berkeley. I want to make a difference in the world, to make something of myself."

"Is that what this is to you, a fantasy world?"

She bit her lip and hurled the stone into the water. It sank, as had all the others.

"No, don't reply. I don't wish to hear it. Chris, you've made a difference to me. I value you: as a counselor, as a friend, as someone who *has* changed my life."

She folded her arms over her head. "I don't know what to think anymore. This all can't be real, but then it is. I know it is."

I interlaced my fingers. "Truly, that's how I have felt since I was chosen and all the way here. That I would wake and it would be but a bad dream."

She lifted her head. "Dang. I was so hoping it was at first and now…now I'm not sure I want to wake up."

I nodded. "It's changed, hasn't it? Nothing is as it seemed."

"And Tristan? Is his dragon-stuckness still playing into your decision?"

"Yes, but more than that. Hugh was right; I was raised to be queen, to rule. I've been trained since I was two to understand my duty. I can't throw away what I am."

"So is that how you're going to decide, the contests be damned? Are you just going to choose based on a title?"

"No, I feel that this must play out, all of it. But it is a part, something to be considered."

The stone tossing started up again.

"Do you mean to date any of them as part of the contests?"

My brows furrowed. "Date? As in, ask when they were born?"

"No, date as in spending time with them individually. Maybe a kiss or two, whatever."

I would have thought my expression of shock would have let her know what I thought of that idea, but she wasn't watching me. Her eyes had a dreamy, far-off look. I could see her contemplating the idea.

"Wow, dating a dragon! How liberating." She looked at me with interest. "Prejudice is so old-world, don't you think?"

I thought back, remembering her earlier comments. Her words were alien, as always, but the meaning was clear.

"Ah, Chris. Remember what you said about dragonette carriers?"

She shook her head dismissively. "Not an issue. I'm on birth control." She sneaked a look in my direction, perhaps remembering that, save James, they were *all* my suitors. "Not that I would do such a thing, of course. Or that I'm interested or anything. Just an observation, nothing personal." I watched her face glow as she dissembled.

Chris plodded verbally on, hiding her red face with a turn of her head. "But I've been thinking. We need to ask the men some questions, pointed questions. You've agreed to marry, but we know little about them, their culture, their country, only what little they tell us. Sure, they implied their women rule. Who knows what that really means? Maybe they shroud their women in black or don't let them vote or, I don't know… bind their feet or clip their wings. Most especially, we need to ask about all the chosen princesses."

I couldn't have agreed more.

During our evening meal, I casually inserted a question into our conversation. "I know so little of your land. Tell me about it."

Rauf answered first. "What do you wish to know, My Lady? It is nothing like this." He spread his hand indicating the rough stone table where we sat. "Our country is large, broad enough that it takes a full three days of flight to traverse it from mountain to sea. Plenty of hunting grounds, fertile crop land, streams in which to fish and forests filled with game."

James interrupted. "That's not what she is asking. She wants to know about the courts, the castles, where she will live."

Hugh looked up. "The land is divided into five dukedoms administered by the princes of Pritorous. Each region has a council where a person from each township has a seat, a way for me to hear the needs of my people. Once a year a meeting is held with all the dukes."

I nodded and was about to ask a more pressing question when Chris spoke. "What about your women? What is their place in your society? How are they treated?"

Rauf stepped in. "We are part dragon and like lovely things. Beautiful ladies, for example." He grinned at me. "And like all treasures, they are handled carefully." He dallied over the words, making them into a caress.

I blushed.

Piers snorted. "You know what Mother would say to that."

Chris looked at him, all attention. "What would she say?"

Piers grinned. "That he had better modify his ways or no woman will accept him. Mother rules our castle since our father's passing."

Rauf grinned back, nodding, "Yes, my aunt would see me properly chastised. A fine, strong woman, your mother; silver-blue scales and the hottest flame in seven leagues."

I ventured a further question. "I am curious about the other chosen princesses. For instance, what happened to Penelope? You mentioned her name before."

James looked up, blinking into the shadows that danced beyond the flickering torches. "She was our eighth princess. When our people came in dragon form, she fled. Fell from a cliff and broke her neck."

I felt blood rush from my face and Chris gasped in horror. Across the table, Hugh and Rauf stilled.

James shook his head. "There was no bride that century. Such a waste. After that, the rules were amended to have the princess sedated and secured. For her own safety. No one could bear to be responsible for the loss of life."

Chris stood up, hands clenched. "That's barbaric. You continued this practice after someone died?"

I spoke through white lips. "A princess's death was but a mistake to be shrugged off as a casualty of circumstance?"

James breached the silence that ensued. "No. It wasn't like that. You don't understand. The princesses are treasured. Our human survival depends on them. These marriages are venerated as the symbol of our commemoration to life and our future."

"They don't sound like happy marriages to me."

"That is not true. There have been many happy and prosperous marriages resulting from these arrangements," Hugh countered.

Chris raised an incredulous eyebrow. "Really?"

"Yes, our chosen women are well-respected. Many of them control land and wield power of their own," Hugh insisted.

I looked from one to the other. Was this true? Women having individual power, not just being the hand behind the throne? As Hugh's queen, I would have respect and power. Decisions would bear my stamp.

If I were with Rauf, or Piers, I would be but a duchess with lands— and if Tristan were my husband, the same, but alone for much of the year.

No, and though my chest ached, I pushed that last possibility away. Hugh was the best choice for me. I spared a quick look Tristan's way. He was watching me, not saying a word through all this discussion. Could he see my thoughts writ upon my face?

Someone coughed and I brought myself back to the conversation, hoping I hadn't missed much.

Rauf agreed. "True. There were ballads composed about the love between Anisette and Kester."

Piers looked thoughtful as he added, "And Rosalind, we have many portraits of her. She always looked happy and smiling, beaming at her husband and four children."

Rauf interjected, "Don't forget Sophia—she reigned after King Ranulf died. Every year she held a festival where couples were married right in the castle courtyard. It is written that she did so in hopes that others would experience the joy that she had in her marriage."

James nodded and then stated, "All true. Wonderful marriages— except for two noteworthy failures: Elsbeth and Victoria."

Hugh snapped his head around with a low growl but James lumbered on, spilling forth his thoughts, as earnest as always. "Not much is known about Elsbeth. She was chosen five hundred years ago. The history books say that she never really recovered after her selection."

Piers and Rauf tried to get James's attention. This was something they didn't want told. He ignored them, obviously lost in story-telling mode.

"Some say her mind snapped. Perhaps she wasn't particularly sound mentally before she was chosen. Still, Justin honored the agreement and made her his queen. I'm sure it was a cheerless arrangement. She bore King Justin two children, but she was never well. The courtiers' journals from that time say that Elsbeth screamed and fainted when she saw anyone in dragon form. King Justin had her protected, confined, keeping her from anything that might cause her distress. The accounts imply she was held almost as a prisoner."

I listened, struck by the bleakness of Elsbeth's life.

"That last day, 'tis said she eluded her guards, said goodbye to her children, walked out of the nursery and jumped from the top portico of the castle.

"There's a statue in the central plaza of her. Shows her with wings. She's hailed as a martyr by some, a sad fool by others."

I shuddered at the image. Chris leaned forward, eager to hear more.

Hugh shifted as if moving to stop James from continuing, but Tristan placed a hand on his arm. "No, let him speak. They have a right to know both the good and the bad." So intent was James on his story that he didn't even notice.

"Victoria, though, well, she was our last human queen. Only eighty-one years ago. Stories and mystery abound about her. Pregnant queens do not just disappear."

He was telling the tale of my great-aunt Victoria. I sat unmoving. "She was pregnant?"

"Yes, with her third child. Two young children left behind; the eldest was our grandmother.

"She and King Leith were like fire and oil. Both hotheaded. By all accounts, Victoria was not a woman easily cowed. According to her journals, she felt betrayed and coerced. Leith may not have made enough of an effort to make her life easier. There were rumors that she had left a lover back in your country. Once she was chosen, there was no going back. King Leith was a proud man. A man accustomed to getting his way. Though I suspect he must have felt guilty for years."

I didn't understand. "But where did she go? Was she lost in the mountains trying to return to her home? Didn't your people look for her?"

"Oh, they searched. But one of the golden cards of magic vanished. It was believed she took it and traveled to a distant land on its power. Whatever the true story, at least one of the four golden cards did disappear with her going."

My eyes opened wide but I managed not to gasp. Chris had been speaking quietly with Hugh, but at James's words she turned, looking first at me and then back to Hugh. Her voice wavered, "What's this about a golden card?"

Chapter 41

She and I excused ourselves and abruptly left, claiming female needs. Now Chris sat cross-legged on the stone floor holding out her card as if it were carrion. "It can't mean that. It's simply not possible. My folks came over from Scotland, not some weird country with dragons!"

Across the cavern, Hugh was speaking to James, apparently chastising him. The others gathered nearby.

I shook my head. "Chris, this makes sense. Your great-grandmother, Ria, was the last chosen princess." I searched for some comfort to hand Chris. "She must have been very brave."

"But don't you see?" Chris's voice rose in a panicked whisper, with many furtive glances toward her newest kinsmen. "She only had one child—my grandfather. They're saying Nana was pregnant when she left, bearing a half-dragon."

She waited for me to say the obvious. Her great-grandmother had not one but three children, two of whom she left with the dragons. The last child, Chris's grandfather, was conceived before Victoria left the dragons. Chris was kin, distant cousins, to these men. I held my tongue. She already knew. It wouldn't do to hold her fingers to the fire.

She looked at me, her face white. "Why didn't I see it before? Ria is short for Victoria. I'm not even fully human, I'm part dragon—part imaginary reptile." Her voice skirted the edge of hysteria. "I think I'm going to throw up."

I took her hand and held it tightly. "Well, yes. But Chris, Victoria was my grandmother's sister, so you are also part of my family." I looked into her eyes, darkened almost to a slate gray, willing her to know that it made no difference to me that she had dragon blood.

As I held her hand, I struggled internally. It was the truth. It didn't make a difference to me. Even in the farthest recesses of my mind, I no longer saw man-dragons as something monstrous.

I understood it clearly then. "That's *why* she sent you. You belong to both worlds. She wanted you to make a difference, to bridge these two cultures. She *believed* that you could. Or at least wanted you to have the chance."

A tear made its way down her face. I wrapped my arms about her shoulders as she wept. Something inside me rippled a small wave of emotion that gathered force as I reflected about man-dragons, about Chris, about Tristan, about differences.

Chapter 42

I sat before the chessboard and faced Piers, who nodded back cheerfully. "White or black?"

Time was running out for me to select a husband. My fourth day. The most important decision of my life, and my parents weren't here to advise me. Nor were the councilors of our country here to list the advantages and disadvantages of each suitor. There was no doubt in my mind that I wouldn't be happy with someone who wasn't a strong leader. I needed someone with backbone, but not inflexible; a razor-sharp mind, but compassionate. Someone who would govern wisely. Someone people would follow. Chris wasn't much help. Though no longer distraught, she still wrestled with her dragon heritage, both drawn to and repulsed by who she was. I had agreed not to say anything; she needed her own time to tell them.

What did I need most? A mate or a crown, power or compatibility? If Hugh was right for me, I would have them all.

Piers did not suit. I already knew this. There was a sweetness to him that inspired protectiveness, but he was so young, my sister's age or just older. Untried.

Three of the men sat sprawled across the rocky landscape, curious, intent.

Piers gazed at the board as if searching for some mystery there. He was not a chess player.

"Um, Piers, it's your turn."

He flushed. "Oh, of course." He stopped then, his hand draped over the table and lowered his voice. "You should pick me."

I looked at him sharply. "I beg your pardon?" The other men looked over at us, wondering what was going on.

"I'm closest to your age. We would be a good match."

I stuttered for a moment before regaining my voice. "I'm flattered that you think so. You might be right." I smiled at him again. "Certainly, any woman would be proud to have you at her side, whether as a friend or a mate." Then I sighed. "But this isn't only for me, it's for your country as well. I have to be fair and evaluate each of you. Don't you agree?"

He nodded sagely and moved his rook one space. "Hugh's hot tempered, Rauf's bull-headed and Tristan's too cautious. I'm the fun one." He grinned as he sized up my reaction. "We'd make a great couple."

I smiled, taking care not to react too strongly, and then I attacked his queen.

Mercifully, it was over quickly. I thanked him and walked outside for some fresh air. I picked my way past the short white mountain flowers—"stomach flowers" my sister had called them, as the only way to see them clearly was to lie flat upon the ground. I thought about the dragons' lands and how different life there would be for me. The men spoke of the power held by women, of women rulers even. I feared I was beginning to think like Chris. It definitely had an appeal.

I had been too long away from the strictures of my land, too long away from the tight boundaries of palace life. Even if I could, I wasn't sure I would want to return to the conventions under which I was reared. I walked out to sit beneath the trees and watch the sun rise over the mountainside. How could I have changed so much in just a short time?

After our midday repast, Rauf and I started our game. He set out to amuse me as we played, regaling me with a commentary designed to flatter and please. He was a decent player but aggressive, taking risks with his men. His verbal gallantry kept me laughing and made it hard to focus.

I chose to play the bright-eyed damsel with him, as he expected.

I moved my knight. Tristan, who had been watching us play with a curious expression on his face, now erased it to a blank.

"Oh," I said, my eyes wide, playing innocent. "Does this mean checkmate?"

I thought I saw the hint of a smile on Tristan's face before he turned away to speak with James.

Rauf stared long at the board. "Ah, My Lady, I am undone." His mouth curved into a smile, but the set of his jaw told a different story. "How about another round? I just wanted to give you a sporting chance." He gave a great laugh deep from within his chest. I reassessed my perception; maybe he was just mocking himself.

I batted my eyes, playing along with this farce. "I don't think that would be fair to your kinsmen, would it? Besides, there is yet another test." From across the room I saw Tristan turn at my words. I pulled away from Tristan's look of amusement.

Chris jumped in. "Remember it isn't whether you win or lose but how you play the game," she said with a wink.

Rauf nodded and winked back. "The only game I truly wish to win is the one for Genevieve's heart. Now I have only the last contest with which to redeem myself." His eyes narrowed. Was that a hint of anger in his eyes or only disappointment well-concealed?

After he left, Chris shook her head. "He's such the flirt."

But I remembered hearing his talk with Tristan and wondered what he had planned.

And Tristan. Even from across the hall I could feel him. Since Piers had embarrassed him by singing his song, he had shown me nothing but measured politeness. No coy remarks or flattering looks. Nothing.

But he had entered the contest. And still I wondered why.

Chapter 43

While I waited for the next game, James examined the remaining detritus of the board in excruciating detail, reinventing our game, walking Chris through Rauf's missteps. I was fond of James in small doses. He was well-spoken, kind, and well-meaning, but long-winded.

Chris milked him all she could for dragon information. She kept directing the conversation to dragons. James's voice became a constant hum above my head as he lectured her with an exhaustive dragon history. It was interesting at first, but as he detailed their lineage back two thousand years I found my mind wandering. I tried to leave twice but Chris was bent on learning any and all minutiae about dragons. In her current state of familial pother, I was hesitant to leave her. As they nattered on about the obscure details of dragon bodily processes, I tried not to listen. I cleared my throat politely, hoping to switch to a somewhat more refined subject. Chris glared at me.

After an evening of despair, she seemed to accept the fact that she had a dragon ancestor. Not that it mattered, of course; she was human. But now her every other comment was about dragons, though she wasn't yet ready to tell the men. They must be curious about her new fascination with them.

I wondered about my lack of interest. How would I deal with a husband like this? Thinking on it brought the reality of my plans into sharp focus. Fear inserted itself in my very core: fire and talons and high flying acrobatics. Not only a husband, how would I deal with a child of these people? Or children? Maybe I would be barren or perhaps I would be unable to love my own half-dragon child.

I closed my eyes a moment, horrified at these thoughts. I opened them quickly enough when I heard the word virgin and my name in the same sentence.

"What's up with the sexist bull? If you guys are so egalitarian, how do you justify insisting that Genny be a virgin?"

I felt my face burst into flame. It must be the color of my hair.

James looked surprised. "Never. Where did you get that idea? We look for someone with honor, with virtue. Someone who isn't already in love. Someone who has the potential to bond with one person. No one ever said she had to be a virgin."

I hoped I might descend into the bowels of the earth before this discussion of my…virtue continued.

He saw my face and misunderstood. "It isn't a problem if you are, though."

I grabbed Chris's hand and squeezed hard. She shot me a glance as if taking in my color, not to mention the anger rising in my eyes. "Mmmm. Got it. Let's drop the subject. We're making Genny uncomfortable."

It was beyond uncomfortable. It was humiliating.

She drew her knees up and wrapped both arms around them. "But what if you're only part, you know, one of *them*, like Genny's kids will be." She blinked, remembering with whom she was speaking. "Sorry, James, part dragon, what does that mean? What traits do the children have in these mixed marriages?"

Was this never-ending? My hands clenched. I didn't want to think about any of this. My decision to marry a man-dragon was sufficiently difficult as it was. I understood why Chris was asking. Her new knowledge caused her to reevaluate who she was, but she was wrong. She was human, even if she was from the land of Berkeley.

James prated on about wingspan, talons, and the color of scales until I could no longer bear it.

I reached forward, placing my hands rigidly on the table. "Will you cease!"

James's mouth dropped open at my outburst.

I sighed. "My pardon, James. The strain of these contests is wearing on me. Might I have a moment with Chris, please?"

He sniffed. "I need to check if the wind has picked up anyway. Hopefully, you will be in a more agreeable frame of mind when I return." He then left with much muttering about women.

I turned to Chris, hissing into her ear. "Nothing. It means nothing. You've lived your life to adulthood and never knew. Nothing will change."

Chris whispered back, "But what if I change into a dragon when I return to school? Trust me, even in Berkeley, people will notice."

I tried to reassure Chris, to get her to stop this fixation with dragons. "You won't turn. Remember you told me about breaking your arm. You tried to fly and you didn't change then. Chris, you're human."

"But flying, can you imagine…? Maybe if I tried again, higher this time."

"Stop. This is nonsense. It isn't wise to think this way."

"Oh, give it up, Genny. You're not my mom."

We both sat in a puddle of silence. I shuddered both at the thoughts of flying and at my fear for Chris. I turned the subject, trying another tactic. "Don't you think you should confide in them?"

Chris pursed her lips, the haughtiest look I had seen on her face. "I don't see any need to discuss my ethnicity with them."

I held my splayed hand toward her, dismayed by her secrecy.

James returned then, anxious, watching the two of us. "Are you two fighting?"

I sighed. "No, James."

Chris smiled her sunniest and adjusted her glass-pieces. "We're just discussing girl things."

I waved for him to sit and rejoin us.

Chris fiddled with the chessmen. "So," she continued to James, like a patient looking for symptoms of some sickness, "are there signs before you change, some feeling of anticipation?"

James opened his mouth to reply, but I glared him down and he quieted.

Piers and Rauf wandered in to remind us that the next match was soon.

James stepped over to his kinsmen with a shrug. "I must bid you ladies good day."

Chris and I began resetting the chess pieces. I whispered to her, "You are looking for something that can't happen. Remember the story you told me—you fell and broke your arm."

She whispered back in my ear. "I *could* turn, I bet, if I had incentive enough." Then she called out to James to wait up for her.

As they left, I rolled my eyes at her silliness.

Moments later, Tristan lounged two arms-lengths from me. Rauf leaned his elbow on the table, spinning me a tale of his exploits, tapping his finger on Chris's glasses to make a point. I stared at them. When did she leave her eye-pieces? And why? She was never without them.

James sauntered in.

"Did Chris not come back with you?" I asked, looking beyond him for her.

He shrugged. "The lady needed a moment of privacy. She wanted some inspiration and incentive, she said. Didn't say for what. She headed up to the tall outcropping across the way."

I felt a tremor of apprehension, a flash of unease. "No! Goddess, she's going to jump."

Hugh's eyes narrowed. "Why would you say such a thing?"

I stuttered, unable to retract my words. "I'm worried about her," I finally managed to say.

Hugh spoke a single word, rolled out slowly, "Why?"

I demurred, "That's for her to tell."

Tristan watched my face. "Something's wrong here. You're white. You wouldn't be this upset over nothing."

Hugh grabbed my arms. "What do you mean?"

I closed my eyes, hoping that I was wrong.

Hugh shook me gently, "Genevieve, tell me, what is going on here?"

"I fear she might try to fly."

"What? That makes no sense."

I spoke the words hoping I wasn't betraying a trust for no reason. "It does if she's King Leith and Victoria's great-grand daughter."

Chris stood high atop a precipice. Surely, she wouldn't leap off that ledge, not her. "Chris!" I shouted. The men followed my gaze.

She didn't seem to hear me.

A muffled curse exploded from Hugh.

I couldn't stop staring at Chris. She wouldn't jump. I knew she wouldn't.

I registered the distress in Hugh's face right before he, James and Rauf took off at a run, changing from men to dragons, wings sprouting as they leapt into the air.

Chris saw us then and stepped back from the edge with a casual wave, a perplexed look on her face at the dragons winging toward her. She cupped her mouth and called across, "Don't worry, nothing's going to happen. I…" The wind gusted then and carried off her words.

She must have drawn back as her foot slipped on the scree, only a bit, but shale gave way beneath her weight. Her arms windmilled. She gave a startled squeak as she tipped headfirst into space. The dragons surged forward, pushing against the wind and sky to reach her.

She fell, careened down the cliff, arms and legs flailing in every direction, three dragons hot in pursuit.

I heard a scream from somewhere close and realized it was me. I covered my mouth with both hands.

She fell so impossibly fast, I feared that the dragons wouldn't reach her before she hit the ground. One of them folded his wings and dove.

Then, Chris's neck stretched impossibly long, wings erupted from her shoulders and a tail ridged with thick spines whipped kite-like in the wind. A small amber dragon, flapping for sky, teetering side to side as she awkwardly tried to coordinate her wings. Her tail swept back and forth like an out of control rudder.

I took a convulsive gulp of air, startled that I had been holding my breath.

Her flight staggered, threatening to collapse into another free-fall, when a gold and coral dragon—Hugh—sailed beneath her, sweeping open huge leathery wings and buoying her up as she held her wings outstretched. Slowly, ever so slowly, they gained height, back up to where I stood waiting, Hugh bearing the weight of a newly-formed dragon balanced on his back. Higher and higher they inched upward, Hugh forcing his wings downward, gaining loft with each stroke.

Piers at my side provided a running commentary. "He's making that look easy, but she has got to be heavy, upward of three tons. You have to give Hugh his due. Not many could fly carrying that much weight. He's going to be one sore dragon." Higher and higher they flew 'til they were level with the plateau. The amber dragon, steadied by Hugh's enormous wings, lifted off and landed with a loud smack.

As Hugh lightly touched his claws upon the earth, they both changed back into human form. Hugh grasped Chris's hand with his. I should have blushed then, seeing them like that, their bodies divested of clothing, standing there, the sun highlighting their naked forms. But it was their faces that held my attention, both stripped bare of pretense, the shock and wonder in their eyes. Hugh released her hand and pulled away—reluctantly, it seemed to me.

Chris flickered—that's the only way I can describe it.

The men shouted a warning to Hugh. Chris's body reverted into a dragon, but Hugh was too close, too exhausted from his rescue flight.

Before he could leap safely away, Chris's wing tip caught him a glancing blow, knocking him to the ground.

"Ouch! Looks like he took a hard hit to the ribs." Piers shook his head. "It could take days to recover from that."

The amber dragon, my Chris, stood over Hugh's body. As I started forward to help, Pier's hand on my shoulder gave me pause. He looking over at me worriedly and warned, "Be careful, sometimes a newly turned she-dragon can be—"

Chris launched herself at the first of the men to arrive, teeth and talons out. A challenging roar came from her throat.

"—vicious," he concluded.

I was so startled that I stepped well away from her and watched James and Tristan continue forward to attempt to calm her.

Piers leaned back against the mountainside. "It must be that maternal thing." He frowned as she rose up on her hind legs and swung a clawed forearm at Tristan. "Oh good, she missed. This might take a while," he said, nodding his head toward me. "Female dragons, in their first turning, are quite fearsome. It can be some time before they adapt to this shape. Not like us boys, who turn from dragon to boy for amusement while playing—" he glanced at me to see if I comprehended. "You understand, for sport."

The Chris dragon snapped and growled, taking a quick leap at James before again hovering protectively over Hugh. Guarding him with her body, I thought. I could hear her soft, distressed crooning to Hugh over the sound of the men's voices.

As we watched, Hugh came to and raised himself up on one elbow, staring into the amber dragon's eyes. She changed again, flickered into her human shape. She looked around, turned very pale and collapsed beside him.

Tristan got to them first, removing his shirt and draping it over Chris. I was almost to her

when Piers spoke behind me. "It doesn't mean anything." At the question in my eyes, Piers continued, a hint of worry in his voice. "She would be protective over a mangy dog in this state. Never know what drives them when they first turn."

But we all saw what happened. It was Hugh she was defending. Hugh, who vied for my hand. She had looked at him in utter adoration.

Chapter 44

"You don't have to say it again, Chris. They understand."

"But a dragon! I can change into a dragon." She looked at me, her eyes big. "And fly. It must be a dominant gene like brown eyes or near-sightedness. Or something. But maybe not." She paused. "My father never changed."

Tristan looked at me for a translation, and I shrugged. Much of what she said was still undecipherable to me. He said to her, "I wish you had told us. It doesn't take much dragon blood to transform, and here in these caves…" He looked around. "It's a magical place for some of us. Many of our historians believe that we came from here centuries ago."

Chris nodded, looking past him. "Where's Hugh?"

I remembered the look on her face from yesterday, wondering if I should feel betrayed. I felt confused. How serious was her interest in Hugh—a passing fancy, some outgrowth of her turning dragon?

"He's off with Rauf." Piers grinned. "Trying to get some of the gravel out of his hide."

"Oh god."

James patted her absentmindedly. "He'll be fine. Interesting, though, about Victoria. This explains why she was never found."

Piers quirked his head. "So are you coming back with us now? Going to turn dragon again and fly with us?"

"I think that's not a good idea, given that I attacked you guys."

She paused as if anticipating the men telling her otherwise. They didn't. Piers and James left to forage for food.

Tristan remained, still awaiting his turn at chess. Chris vacillated between exhilaration and horror. "So, tell me truthfully, what did you see? My memory of it is all so fuzzy. Did I really attack the men?"

How to say this politely? "You seemed agitated but you didn't harm anyone. Not really."

She shook her head, refusing my comfort. "Hugh is scratched, bruised, splotched in colors of blue and brown. Did I do that? He won't say."

"Well, yes, but it was an accident. I suspect it was difficult for you to know where the edges of your body were. Something like wearing a formal court gown with all your hoops. Last winter my sister was practicing and she knocked over a large porcelain vase."

Chris put her knuckles to her mouth.

Tristan leaned forward. "But you were beautiful, amber and gold and every color of the sun. One of the loveliest dragons I have seen in a first turning."

Chris grinned at his words. "The loveliest woman also?"

Tristan's eyes met mine for a second; a bolt of lightning leapt the distance between us. He grinned back at Chris and I wondered if it had even happened. "Certainly one of the loveliest," he said, sitting across from me. He stretched his legs out before him and flashed me a complicit smile, as if he and I were a team.

I felt my face redden as I held out my hands, a pawn hidden in each. "Choose."

He pointed to my left fist.

"White."

He would move first.

A loud roar of annoyance came from outside. Chris jumped up. "That's Hugh. I need to say I'm sorry and see how he is."

And Tristan and I were alone.

He met my eyes for a split second, and I looked away. I sat up a little straighter, trying to compose myself. It must be warm, I thought. My cheeks were definitely hot.

Tristan moved. A classic double king's pawn opening. I used my pawn to counter.

After four moves apiece, we were locked into a tight game. I watched his hands, a musician's long, slender, callused fingers. My mind drifted as I wondered what they would feel like against my skin. I jerked upright and saw him staring at my bodice, lips almost pursed. I breathed out quickly and moved my bishop. A careless move, one that even an intermediate player would be ashamed to make. Now he would corner my castle. And from there, two more moves and it would be over. He hesitated, fingers caressing his knight. Then he removed his hand and pushed a pawn but one space forward. My heart raced, fingers frozen in my lap. A throwaway move.

I looked up then and met his eyes. We both turned away. I corrected my move and we were back to even, a balanced board, neither of us with an advantage. There was quiet for the space of four breaths, maybe more. His hands rested on either side of the board. I listened to the sound of our breathing. With his next move, he pinned my castle with his knight. I countered with my bishop and around we went, both of us determined to win. He would attack my men and I would respond by attacking his. A carnage of chess pieces stacked up on each side of the board. The other men gathered around. I didn't notice at first; my head was down as I focused on the board. Finally, James spoke up. "It is over. You are evenly matched. It's a stalemate."

How much time passed after that, I don't remember. James and Piers drifted away soon after. Rauf left with a sour mouth and no words.

We sat at the table unwilling to part but neither of us able to break through our reserve. I believe it was I who finally stood. Tristan offered to walk me outside, and I accepted. So conscious was I of Tristan's hand barely skimming the small of my waist that nothing else mattered.

As we stepped outside, the glorious blue sky called me back to my surroundings. A few gray clouds rimming the northern mountains and a handful of leaves scooted by as if on an important errand. All my thoughts were of Tristan. His hand left my back, and I felt bereft.

We looked out over the southern landscape, watching a formation of geese winging through the sky, listening to their calls. My whole body tingled from Tristan's closeness. I wondered if he felt the same.

"Genevieve?" His voice was so soft that it might have been the wind calling my name. I turned and saw his hand extended toward me. Our fingertips touched. I felt the ridges on his thumb as it caressed mine. We were standing so close, our lips neared; I could feel the heat from his face. Was this what all the ballads were about, all the love songs I'd heard sung?

A gust of wind brought a sudden chill down my back. One gust and then another. My skin prickled with cold. I ignored it. Tristan's chest rose with his breath. I saw his nostrils flare as if scenting something in the air. A branch tumbled by me as a freezing breeze raked my skin. I shivered with cold. Tristan lifted his head to the north, his body tense.

Something hit me and then again. Ice. A torrent of hailstones dropped as a freezing wind encased us.

From the cave mouth, James's voice called out, "Tristan, Genevieve! A storm, a freak hailstorm."

Tristan's sharp exhalation caused me to look up as the hail continued showering down. He pulled away, but beneath my fingers I felt the first changes: claws that lengthened to the size of my hand, scales erupting across his arms. A piece of ice brushed my cheek, others hit my arms and shoulders. Tristan's scaled arm stretched over my head.

His face elongated. His jaw pulled forward out of his body, the forehead ridges protruding, his neck extending far above. A tail uncurled and slithered across the ground. In seconds, no more than that, a dragon towered over me. I froze, a rabbit beneath a falcon on a ground white with hailstones.

I heard the pounding of the ice stones as they bounced off Tristan's body. He shielded me, but with one careless move of that wing, I could be dead.

This was Tristan. Tristan, I kept thinking, even as I trembled. But as his dragon head snaked downward, I could see myself mirrored in his eyes, my body shivering from the icy storm, my look of fear at the silver and emerald wing above, protecting me. This was too sudden, too close.

I picked up my skirts, ducked and ran.

Chapter 45

By the next morning, it was as if the storm had never happened. The day was so hot and humid that we were hard pressed to step outside the cool of the cave. I hadn't seen Tristan since, well, our interaction. With the high heat, James had told me Tristan was back in his human form, but I don't think either he or I were ready to face the other. I shouldn't have run, but it had all been too abrupt for me. Before, the dragons had been never been near, almost touchable, when I had seen them. I could always pretend that it didn't matter. I no longer knew how I felt.

Chris thumped down, tucking one knee under her chin. "So what happened with you and Tristan? Yesterday I thought you guys would climb in each other's pocket and today both of you are avoiding the other."

"Nothing."

She looked at me dubiously. "Must have been a whole lot of nothing, then."

I tried to tell her what had happened. No words came forth. None that wouldn't sound like the babbling of a frightened child.

I finally braved the question, "Is Tristan angry?"

"Don't know. Maybe you should ask or apologize or…"

I winced, shaking my head. "No, let it be, Chris. It's for the best."

It was. I had let my emotions control me. This couldn't happen. His shift brought me to my senses. Though I had been startled the previous evening, I realized Tristan would never deliberately harm me in whatever form he took. But it did remind me of what the consequences would be for my choice. This marriage would be difficult enough for me. I couldn't choose a partner who was not at my side to smooth the way. I had to do what was right for my future and for my children's future. I was no farmer's daughter who could afford to be swept away by passion.

Chris acted as if she could read my mind. "Genny. I've got that you're planning on marrying here. But let that be your only sacrifice."

I steadily met her eyes, unflinching in my resolve.

She put her hand over mine. "There is no looking back. This is your life, you need to grab hold of it and do what's best for you."

I refused to answer. But her words niggled at me and I couldn't let them go.

Hugh took the seat across from me. We all were uneasy since the hailstorm, anticipating the next storm. Tomorrow was day six, my last day. I could see they were eager to leave soon, so we wouldn't be caught in the winter weather.

Since Chris's transformation, Hugh had grown more somber, and the hailstorm only increased the burden he appeared to carry.

Hugh's stance seemed to soften, to melt, whenever she entered the room. Now, sitting before me, preparing to begin our chess match, his eyes reflected a certain distraction. I wondered if he thought of Chris or of the storms. I knew what my father would say, that his thoughts weren't my concern. His behavior was. And nothing had changed there; he was here before me competing for my hand.

Hugh raised his head. "Genevieve, I wish to speak honestly to you and brush aside any false perceptions. Your path here was harsh, I don't deny that. But neither of us came here by our desires alone. Both of us are bound by duty. But this doesn't mean that we can't learn to love."

I met his gaze.

"I've made many missteps in courting you. I offer no excuse. But I do offer a new beginning."

Hugh was reaching out to me. He was much like my father, loyal with a deeply caring heart buried under a hard exterior.

I nodded for him to continue.

"I have taken you for granted. I have ignored your desires and feelings. From here on, I promise that I will make every effort to listen, to honor and value your words."

He beguiled me with his direct stating of where we stood with one another.

"I would be proud to have you as my queen. Not only are you beautiful, but you have a deep intelligence and emotional strength that I admire and respect. I only hope that you will consider this when you choose."

His honesty dazzled me. I reached out and clasped his hand in a

192

gesture of respect, understanding what it took for him to say this.

This was a man willing to marry me for the good of his country and his future children. He was the one I was chosen for. Someone who carried his kingdom's responsibilities on his shoulders.

No matter what Chris thought, perhaps as queen, as Hugh's queen, I could begin some discourse that would ease the centuries-old tensions between our lands. It could be a good match.

Hugh smiled at me, giving my hand a squeeze as we re-evaluated each other. He pointed to the game. "Shall we begin?"

He opened with his knight to queen-bishop three. I countered. The others collected around us. Chris came in to sit by my side. Hugh, after a quick look, bent his head down and didn't look her way again. Back and forth we moved. He was a careful player, each move decisive. His attention seldom wavered from the board. I, too, watched the board, but I watched him also. Duty aside, did he want me? Did that matter?

Hugh moved again. I examined the board. I was bounded on all sides. I stared at the board searching for an escape, but there was nowhere I could move safely. I pushed rook forward hoping to buy time. Hugh cocked his head at me as though in confirmation of something he already knew. "Checkmate," he said as he moved his knight to take my queen. He wrapped his fingers around my queen, cradling her carefully in the palm of his hand. My king was cornered.

Hugh slanted his eyes to me, and I thought this is what our marriage would be like: respectful, considerate, safe. I looked back at him and smiled, wondering what it would be like to kiss Hugh.

He must have seen something in my eyes as he gave me a quizzical look, then bowed before leaving the table.

Chapter 46

Laid out before me was a fine emerald ring from Hugh and one bunch of fast-wilting daisies coupled with a scratched out poem to my beauty, courtesy of Piers. There were two more gifts I awaited, Rauf's and Tristan's. Nothing from them yet, and this day was almost over. My final day. Perchance both had decided to withdraw their suits.

That was their choice.

Tristan was still avoiding me, refusing to meet my eyes, so perhaps that might be the case for him.

My heart sank, pulled into a whirlpool of disappointment. I steeled myself not to care, not to allow my heart to lead on this. Enough. I turned my mind from him.

Rauf had left soon after I rose the previous morning, and hadn't been seen since. He had appeared bent on winning. I was fond of him, though his teasing was somewhat aggressive. A few evenings before, Rauf had cocked his head toward Hugh, taunting him, and said that he knew the perfect gift for me. Hugh had glowered, as we both knew he would.

I fervently hoped that Rauf would not bring me a prize steed or bullock or something equally unwieldy.

I had to choose. And soon.

Chris was out somewhere, talking to Hugh, asking about her newly discovered nature. I worried about her. How would she fare when she returned to her world knowing her heritage was part dragon and part human?

Which one to choose? In my head, I leaned toward Hugh. He was admirable, smart and capable. I could be his queen. I could see us together, ruling the land, conferring on arbitrations and judgments. It could be a good marriage, one of respect and mutual understanding.

But even as I thought it, I heard what I was saying: a political marriage, one like my parents' and their parents' before them.

It could work. All noble marriages started so, and many, many moved into a close, affectionate union.

My thoughts turned to how my life would be with each of the remaining men.

Rauf was too impetuous, too willing to risk all to win. I tired of his desperate need to shine. His pride often overrode common sense. Even more to the point, I had no interest in being the trophy for his mountain home.

Piers was charming, but lacked the intellect and depth that I needed in a husband.

I was grateful that James wasn't a suitor, though he was a good man and learned, because every conversation turned into a long-winded treatise. I simply wouldn't have the fortitude to listen to him for a lifetime.

That left Tristan. I had to trust my head, not my heart. I remembered my mother's words: passion is fleeting and intellect enduring. He would be locked in dragon form snowfall to snow melt. It would mean being alone all winter, this first winter, then every year after, in a realm where I was the outsider.

Who made decisions for his people while he was incapacitated? Could I be that person?

I pushed the thought away. It wasn't for me to reshape his life. Still, part of me yearned that he would come to me, do something that would sway my choice.

The sun was lowering, and I had promised to choose before this day ended.

Only a few more hours remained.

I heard then the trumpeting of a dragon. It was an odd cry, almost a yelp. The men streamed out from the caves, searching the western sky. The air around them spun as they prepared to change, sending up showers of dust. What was it? Swarms of fire boar? Were they coming? What danger could alarm this many dragons?

There, winging toward me, backlit against the bright afternoon sun, was a bronze and turquoise dragon, Rauf. He swerved midair, then leapt forward in a surge of flight. Still flying erratically, he circled once, sailed into the clearing and landed, bouncing and shaking himself like a big dog. Something rode upon his neck, something small and agitated, clinging to what appeared to be a rope or leather harness. I leaned forward, trying to identify it. Rauf in his dragon form reached his foreleg back and grabbed the creature, but even from this distance, I could hear him.

"Genevieve!"

I picked up my skirts and took off at a dead run.

It was Harold. My brave little brother.

He was half-hidden by the boulder-strewn ground, dragon talons pinning him in place. The dragon's head snaked around. His lips pulled back into a snarl. Harold had one arm out, reaching between the black claws, swinging his wooden practice sword toward the dragon's head, a splinter catching the tip of one nostril. The beginnings of flame seeped from the beast's nose. I screamed and the dragon swung his head toward me, transforming into Rauf. Not dragon fire, but blood trickled from his nose. Both his hands stayed wrapped around Harold's shoulders as he shook my brother like a small rodent. Even above the wind, I could hear Rauf's roaring. "Don't ever, I mean *ever*, use spurs on me again!"

Harold wriggled out from Rauf's grip and launched himself at me. "Genevieve, did you see me? I rode a dragon. I flew!"

I held him tight, crushing him to me, my little brother, heir to the throne, whom I never thought to see again. "Harold." His whole face brightened with a grin, and my eyes welled with tears.

"I came for you, to rescue you, as I said," he told me, wriggling in my arms.

I hugged him again, drinking in his scent, pressing his head still warm from sunlight to mine. Until Rauf's words sank in. I lifted my head. "You used spurs on Rauf?" But for Harold's wind-chapped cheeks and tangled hair I would not have thought him just down from the skies.

He nodded vigorously, looking back over his shoulder and confiding, "He *was* going too slowly."

My happiness was short-lived as I thought about my parents searching for the heir, perhaps hearing of a dragon that scoured the sky. I was beyond delighted to see him, but now everything was changed. "Harold. Rauf. What have you done?"

Harold scowled. This was not the hero's welcome that he obviously expected. "I left a note. Just like you told me. I wrote to Mommy saying I was leaving with the dragon to get you and that I would be back when I rescued you."

I looked at him in dismay.

"Remember, I'm your protector. Sir Harold, the dragon slayer."

Rauf came out from behind the boulder, clad in breeches and

pulling on his shirt. Harold pulled out his wooden sword and took another swipe at Rauf. "Back, back, foul beast." There was a crack as the sword made contact with Rauf's knee.

Rauf grabbed the end of the sword and yanked it from Harold's hand. "The perfect gift," he snarled. "And I have a perfect gift for you, you little monster. A little discipline and a strong hand."

I placed myself between the two of them. "No, please, he's trying to protect me. Truly, it is a lovely gift, Rauf."

But it wasn't. Mother and Father would be frantic. I imagined Father ordering up his men and heading up the Perpinans and onward toward the Fandrites. Any fear of dragons would be overridden by this second abduction, first me and then the heir. This betrayal of the agreement between humans and dragons would be the break in the dam. My father wouldn't let this lie. Dragons would be the enemy, no restraint. My country would be at war. My country? My two countries. Whichever won, I would lose.

I had to return Harold myself. Any dragons would be shot on sight if seen within the borders of my land. No one would believe they were there to return my brother. My mind scrambled for strategy. Without thinking, I turned toward Tristan.

"I have to leave immediately. Father will be amassing an army. Mother—I can't bear to think about her fears. She'll believe that another of her children is lost to the dragons. I have to start back now. There's no time to waste."

There was silence among the men. I had promised, promised to decide on this day.

Rauf moved restlessly. "What about the treaty? Who have you chosen?"

I looked at him in disbelief. "That has to wait. My parents will think Harold dead. War between our two kingdoms will result. Bloodshed. Perhaps years of conflict. Can't you see that this is much more important than whom I marry?"

Rauf got a stubborn set to his mouth. "Naturally, but you could still choose. You must have decided by now."

Piers stood by his side. "No one has ever returned after they were chosen. Not in the history of our land. And now that your brother knows that we are man-dragons, he also cannot return."

Hugh's back was straight, his brows lowered in anger, all softness gone. "He's wrong. Your brother must go back. All these centuries that we protected our land by keeping it hidden and inaccessible are now undone. Rauf, you have destroyed our isolation by the careless strokes of your wings."

Chris looked at Hugh before speaking. "Is this such a bad thing? Is change so hard for you? Doing the right thing?"

For the longest time they looked at one another, oblivious to the heated discussion that raged about them—I, defending my decision to return with Harold. Piers and Rauf insisting that I choose. My attention was torn, so I didn't see his intention until Hugh stepped forward. He placed his hand beneath Chris's chin, lifting it up to place a gentle kiss upon her lips.

There was silence as if in church. Chris looked too stunned to speak, her mouth half open as if she had been cut off in mid-argument. James looked unsurprised. Rauf looked on with glee—one more suitor out of the running. Piers turned to Rauf, asking what had just happened. Tristan seemed deep in thought.

Chris still didn't move, standing as if tied to the ocher stone beneath us.

Hugh turned and walked over to the presents that lay next to me. He picked up the ring, turning it around and around in his hand. He looked through me, as if I were made of gossamer lace, and seemed to come to some determination. "I'll help ease your choice, Princess," he said, staring out at the setting sun. He was outlined in light, by the sun moving down the mountain, its last rays striking his hair and creating a nimbus around his head. "One less for you to choose from." He turned then, placed the ring in Chris's startled hand, and walked off.

Chris stood as if a statue, hand curled around the ring.

I prodded her. "Go, go after him."

She blinked twice and then stumbled off toward the tall trees where Hugh was disappearing.

Relief whirled though my mind now that this choice was removed, and I only felt joy for them both. No matter his political appeal, Hugh had never been for me. Somehow I'd known that all along.

Everything seemed to move too fast then. Chris was gone after Hugh. Tristan looked at me, watching my reaction. Harold bounced around like the half-grown pup he was.

It took only a moment before Rauf leapt back to his insistence that

I make a decision.

His attitude was tiresome.

Piers and James seemed to feel the same, as I saw them roll their eyes at his persistence. James commented to Rauf almost below his breath, "If you hadn't dragged the king's heir to the Crystal caves, we wouldn't be facing this crisis, would we?"

I nodded, happy that someone else could see this from my point of view. Then I realized what this meant. "Wait! You've broken the contract. I'm no longer bound. I don't have to make a choice. I can do as I wish—and I wish to be taken home."

Harold sidled over to me, placing his hand in mine, a small furrow of worry crossing his brow. It must have occurred to him that Mother and Father were likely to be upset despite his note.

Rauf's head drew up. "No. This affects nothing. You are still bound by the contract."

I stared him down, not willing to let this become a shouting match—but he was wrong. Tristan spoke up. "No, you stole the heir to her land, an act of war."

No treaty would withstand that. Our contract was broken.

James sighed. "Rauf, she's right. This was not well done."

Furious that his gift, his hard-won gift, was his own undoing, Rauf snarled, "Since my gift is of no value, I will take your brother back. A few days' rest, and I will be completely restored to make the journey again."

I ignored him. I had neither time nor patience for his bluster. Things had changed too fast for me. I held Harold's hand tightly in mine.

Braced with my knowledge, I confronted Rauf. "I'll not send him back without me. He's barely eight. It's too dangerous. Harold is so small he would be easily overlooked. If my people saw a dragon now, they would shoot their arrows first, and never notice a small boy."

I could feel Harold quiver with indignation at being called small. Two steps behind him, Tristan stood staring at the horizon where Hugh and Chris had disappeared. He leaned forward and whispered to James. James nodded and shrugged.

Tristan shifted uncomfortably. "Genevieve is right. She should be returned."

All heads turned.

"James and I could leave within the hour carrying both Genevieve and Harold. We could have them back before dawn. Our night vision is sufficient for such a thing."

I gasped, as did both Piers and Rauf.

Rauf said, "Return the princess? You would compromise our secrecy? Put our land at risk?"

Tristan spoke then. "It's already done. By taking Genevieve's brother, you have exposed us. The heir apparent must be returned. Taking him was a blunder. Keeping him would be an act of war."

James came forward to stand shoulder to shoulder with Tristan. "It may be that by traveling by night we won't be seen when we change to human. But if we are, then perhaps it is time to reconsider our secrecy, to parlay with the Verdeux king."

Tristan nodded, continuing. "It is time we revisit these traditions. It may not be in our best interest to continue in isolation.

"This is something Hugh and I have been discussing. It is time to reevaluate these rules. This is Hugh's decision; he is king. When Hugh returns, we will have a meeting of the council." Tristan looked at his kinsmen, getting a nod or head shake from each. Even Rauf, after some muttering, slowly nodded.

He turned to me then. "If Hugh agrees, you would have to travel in the sky."

I blanched. Riding a dragon? I hated heights, hated the thought of not having my feet on the ground. I thought of how ill I got even near the edge of a mountain. Then I thought of Tristan, of touching body to body, of the warmth of his hand on mine. I willed my heartbeat to slow as I attempted to speak. I opened my mouth and nothing came out.

Rauf pointed off in the distance toward Hugh and Chris. "Why can't she return with the boy instead of Genevieve?"

I stood up, my head forcing the words out one by one. "No. It has to be me who takes Harold back to my father. Even if Chris traveled as a human, they would deem her a witch in league with the dragons. My countrymen would shoot before she had time to explain. It has to be me. No one else would be believed." I raised my head, perhaps hoping for divine intervention to avoid flying home on the back of a dragon. "Yes, of course. I'll do it. There's no one I trust more than Tristan." But I found myself unable to meet his eyes when I spoke.

Chapter 47

"Chris, I'm not certain I can do this."

"Yes, you can. Think of your mount as a big horse."

I averted my eyes. When I looked back, Chris was looking at me in astonishment.

"This is to save your people, the dragons and return your brother. Are you that afraid of heights, of flying? Your own little brother did it, Genny. Or are you still afraid of dragons?"

"No, none of those. In whatever form they take, dragon or man, I know who they are. But this is an issue of propriety. My little brother is not female and unwed. It's…unseemly."

Chris rolled her eyes. "Oh for heaven's sakes, you've got to be kidding. You can't be that much of a dainty darling. After all we have gone through, after icky men and wolves and dragons, unseemly is what worries you?"

I nodded.

She placed her hands on either side of my face, unable to understand my hesitation. "Just let it go! You are so past this."

I looked long into her face and blew out a sigh. "Well spoken." She and I held eyes then, recalling the changes that had occurred these past months, changes for both of us.

"And where do you go, Chris? What do you choose?"

She stepped back, clasping her arms about her. "I don't know. I need time to think. I'm still coming to terms with my…ethnicity. But to leave my folks, my friends, my education and career goals to live in an unknown land? I have responsibilities."

I couldn't help teasing her. "Responsibility to those you love, perhaps?"

"Well, yes, sort of." She twitched her shoulder in acknowledgement. "I guess we are a bit similar. Bottom line. I can't up and abandon my future because of a guy. Not in my world and not here.

"I won't turn my life over to anyone. Not even to Hugh."

And what was I choosing? My life to return the way it was or to step forward and claim what I now knew I wanted.

Chapter 48

Night was upon us, the last rays of the sun gone. Tristan and James conferred with the other men, finalizing the details of the trip.

"Don't get too close to the castle," Rauf warned. "You never know what humans will do if they see you."

Tristan nodded, busy packing a small satchel with supplies.

James added, "We'll have to be careful of the updrafts over the front edge of the mountains. They can be nasty. I believe it was Kester the Fifth who died there, and he bore no rider. A bad ending."

I lifted my head, trying to disguise the fear running through my veins.

Tristan shot James a look as he discarded unnecessary items. "Ummm."

If that wasn't enough to cause me to fret, Piers pushed in, "Maybe we shouldn't return them right now. There's a nasty storm forming up in the west. It might be better to head home now. Next spring we could bring them back. It's a better season for traveling."

I held my breath.

Tristan kept packing, speaking with no inflection in his voice. "We've been over this. It's been decided at our meeting. We must return Harold. Genevieve wants to go back now. We will return her too. No more will we take a princess this way. This treaty, this process will be renegotiated."

I tried to examine my feelings. I should be happy and relieved. Tristan was doing what I said I wanted. What I did want. But I was choked by sorrow.

I spoke not a word to any, but for me, I had selected whom I would have wed.

The only one who had not given me a gift. Not offered for me. Nor did I blame him. After I had run, how could he feel otherwise but distant? Of course, it no longer mattered. I was returning.

I held my peace, hoping he wouldn't guess and see me as a fool.

Did he suspect? What would happen if I told the others? Would they be sympathetic? Insist that Tristan marry me?

Would I still be able to return Harold? No matter, I couldn't risk it. The kingdom's safety and Harold's safety were too important to risk for my own longings.

Tristan looked over at me as if sensing my indecision. "We could wait a day if you choose. There is rain in the air. James and I are strong and careful fliers, but it might be wise to wait for this storm to pass."

I studied Harold, slightly bedraggled, trailing after Piers and Tristan with star-struck awe in his eyes. Prying him loose from these exciting man-dragons would increase in difficulty with each passing day. And my father could be gathering his troops at this moment, my mother distraught.

"No, please. Tonight if it is at all possible. I don't wish to risk your safety, nor Harold's, but we need to get back quickly."

He nodded, his eyes serious. "It shall be as you wish." And he smiled at me, that smile that melted me each time. I smiled back and our eyes held. Should I tell him? I yearned to reach over and touch him.

Harold ran up and tugged on my sleeve. "Genevieve! Genevieve! Can we go now?

I pushed down my feelings.

"Yes, love, soon."

He leapt up. "I'm going to fly again. Harold, the Dragon..." He looked around revising his words mid-speak. "Harold, the Dragon Rider, flies again!"

I patted his head, straightening his curls, and then continued speaking to the men. "Not one more day. My parents can't bear this."

James and Tristan exchanged glances.

Tristan looked to the west, nostrils flaring. "I can smell the rain not far off. It can be cold for a human. We will bundle you up as best we can."

Harold stood with his feet apart, looking every inch the miniature monarch. "I'll protect you, Genevieve. The storm won't come while I'm here. Sir Harold, the Storm Turner. That's what they'll call me."

Tristan reached out and ruffled Harold's hair. "Perhaps with you astride, we can outfly the storm, small king."

Harold tilted his head up, glowing with pride.

Tristan continued, "Let us be gone now, and perhaps we can miss the worst of this storm."

James motioned Harold to him before changing into a brilliant purple and umber dragon. Piers and Hugh fashioned a makeshift harness on James's back with sturdy straps for keeping Harold secure.

Tristan crouched before Harold, inspecting his boot heels. At my look, he explained with a grin, "Just checking for spurs."

He lifted him up onto James's wing and Harold scrambled up onto James's back. Tristan tied him in securely, checking the straps and knots twice.

I prepared myself. Steeled my body not to shake. Chris stood near, holding hands with Hugh, both lost in the other's eyes.

"Chris, I can't say goodbye. I can't bear to leave you."

She came over to me and put her arm around my waist. "This isn't about goodbye. I'll find you, you know I will. This isn't over. We have a bond that has crossed worlds. Look for me. We have unfinished business."

Behind me I felt the air move as Tristan changed. I gave Chris a hug and took one last look at the Crystal Cave glittering in the slanting sunshine. Hugh and Chris wrapped a great felted cape about me before lashing me tightly into Tristan's harness.

Muscles flexed beneath my legs. I was afraid to breathe, to move. My fingers clenched the leather straps, hoping they would keep me in my seat.

Tristan's wings extended and with a huge leap we were in the air. I squeezed my eyes tight, unable to watch the ground disappear.

Chapter 49

The winds pounded against me, straining at the leather that held me safely strapped on the back of the man-dragon, Tristan. That first hour had been exhilarating, my fear of heights unfounded, but now, as the night dragged itself across the moonless sky, I concentrated on enduring. Never had I been so cold. Icy rain trickled down my back, sneaking past the thick folds of my woolen cape. Flying beside us and slightly above, was James, carrying Harold. From here I could see my brother's face, usually so cheerful and determined, his lips now blue with cold and exhaustion. He saw me, and his face crumpled into a look of misery.

He couldn't survive this weather much longer. I tried to control the tremors of cold that racked my body. I wasn't sure I could take much more either.

A muscle rippled beneath me, as Tristan called to James with that eerie trumpeting that had caused me such fear so long ago. I could barely feel it for my own shaking. They started downward, moving through more moisture-saturated clouds, lower and lower until we settled down with a neck-jarring thump on the edge of a small copse of wood. My fingers clumsy with cold, I released the leather straps that held me tight to Tristan, sliding down his wet slick scales to land in mud that covered my shoes and the hem of my gown.

More mud spattered across me as I struggled through the rain-drenched landscape to Harold, untangling his harness and removing the stiff water-soaked leather straps before pulling him down from James's broad umber back. I hugged him to me. His teeth chattered. The rain continued pelting us as I looked frantically around for shelter. Anywhere we could get out of this weather.

Tristan crouched by my side, his silver and emerald wing outstretched, a haven from the storm. I ducked beneath, guiding Harold before me. Within the cover of this living leather shield, the wind ceased. I stood adjusting my eyes to the shadows. A clicking sound quickly resolved itself. Harold's teeth were still chattering with cold. I pulled him beneath my cloak, kissing his cheek and tasting his salty tearstained face, smelling the soft wet sheep scent from his woolen felted coat.

James, also in his dragon form, dragged boughs of dry pine and fir upon which Harold and I scrambled, ignoring the resinous sticky sap that clung to our skin and clothes.

Tristan's wing lifted slightly and his head crooked beneath, breathing hot air back to us, warming our sheltered enclave to the heat of a summer's day.

Harold relaxed in my arms. He stirred, putting his hand up to my cheek. "I don't want to be Harold the Dragon Slayer anymore. I want to be named Sir Harold, the Dragon Friend."

Soon after, he fell into a deep sleep nestled tightly against me. I remained awake. Early morn we would fly again, return to my home, my life.

My emotions felt raw, scrubbed to the skin and scoured layer upon layer, until all that was left of me felt like a thin parchment written in deeply cut lines, brittle and fragile. No longer the soft, clever princess, sure of herself and her world. I didn't believe I could seamlessly walk back into my life, taking up my cards in the game of royals as if I had merely stepped away.

Slowly, exhaustion overcame me. I drifted to sleep holding my brother in my arms and my own thoughts at bay.

I woke gradually, struggling out of my dreams, unsure where I was. A lark trilled the coming dawn. Harold lay beside me, curled up tight against my side in peaceful sleep.

The smell of pine infused the snug space and something else, the rich smell of newly cut hay and sage; the warmth and coziness of a well-hearthed room. I reached out. My fingers brushed against a wall and felt the softness of watered silk. The wall shuddered at my touch and I remembered where I lay, sheltered beneath a dragon's wing. Tristan's wing.

Chapter 50

Almost home. Joy and anxiety roiled inside me, drying my mouth.
It scarcely helped that Tristan, as a man, was walking beside us to the
edge of a meadow. Beyond a small hummock to the west, I could see
the tops of the castle's turret banners flying in the stiff breeze. James,
in dragon form, watched from within a stand of tall hemlocks. Harold
bounced ahead like a spring lamb, still pleased with himself for rescuing
me.

Tristan motioned to the path by our side. "Here we must leave you,
only a half mile to your castle. We may already have been seen in the sky,
but there's no reason to inflame your people's fears further."

I nodded. Tristan must have seen the regret on my face and
mistaken it for fear, for he stared across the fields as if reconsidering.
"Maybe I should walk you the rest of the way, to be safe. The cat's out
of the bag, as it were, or will be once you and Harold are returned. Our
secrecy is a thing of the past."

"No, it's too dangerous for you. It's naught but a short walk."

I looked down at my feet, suddenly shy. "Thank you, and say thank
you again to James if you would."

I half turned, unsure what else to say.

He reached out as if to take my hand, then pulled back. "Before
you go, wait with me for a space."

Tristan appeared stiff and uncomfortable, as was I. He finally
shrugged, slowly reaching for my hand. "Perhaps I'm overstepping, but
I can't leave without telling you. I did not fail to remember, nor did I
plan to forgo the last test. And though the treaty is broken, you deserve
to know what my gift was. It wasn't gold or riches, but it was what my
mother said should have been given to the princesses."

He took a breath and blew it out. "I would give this gift to you
with my respect and love. I had planned on giving you your sovereignty,
the freedom to choose."

He shook his head with a wry smile, lifting my hand close to his lips. "No, that's wrong. I would merely be acknowledging that which is already yours, which you have so aptly proved to us."

"That was to be your gift?"

He nodded slightly before reflecting for some moments, as if he was deciding something. Then with a dismissive shrug, he spoke, "No, not anymore. It was my way of undoing a wrong. A wrong in which I was a participant.

"You are not a pawn. Not a chess piece to be fought over."

I studied his eyes, seeking for the truth there.

He continued. "You have a right to happiness. So I leave you here with this pledge. We won't return to take you by force, and no harm will come to your kingdom. Nor will I press my troth." He pressed a gentle kiss into the palm of my hand. "My gift to you is my heart." He turned and I heard him whisper, "If I don't leave you now, I might not be able to keep my vow."

Startled, I watched as he crossed the field, unable to pull my eyes away from him. The air spun about him as he started the change into a dragon. For a short time, both Tristan and the shadow of his dragon self overlaid one upon the other. Impulsively, I called his name and he turned, smiling at me with his blue eyes. I blew a kiss, trying to let him know I cared. That I chose him. That it was him I loved.

His face broke into a grin. The air slowed around him, stopping his change. The dragon shadow disappeared as he stepped toward me in human form.

A great clatter reached my ears as my father's soldiers rode up from beyond the hill, flung themselves from their horses and raised their bows. I heard the call, "Loose the arrows," and before I could stop them, arrows struck Tristan and he fell.

"Tristan!" The scream ripped from my lungs, hurting, carrying my heart with it.

James flew out from beyond the forest edge, scooped Tristan up in his talons, spread his wings and rose into the air. In the distance, my father sat on his war stallion directing the next volley of arrows. I shouted, called out. Ahead of me, Harold struggled against two soldiers who had leapt forward from behind a small stone fence.

I ran back toward where Tristan had last stood.

Far away a deep voice shouted my name, but I didn't even turn my head. All that filled my mind was Tristan. Beneath my feet, the golden grasses were splattered with bright red blood, Tristan's blood. High above, out of reach of the longbow arrows, a dragon carried away his limp body. I stretched my hands upward, reaching through the tips of my fingers, my heart beating, overflowing with loss.

I remained there, unmoving, until my father approached me, gathered me up in his arms and carried me, sobbing, away.

Chapter 51

The picture of Victoria, my grandmother's chosen sister, looked down at me. "So how did you fare in Chris's land?" I asked, leaning my head against the wall opposite her painting. "Twice you were uprooted. Once chosen and sent to the dragons, and once to leave them. Did you go because you were afraid, in despair or merely a fit of temper? Did you regret leaving the man-dragons, your husband, your children, your life?

"Is that why you sent Chris to me across worlds? Was it to mend the rift?" I knew she couldn't answer, not a painting of a deceased woman.

"I owe you much. But what was this all for? I'm back with my family but so confused and torn. Should I have stayed and sent my brother back alone? And Tristan. He defied his kinsmen to bring me back and then was shot." Tears threatened to come. I rubbed my hand across my eyes, banishing them.

"Winter has come and gone but there is no sign of Chris. She promised to return. I need her counsel.

"I am no longer who I was. But who am I now? Who do I want to be?

"I've no patience with my life here. Hopeful suitors have started paying their respects, and I can't bring myself to feign interest. Their posturing bores me. The mindless pattering of my ladies-in-waiting sets my teeth on edge. If Clara titters once more, I don't believe I can prevent myself from smiting her with my fan. This can't go on. I need to know if Tristan is alive." My voice trailed off. "If he still cares for me." My fingers trailed down to the token around my neck.

"I need to put this to rest."

"Take me too," a familiar voice called.

I flinched. Harold clattered into the hall, rounding the corner from where he had clearly been eavesdropping. When my heartbeat settled back to normal, I realized he couldn't know my plans.

"Please, please take me with you."

I looked at him with love and exasperation. "You have to stop sneaking after me and listening to everything I say."

"But how else will I know what is happening?" he countered. "I'll get left again. You'll have no one to defend you."

"Harold." I could hear how testy I sounded, but I couldn't have him nosing about.

A rustle of silk interrupted us, and my mother appeared behind him. "Genevieve, I wish to speak with you." She looked at my brother and spoke firmly, "Harold, your tutor is searching for you. Go back to your lessons."

"But I'm a hero, Sir Harold, the Dragon Friend."

"Yes, dear, you've spoken of nothing else since your return."

He frowned and hunched his shoulders. "But Gen…"

Mother reached out and turned him around. "Harold…now!"

Harold slowly turned and walked dejectedly down the corridor. Mother raised her voice, calling after him. "If you aren't at your lessons by the next bell, you will be cleaning the stables for a fortnight." Harold leapt to a trot.

My mother sat silent for some time. She was not one to force a confidence. She could wait out a confession from the most taciturn of people. She arranged one of the green brocade cushions from the wooden benches that lined the hall before sitting down and placing her hands in her lap, as if she had all the time in the world.

"It's a very expressive portrait." She nodded toward the picture of Victoria. "The artist captured that same look of pride and will that my grandmother had—Victoria's youngest sister." Her lips curled into a knowing smile. "That all the women in our family have.

"Victoria was your age when she was chosen. They all were. I never mentioned it to you. Every royal family fears when they birth a daughter within the end of a century. No one ever knew exactly when they would come. Seventy years, ninety, one hundred. Once it was one hundred and twenty. And always, ever so coincidentally, when the girl of their choice turned seventeen; always the best and brightest. Each time a gold token arrived." She looked at my neck where the dragons' token lay against my skin, tied in place by a gold chain, and then continued on. "I never understood how that could be. It was too convenient for coincidence. It makes sense now that we know they were men, that our priestesses were involved." A hard look crossed her face.

"I kept hoping the dragons might not come when you turned

212

seventeen or that some other royal female would catch their eyes. I couldn't see the value of burdening your childhood with the weight of something that might never happen." She was silent once again.

"Perhaps I was wrong. Perhaps I should have done more."

I shook my head. She stopped and looked long into my eyes before continuing with her story.

"At every court gathering I would count the princesses, those within three years of you. Weigh their qualities against yours and come here to this gallery to brood.

"Even from my view as a doting mother, I knew you were special." She reached over and caressed my cheek. "That if they came, you would be their choice. You were far and away the prize of the young princesses. I told myself that it was only my fears speaking, my motherly pride clouding my judgment. But I knew."

She curled both of her hands around mine.

"You were chosen and then returned, the only one in eight hundred years. I rejoiced when you and your brother came back." She stopped there, a catch in her voice. "But it has been five months and still you wear the token. I find myself questioning why."

Still I said nothing. How to explain how I had changed?

She sighed. "You've said little about your time away, and I have honored that, trusted that you would come back to yourself. First you mourned, and while I didn't understand, I granted you that time. But since snowmelt you've changed again. You've retreated. It isn't that you are still in suffering from your ordeal. I could read that."

I closed my eyes, unable to view the sorrow and concern in hers.

"Genevieve, what is wrong?"

I sat beside her and leaned my head on her shoulder. She held me while silent tears slipped down my cheeks. I couldn't speak. If I did, she would try to stop me. Harold had guessed right. I couldn't tell her how I begged the guilt-ridden Captain Markus to help or about the horses waiting or the two months of supplies cached away. I feared I would confess that I was leaving for the Fandrite mountain to hunt a dragon, one that I had chosen out of the best princes of Pritorous to be mine.

Chapter 52

The music was pleasant enough. My ladies played a soothing medley of tunes prepared expressly for a string ensemble. Clara was on the harp, Felicity and Melody viol, and one of mother's ladies played the lute. Banal entertainment to while away another spring evening. Father sat, one leg crossed over the other, relaxed and content in his favorite blue velvet chair. Mother, beside him, leaned over to whisper in his ear.

I picked up my fork, trying not to think of their pain. Soon they would lose a daughter again. This time of my own volition.

I sat between a prince from the next kingdom over, who was the most dandified man I'd ever encountered, and Neville, the crotchety duke from two kingdoms south of us.

Both bent on wooing me. Both with no chance whatsoever. No longer was I a prize for some lucky royal to win. My life belonged to me.

Two servants circled, offering a small repast to those in need of fortification to endure the evening. I was pretending to listen while lost within my thoughts when the air spun between two tall braziers. My heart jumped. And there she was, Chris, looking a little unsure of herself, standing halfway across the room. Her eyes wide as she searched for me. She was almost unrecognizable in a court dress of amethyst with long vee-shaped sleeves decorated with buttermilk colored inserts. Her hair was braided into a hundred plaits and coiled about her head. Beneath the dress, I could just see the hint of sandaled bare toes tapping against the court's white onyx floor. I was comforted that some things never changed.

The musical interlude ended in a cacophony of strings as Clara registered Chris's presence. Clara screamed, just as she had months ago when Chris first appeared, and leapt away from her harp.

I pushed back from the table, silverware clattering around me as I rushed to her side. "Chris! Chris!"

Clara's voice shrilled across the room. "It's the witch! She's one with the dragons. They're going to take our princess again." Father was up in a moment. I heard the snick of several knives being drawn. Mercifully,

I was between them and Chris.

Two guards burst into the room and raced to surround Chris. I stood braced, shouting at them. "No, she's my friend."

The guards looked from me to my father. He sat slowly, unruffled but for the paleness of his face. Mother had her hand to her throat. Felicity, after a sudden squeak of surprise, collapsed heavily against Melody.

The guards inched closer, swords out.

Father's voice rumbled above it all. "Leave her."

Behind me, I felt Chris shudder in relief right before she whispered in my ear, "Genny, I have to talk with your dad."

I looked at Chris in her dress that dipped too low in the bodice and her face unadorned by any proper cosmetics. She was not properly attired to be presented to my father. Chris noted my uncertainty and pressed me again. "Genny, please, this is important to me and to you."

I shook off my hesitation, took her hand and led her forward slowly, the guards making way before us. The whole room stilled.

I proudly presented her. "Father, I would like to introduce my friend, Chris." I hesitated and then corrected myself. "No, my friend and kinswoman, Crystal of Berkeley, great-granddaughter of our own Princess Victoria. She stood by me when I was chosen, stood by my side before the dragons and was instrumental in my return."

Gasps came from somewhere, perhaps Mother, but when I looked to her, her face was composed.

"I would beg an audience for her." I dropped into a low curtsy.

"Rise, my daughter."

Father looked at me, and with a small twist of his hand, indicated that the room was to be cleared of visitors. The two guards leapt to do his bidding, ushering all out, the duke still clutching his platter of meats. Before Felicity could complete her elaborate faint, they gathered up my ladies and escorted them out of the room. There was some resistance—Clara put up a good show of refusing to leave me with this woman, the one aligned with the dragons. Father had the seneschal close the door firmly against her remonstrations.

Chris took a deep breath and collected herself. She looked at me one last time. "Okay, I can do this. Give me a few minutes alone with him and then we'll talk." With her normal lack of decorum, she shot a wink at me. I stepped to the side as she walked the remaining steps to my father.

She executed some posture between a bow and a curtsey, her glass pieces glittering in the candlelight. I laughed aloud. I knew I should have taught her to curtsey.

My family, the servants and the guards turned to look at me. My mother signaled that I should rejoin my siblings at the table and wait this out.

From outside the iron-clad oak doors I heard noise, voices raised, and a bugle call to announce visitors. But I was immune to anything except what was happening before me. Chris was here. I wouldn't have to travel alone, with just the men I'd begged to go. She could accompany me to the Crystal Caves.

She spoke quietly with my father for what seemed an interminable time but couldn't have lasted more than a few minutes. Father pointing an irate finger at her, and Chris pointing hers right back. My father's eyebrows came down and his nostrils flared in anger. I started up to assist, but a small headshake from my mother held me in place.

Strain as I would, I couldn't hear their words, what with the guards nervously shuffling about and the servants' low whisperings. Once, when father's angry voice rose and bounced off the ceiling, a maid overlooked in a shadowed corner dropped a platter of sweetmeats. So high was the tension in the room that I may have been the only one who noticed.

After smiling encouragingly at Chris, Mother remained calmly in her seat. Her left hand rested firmly on Harold's shoulder as he wriggled to get up. My sister, Danielle, sat a mere three seats from me, vacillating, it seemed to me, between trepidation and excitement. Her eyes caught mine and we both winced as Chris waved her hands in the air, making some point. Father glared at Chris, eyebrows drawn down even further. His hand slammed down on his chair arm as he leaned forward, pressing his face almost into Chris's. His left hand, knuckles white with restraint, latched onto the arm of his chair as his back stiffened in anger.

Chris froze, finally realizing that she may have overstepped. Father didn't move again. So fierce was his expression that we all watched, waiting for Chris to be ordered away—I feared to the dungeon.

Casually, my mother leaned over and whispered in Father's ear. He scowled, looking first at Chris and then me. His brow cleared. Mother whispered again. He snorted. The glower on his face relaxed into a half smile. Chris started to back away, but Mother spoke to her, and Chris, after a quick wild-eyed look at me, knelt.

Father raised his hand up for Chris to kiss his ring. Chris grabbed his hand and shook it firmly. Father appeared startled but recovered himself with no further ado, acting like that was how he concluded all his interviews.

I jumped as his voice rang out. "Done."

Chris delivered her combined curtsey/bow again. Father dismissed her, shaking his head in amusement as if watching a small child cartwheeling in the throne room.

She danced over to me, obviously pleased with herself, her arms clasping mine as if I were a lost treasure.

"What did you say to Father? What did he agree to?"

I pulled her toward a quiet alcove, seeking some privacy from the gauntlet of stares. Chris ignored my questions, clasping my hand in a tight grip. "So what do you think of the dress? Cool, huh? Does it suit?" She spun around, then took hold of both my hands.

I nodded, unwilling to draw attention to the daring cleavage. I wondered how many of the ladies in the court would imitate that look within a fortnight. "You look lovely. But what happened with Father? Why are you here?"

"Oh, you'll see." She winked, and then her face turned serious. "I had to come, of course. Had to see if you were happy and safe with your family." Chris looked hard into my eyes, all girlish folly pushed aside. "You're not, are you? What's wrong? Why are you crying?"

I smiled through the sudden tears. "Nothing is wrong. It's just that I feared I wouldn't see you again." I reached out my arms and enclosed her in a hug. "And Tristan? Is Tristan alive? Is he badly hurt?"

"He's fine. Oh, right. He said you saw him shot and would be worried. Dragons are very, very tough. A few little arrows didn't cause him much grief."

I brightened and then realized that he wasn't here. He hadn't come back for me. I brushed my hurt feelings aside. I smiled, trying not to let Chris know how disappointed I was. I changed the subject. "So what happened after I left?"

"Oh, lots! I went with Hugh to give Tom Mastin what was coming to him. I understand that he had received gold from the dragons as well, and that neither side knew the other was paying him. Tom and I had some unfinished business. We had a little chat about women and ethics. He was eager to see my point." She looked at me. "It's all about framing the question properly, isn't it?"

"What did you ask?

Chris checked her newly manicured nails as if looking for flaws.

"I asked him if he wanted to live. Then he and I took a joy ride three hundred feet in the air. With him dangling from my claws."

Chris grinned at my look.

"I offered your father the same diplomacy for your Priestess, but I understand your Mother had dibs on that."

I burst out laughing. "And what did Tom choose?"

"Oh, disappointingly, he wanted to live. Still, I felt there was stuff he should think on. So I decided he needed a contemplative retreat. I left him in the middle of a huge lake, on an island with just enough room to walk a pace or two. Poor man can't swim. He was already looking downright meditative when I left."

I couldn't bear not to ask.

"What happened with the man-dragons? Did you return to their home with them?"

"Oh, that. Well, we started talking—Hugh, me and the others—and I…" She took a deep breath, her eyes twinkled with delight. "I flew with them. It was so amazing. And now I'm trying to re-establish relations between countries, er, kingdoms, like China and the US, like the three kidnapped princesses did, same kind of thing.

"You know, like John Lennon, 'Give Peace a Chance.'" She almost danced in place at my blank look.

"Oh, you'll see in just a bit; you won't have to wait for the movie."

I was dizzy with Chris's thoughts flaring up like fires at Beltane.

But she seemed so pleased with herself that I changed the subject to let her enjoy this mystery. Mother would tell me soon enough. "Have you decided to stay with the dragons? Or are you leaving for the world of Berkeley?"

Chris twisted her mouth in a wry smile. "I'm not sure. Hugh and I are working on a compromise. I can't just walk away from my world and jump into this one."

Outside, the clatter swelled to a shout.

She grabbed my hand. "Ignore it. Give me a few more minutes."

I put my hand on hers, thinking to reassure her. "Chris, I owe you a debt. I would give you much more than a handful of minutes. You must know that. Why would you doubt it?"

"Mmm." She smiled, a look of one well-pleased with herself. "Well, just bear with me while I fill you in." And, again, a smile of a fox that had captured a hare.

I cocked my head, listening.

Outside, the cacophony was getting louder. Whatever it was could wait. Chris was here with me and I rejoiced.

The seneschal, Samuel, after confirmation from my father, went back to his station. Through the half open door, Captain Markus, in full dress livery of blue and gold, conferred with him. From my vantage point, I saw Michael right behind him. I paled. Were they here to betray my plans?

Chris spoke faster now. "So we came, or rather we planned when to come. I had to return to Berkeley to finish the semester, but we planned the timing pretty carefully." She grinned again. "It looks like it worked."

"We?"

"Hugh and me."

"Hugh's here?" My mind went blank for a moment, bewildered and confused. "Are the other dragons here also? Is Tristan here?" I started to pull away, but she nodded her head.

"They all are."

I thought I hadn't understood at first. I didn't believe it. Couldn't believe it. Tristan was here and hadn't bothered to see me. I was surprised at the intensity of my joy and disappointment.

Then the ever-increasing noise outside made sense to me. My heart leapt and I felt my feet freeze in place.

The seneschal stamped the floor with the royal staff and announced the visitors.

"King Wilheim and Queen Camille, may I present, King Hugh Buchan—"

He didn't get any further. He stopped and questioned Markus again, trying to get the pronouncements right. The seneschal looked confused. Markus repeated their names and titles. I heard the word dragon. After a panicked look behind him, the seneschal's eyes rolled up into his head as he slumped to the floor.

My blood chilled. I felt goose-bumps on my arms as one by one they entered the room.

Man-dragons, five of them. Dressed in formal court attire. My eyes flashed to Tristan and my breath caught. There he was, standing just inside the timbered doors with his chestnut hair braided neatly, dressed as if for a meeting with the king, a white linen shirt, topped with a gray overtunic and high black boots. His sword slung by a wide leather band on his left side.

Chris could barely contain herself. "Think about it." She squeezed my arm. "You've changed the dynamics of two countries. It's just like Gandhi said, 'Be the change you want to see in the world.' Look at them. No longer are they hiding behind legend and mountains. They came, all of them. Prepared to play ball." At my quizzical look, she added, "To talk."

Still I said nothing. The enormity of their presence overwhelmed me. The man-dragons proceeded forward in an orderly fashion, long legs striding across the floor, the click of their boots' heels reverberating off the walls, to stand before my father. Tristan stepped forward, bowed and then spoke in low tones to my father.

Finally, I found my voice again, my emotions in a tangle.

"Why, Chris? Why are they here?"

"Negotiating a new treaty, one where all the cards are on the table, totally up front."

I felt my body sag. Not for me. Tristan isn't here for me.

"Yes, of course, he said I was free. That they wouldn't come for me." I was trying to make it sound like something I desired.

She watched me, my face flushing. I looked over at Tristan intent in his conversation with my father. Should I go to him? Could I even talk with him? All my brave plans to force an answer blew away like fleece.

"How nice that they all came to parley a pact, even…even Tristan." I bit my lip; I sounded inane even as the words slipped forth. I couldn't say his name without tears welling up.

Chris looked at me as if my crown had fallen lopsided. "Oh no! Is that what you think? Tristan just came for the treaty? Tristan has been pining like an abandoned puppy, er—a rather big one in dragon shape, for sure. But once spring came, you're all he talked about. He's here, we're all here, for you." She stopped at my look.

"Not by force. Never again will they do that," she amended. "You have to go to him. He's being silly over some ridiculous promise he made to you. Go."

Could that be? Did he truly care?

Chris stamped her foot. "Oh, for criminy's sake, Genny, you know you have a case on him. Are you going to go or not?"

My mind whirled. Since I returned, Tristan was whom I thought of, whom I dreamed of. And there he was.

Chris was still talking, babbling in my ear.

She poked me, nudging me forward out of the alcove.

Both Father and Tristan's gaze turned toward me. Father, anxious, and Tristan with such hope and love in his eyes that I couldn't look away.

"He's waiting for a signal from you, Genny. He's such a stickler for protocol and manners," Chris said with a dismissive shrug of her shoulders.

"I can't." Now that he was before me, I found my tongue glued inside my mouth and my feet locked to the floor.

Chris looked at me and we stood in silence for what seemed forever. About me there was a world that continued as my mind circled around. Was I a pawn or was I the player?

Chris waited expectantly. "Did you learn nothing?" She slammed her elbow against my side. It's your life, isn't it?" she whispered.

Worlds collided in my brain. One where I was the dutiful daughter—clever, protected and mannered. One where I had stood strong and defied five dragons. One where I braved my fears and flew high above the land strapped atop a dragon. One where I had plotted and planned for months to return to the Crystal cave to force an answer from a dragon. And one where I loved Tristan.

Demonstrate, I remembered. That was a term Chris had used long ago. A word from her world, a way of standing up for something important to you.

I looked at the men, the man-dragons, aligned before my father.

"They, too, are demonstrating, are they not?"

Chris quirked her head. "Yes, absolutely." Her face broke into a grin. "Nana would be amazed! It's just as she wished, a demonstration, a demonstration of dragons."

I looked at Tristan. His eyes glowed as they connected with mine. I started forward slowly, then ran as he opened his arms for me. Perhaps it was, more truly, a demonstration of love.

Acknowledgements

So many people have been a part of Dragons. Each time it has morphed into another version

Josh Schimel, my husband and love, who has read and critiqued draft after draft of Dragons.

Kate Epstein, who critiqued so many, many revisions.

Val Hobbs, Sherrie Peterson, Kim Hernandez and Lori Walker, my current writing group who cheered me on each step of the way.

Rebecca Finley, Sarah Potok, Denise Fitolas,Helene Gardner, Lori Walker, Nicole Archambeau, Sigrid Erro, Kerstine Johnson, Beth Taylor-Schott who listened to early versions of Dragons as it took form.

Dianne Salerni, who helped me strengthen my writing.

Cynthia Bates, Sidonie Weidenkeller, Kate Schimel, Nancy Tubbs, Jeannie Meekins, Michele McGrath. Judith and Michael Thompson, Heather Latham and Joseph Grayson. Readers extraordinaire.

Jeanne Panek, for convincing me to change the ending.

Phyllis Schimel, for laughing in all the right places.

Anne Lowenkopf, who gave me the courage to write.

Gwen Dandridge is the author of
The Stone Lions and *The Dragons' Chosen*.
She lives in California.

You can visit her online at
http://www.gwendandridge.com

www.ingramcontent.com/pod-product-compliance
Lightning Source LLC
Chambersburg PA
CBHW022014170626
46808CB00001B/407